"Zani's storytelling instantly connects the reader to the charac-ters and makes the reader yearn for more. *Hope Rising* is a soulful story filled with hard truths, family ties and bonds, and the reality that we are all on our own journey to find our heart's path to self-love and healing."

—ANITA CELLUCCI, Librarian

"The third installment of a thought-provoking fiction series, an exploration of love, loss, enlightenment, and self-discovery written by self-described 'intuitive medium' Zani. New Age philosophy deepens this touching but sometimes mysterious coming-of-age story."

—KIRKUS REVIEWS

I0526622

PRAISE FROM READERS

"Honest, hopeful and quietly powerful, *Hope Rising* is a story about what it takes to trust again after trauma—and how love, time and the strength of family can slowly piece a heart back together. Set in the world of equine therapy, it explores how the past can wound us, but doesn't have to define us. With human, heartfelt prose that begs to be read aloud—and a twist that keeps us hooked—this novel reminds us that healing is possible, even when it feels out of reach. With the same touching connection to nature and all things horses as *Where the Crawdads Sing* by Delia Owens and *Chosen by a Horse* by Susan Richards, this is a story that speaks to the quiet power of empathy, animals and second chances."

—SCOTT BALDYGA, Screenwriter and Author of the #1 Amazon true crime release *Frozen*

"Tender and uplifting, yet compelling, *Hope Rising* is fully charged with emotional depth and illustrates how the 'coincidences' in life can lead to connections we never knew existed and through them, healing. With prose alternately lyrical and then harshly grounded, *Hope Rising* will stay with you long after the last page. An engrossing read!"

—FRAN G THOMAS, JR., Author of the *Silent Justice Series*

"*Hope Rising* is a beautifully layered story about healing, legacy and finding strength in unexpected places. I was pulled in by Hope's quiet determination and the way her journey unfolded—with grace, grit and just the right touch of mystery. Zani captures the pain of the past and the promise of what's possible with tenderness and depth. If you've ever had to rebuild, or learn to trust again, this story will stay with you."

—GINA CLAPPROOD, Intuitive Advisor and Author

"In a multidimensional sense, this book is about soul retrieval, remembering the parts of ourselves buried under bloodlines, pain, and silence. The land, the horses, the shoreline , all play conscious roles in this unraveling. Nature herself becomes an oracle, reminding us that healing comes in waves, not resolutions. The past lives in the soil. The future waits in the breeze. And the present, the now, is where miracles unfold. If you are a seeker of truth, a feeler of subtle frequencies, or someone who listens for the voice beneath the voice, this story will resonate deeply. It reminds us that love is not just an emotion, it is a path, and sometimes, we must lose our way to find the soul of who we've always been. A beautifully written novel that will live within your heart."

—JACKIE WAITKUS, Spirit Medium at Blending Two Worlds

"Zani pulls you into her stories and makes you feel like you are living in Maine, right next door as a neighbor, a friend. You get to know the characters and feel all of their emotions. More than anything, as you near the end of the book, you will not want it to end."

—EILEEN BERNIER

"Zani masterfully blends her intuitive mediumship with her natural storytelling gifts, breathing authentic emotional depth into her characters. Her prose feels approachable yet profound—like listening to a close friend who understands exactly what you're feeling. Each page brims with sincerity, empathy, and insight, a testament to Zani's connection to both the human heart and spirit. Fans of her earlier novels, *Piper, Once & Again* (2016) and *Waiting for Grace* (2020), will find *Hope Rising* a satisfying and uplifting conclusion. But newcomers, fear not: Zani skillfully weaves enough context throughout that the novel stands beautifully on its own. Zani leaves readers with a heart full of hope and perhaps a renewed trust in life's unpredictable beauty."

—BETTERAUDS.COM

Book 3
ECHOES
PAST & FUTURE

HOPE RISING

a novel of reclamation

CAROLINE E. ZANI

Wyatt-MacKenzie Publishing
DEADWOOD, OREGON

Hope Rising
a novel of reclamation

Caroline E. Zani

ISBN: 978-1-942332-54-6

Library of Congress Control Number on file.

Dedication

In memory of my mother, Carol Ann Zani who modeled
for me what it means to be a salt of the earth mother.

In memory of Giuseppe Struppa, the best boy,
who lights the stars each night, reminding us
that we will all go home one day.

Acknowledgements

THIS STORY, THE THIRD IN THE ECHOES PAST & FUTURE SERIES, is a story of reclamation. It's the culmination of many experiences, some mine and others not, that challenge our spirit to overcome the cards we've been dealt as humans while learning to reclaim our own place in the world.

It is, at its roots, a story of trust, insight and perspective. Allowing life to unfold while also being open to a history we might have only learned from a single perspective, is a skill that surely takes time to learn and discipline to practice. It can change everything.

Every person we meet is here to teach us something, while we, sometimes unaware, are the teacher. *Hope Rising* was born from this belief and the truth that our intuition is a trustworthy compass. Finding your true north is, undeniably, a gift.

I would like to thank my publishing house, Wyatt-MacKenzie Publishing, for their expertise, talent and never-ending creativity in an ever-changing literary landscape. Nancy Cleary is a visionary who understands that characters are more than a concept and that a story comes from a place that doesn't always originate inside an author's head.

For my Thursday night development group, thank-you for being the wonderful souls who come in disguise as students and prove to be some of my greatest teachers. Always remember to "say everything."

For my sisters Lisa, Nicole and Monica for getting us all through the last year of our mother's life with dignity and grace.

And to my daughter, Amanda Lucia Zani, for being a true inspiration. I love you more than words can capture. Keep moving.

And for Chris Conaty, thanks for showing up when you did. I owe you three tacos and a beer.

I would be remiss to leave out Honey and Bee who sprung from the pages of *Waiting for Grace*, like magic and have edited more of my copy than I'd like to admit, with the swipe of a paw. How much has been lost, only God knows.

And for all of the horses who shaped my life, taught me about boundaries and reaching potential, caught my tears, listened to my dreams and gave me Hope, especially Sergeant Budweiser Jones, Colonel, Shadow, Dragonslayer, Chianti, Big Ben, Chubby, Patton, Missy, Piper and of course, Oliver.

"O Shepherd. You said you would make my feet like hinds' feet and set me upon mine high places."

"Well," He answered "the only way to develop hinds' feet is to go by the paths which the hinds use."

Hannah Hurnard, *Hinds' Feet on High Places*

"Moose! Help me! Moose!"

He might have been underwater or on the other side of the Hindu Kush mountain range for all the muffled sound he could barely make out. His head was still in his brain bucket and attached to his body. He knew this for the simple fact that it would have to be, in order to hear anything. The sun in his eyes was as it always was. Blinding. Blinding and hotter than anyone should ever have to feel.

"Moose! My leg! Find my leg! Moose. Please. Find my leg."

Suddenly the sound returned like it did back home when he would hit a spot on a back road and reception was lost, found, lost again. He and Ash would keep singing even if Cash or Springsteen could only stutter a word or two between signals. Now it came roaring back, all the missed lyrics at once. Full of pain.

"Moose! My goddam leg!"

He looked across his shoulder, head just far enough off the ground to do so but not high enough to have it blown off his neck.

He could see the leg. It wasn't close. It wasn't close to him and it wasn't close to Hemi.

Moose looked up as if just willing a bird to appear could make it happen. He thought about home, his parents, his dogs and though he tried not to, he thought about Ashley. He had to get home to her. Moose was twenty-two and Ashley, eighteen when they married. They celebrated their tenth anniversary by sat phone a week after he arrived in country. He had promised her that when he got back they would fix up the house his grandfather built after World War II and they would raise their kids there. "Yes, of course we are havin' kids! Make an appointment. See what the doc says. I'm serious. We are gonna make this happen!" Ashley wanted a swimming pool and Moose promised she would have it, just as soon as he got back from this deployment, his third. More than a pool, she wanted kids but they hadn't come as easily as one expects.

"Third time's a charm, Ash. Nobody is gonna keep me from our dream."

"Moose. My leg."

This time, the sound was fading, desperate, tentative in the way someone might mumble their way through pizza toppings while scanning a menu that's a little too far away on the wall behind the cashier. It was too non-committal and it scared Moose. It was the sound of someone who didn't have a lot of time. Without another thought, he crawled, all belly and elbows in full battle rattle on the baked earth toward Hemi. He knew the grunt from podunk Massachusetts wouldn't have much use for what was left of his leg but if he could get to Hemi, keeping his M27 off the sand, and get a tourniquet on him, he might make it, send the brother home to his girlfriend. The kid turned twenty not even a full week before.

All the movies Moose watched as a kid, the ones that made him want to join the Marines just as soon as he turned eighteen, seemed so oddly comforting right then as though this was a script and though it sucked, soon they'd demob and he'd be going home.

Behind him, another IED tore into the convoy and all the chaos started again. The concussion, loss of hearing, heart exploding in his throat, twisted metal and flesh. He knew it was now or it wasn't going to happen. He had sensed the moment he shipped out of Pendelton three months ago things would be different this time around. The Taliban had gained far too much ground, the US had gotten tired of this never-ending war and he was twelve years older than he was when he first kindled the generational military fire in his one hundred percent red-blooded American heart. He wondered before he had boots on the ground if the third time wasn't the charm after all but taunting fate. Either way, here he was, a 1st Sergeant under heavy fire in Mosul a few yards from this kid who now was going home, at best, with one leg and it was his responsibility. The Hollywood movies were great but the real deal was many hundred shades darker and a lot of what he knew was to come would be unscripted and far more complicated if he didn't move. Now.

"You're okay, Hem. I got ya. You have to listen to me. I'm gonna get us on a bird as soon as I can. You just keep breathin'. He cranked the tourniquet again and knew the color coming back into Hemi's face was a good sign even if the screams belied the progress. "Moose, you're killing me, man. Stop. Let me die. Let me die. Just stop the pain." Moose ignored his pleas. "You and me are gonna get our girls togetha when we get home. The four of us, we'll go canoeing down the Kennebec all summer, fishin' and drinkin'. In fact, we'll do it every summer. And when we have kids, they'll be friends and we will take a trip every year. Got it? You just gotta get home first."

Moose bent down, sweat running off his brow onto Hemi's face. "Ya hear that?! Do ya? That's our ticket out, Brotha!"

He knew Hemi didn't really comprehend what he was saying. He was too far away, over the mountains, under water. He moved himself out of Hemi's way so he could see the Blackhawk.

"Ain't that bitch the most beautiful thing ya evah seen?"

He leaned back over Hemi to shield him from the blowing sand and brutal sun. "That's our bird. Dennis. That's our ticket out."

He stopped, aware he used the Marine's first name. It wasn't a bad thing but it certainly made everything more real.

Hemi was a grunt, Dennis was somebody's son, brother, uncle, boyfriend.

"I hope so, Moose." Hemi smiled, eyes just pale blue slits on his sunburnt face.

"Yea, Brotha. Me, too."

1

"They will never believe you anyway. I'm his real daughter, I mean, let's be real. He felt bad for you and that's why you're here. Doesn't that embarrass you? Even a little bit?"

Grace was every bit as dramatic as she was when she first showed up in Bar Harbor nine years before. Entitled, angry, manipulative and unapologetically demanding compensation for her woes, Grace was anything but. She was more tempest than tide, her name a prayer whispered in vain.

She walked to the bedroom door and closed it quietly. Turning back with her finger pointing directly at Hope, she walked slowly and deliberately, avoiding the floorboard that squeaks. "But you're not going to say a word in the first place. I know I'm right about that." Hope looked past her, ignoring the cloying perfume and obnoxious squirrel tail lash extensions, to the gently swaying arms of the weeping willow in the center of the pasture.

"You'll never get into it," Hope said without emotion or even inflection. This wasn't her first rodeo with Grace Cranston but by the conversation she'd overheard earlier, she was pretty sure it'd be the last.

"Oh, yes, I will. You don't know me and you don't have any idea where I've been or what I learned there."

Hope tried not to laugh. She knew exactly where Grace had been during her late teen and early adult years but didn't think it was something to brag about.

Grace stepped in Hope's line of sight, forcing her to look in her eyes. Grace would not be ignored.

"Listen. Very. Closely," she demanded. Her breath reeked of garlic and breath mints. "Go out to the store, grab Rebecca's phone and open her Notes app. It's there. I've seen it. Take a screenshot, send it to me and then delete the message. Got it, Hope*less*? Do *not* forget to delete the message. Now go! You've got ten minutes and if I don't get the text by then, I'm telling them about your Only Fans account."

Hope looked to the side, stunned. "What? I don't have an account." Grace's head tilted backward like a Pez dispenser but instead of sweet candy, all that came out of her mouth was vitriol. "Yes, you do, Sweetheart. I've been making bank with your pics. You'd be shocked at how many men love watching a girl on a horse or sleeping in pink pajamas. You're a freaking goldmine."

Hope wondered if she was bluffing but based on the last three years, it was best not to undermine her stepsister.

As if Grace could read her mind, she swiped her phone open, her long, pointy acrylics tapping the screen like morse code. The light from her phone spun around to face Hope and there it was. Proof.

"Get your skinny ass out to the store, get me those digits and do not get caught and I will delete the account when Grayson and I are on our flight back home in a few weeks. Don't fuck up, ye of little, little Hope."

2

Eli stood, unaware of both the drama unfolding at home and the fact that shoots can emerge from a wisteria chopped to the ground, grow rapidly from a deep taproot, its insidious nature sneaking under clapboard and shingle, breaching the tiniest spots to run rampant in all the places you never wanted it. He rested the loppers on his shoulder. "Wow, that looks so bare. I don't know why the realtor insisted it be taken out but it's out now," he said to the ocean breeze that might have known more than he about what was to come. He dragged the twisted vines and splintered branches to the pile of refuse to be picked up. Last chore. I can't believe this is it, he thought. "We'll go soon, Pep, I promise." Eli wasn't sure bringing the old dog back to the only home he had ever known was confusing or comforting but he seemed to be okay as long as Eli wasn't too far away. Settling in at Eli and Rebecca's didn't take long, so Eli hoped bringing him down to Camden on the handful of times he needed to prep the house for sale, seemed like the right thing to do.

The wind picked up, making his ears numb as he walked across the patio and in through the French doors to Otto's study, cavernous, spotless. Trying not to think about the hundreds of books that once lined the shelves that would soon hit the auction block, historical society and, sadly, thrift stores. Eli didn't linger there. He had made peace with these changes throughout the previous months.

In the meticulously appointed kitchen, the legal-size folder seemed completely out of place and yet Eli held it with one hand and methodically tapped it on his opposite palm. He realized he hadn't touched many of these in the last twelve years but his mind and hands instantly collaborated on how he should handle it. Muscle memory.

When he became conscious of that, he gently placed it on the marble countertop briefly and smoothed the surface with both hands before tucking it under his arm. In doing so, Eli Cranston closed a chapter of his life, again. *So many chapters,* he thought.

Otto and Elise had acquired an estate the size that Eli's firm would have been more than happy to handle back in Los Angeles. The Gunthers were meticulous with their wishes and detailed every aspect of how their assets would be dispersed and settled. Otto had entrusted Eli as executor of the will not just due to his legal background but because he was the adoptive father of Otto's great granddaughter. "Gott's plan," Otto had told him. "It's all God's plan."

Eli closed his eyes and nodded in agreement. He could see it now, clearly; with that came closure, not just for him but for so many people around the world who loved and admired their journey. From Ravensbrück to America, and into the annals of both medicine and psychiatry. Who better to heal others than those who have suffered so greatly?

Peppercorn stood up on his frail hind legs and planted his furry toes on Eli's shins as if to say, "It's just us now, isn't it?" Eli reached down and very gently stroked the top of the old dog's head, noting how little there was between his hand and his old friend's skull. He had only been a few years old when Eli first visited Dr. Gunther. Once very spry and springy, able to hop onto Eli's lap without a second thought, Peppy as Eli nicknamed him, now creaked like old floorboards when he moved.

Scooping him up off the floor, Eli held him close and could feel his tiny heart beating with love and excitement. Eli closed his eyes and recognized the sadness, too. His therapy practice had taken on a completely new branch since Hope moved to the farm with Rebecca and him. Eli, who had never had any pets growing up, was absolutely stunned at the healing power animals have on the human heart and psyche. In fact, only one thing struck him more and that was the fact that animals asked absolutely nothing in return.

The phone on the wall screamed in the silence, making Eli jump comically, Peppercorn ducking his shiny nose under Eli's chin.

Walking toward the phone, Eli slowed, deciding to let it go since there was still an old answering machine attached and he would be able to hear his old friend's voice.

"Hello and thank you for calling the Gunther home. We can't take your call right now but please listen carefully and choose the option that suits your needs. Press one to reach the family mailbox, press two to reach Dr. Elise Gunther, and press three to reach Dr. Otto Gunther. If this is a medical or psychiatric emergency, please hang up and dial 9-1-1."

His eyes closed, Eli imagined Otto there in the kitchen with him, offering him banana bread and coffee. When he opened his eyes it was like he was standing in the kitchen for the first time. Everything was so clean and bright, and though there was nothing in the coffee pot, he could smell it. He could smell the special coffee that Otto bought at every German open-air market in New England at Christmastime. Being a Jew made no difference to Otto. He loved the season and he loved what it stood for.

Hope.

Beep.

"Hello, this message is for Doctor Otto Gunther. This is Kiersten at Camden Town Hall with a question about your tax bill. When you get a moment, please give us a call. Thank you."

The water rimming Eli's eyes was a surprise to him. Otto had been gone for almost a month, but Eli hadn't allowed himself the time or the space to grieve. He sighed deeply, emptying his lungs and thought how amazing it is that a man can die shortly after his wife, clearly from a broken heart and Town

Hall still wants his tax money.

Eli and Peppercorn made it out to the truck and with one last look, Eli recalled the first time he had walked up this brick pathway to the door, nervous, excited, and with disbelief that he was about to sit with the man he had idealized throughout graduate school and the start of his own practice. Now a decade later, Otto was like a father to Eli. The wisdom and compassion and love for humanity was unequaled in Eli's eyes. For a young boy to suffer the pain and deep, desperate sadness of losing his entire family and while being about a day and a half from losing his own life, young Otto had allowed the love of Elise and her mother to heal him first physically and then emotionally and many years later, spiritually. Eli often thought, *What if every person who survived the Holocaust let hatred and revenge fill their heart and seal the fate of their future? How many fewer doctors, therapists, and leaders would there be in the world?*

The sun reached through the windshield, warming Eli's hands, and as he scanned the landscape, something caught his eye high up in the lookout tower, the most beautiful place he could think of at the moment. It was the small room above Otto's office. Eli had been invited up there on several occasions, the last of which was when Otto was mourning Elise's death. Eli had come to console the man who had helped thousands of people work through the worst tragedies of their lives throughout his career. He distinctly remembered what he had been wearing that day, and what Otto was wearing, the smell in the room and how it meant what it meant. Eli had peered into the bed which he and Otto's son Nathan hauled up the steep stairway. Hope and Clem had helped get Otto settled with his books, tea and blankets, medication on the bedside table. In the bed lay the diminutive version of the man Eli had come to know. Otto peered out over Penobscot Bay, his eyes as watery as the gentle waves that tickled the craggy shore. Even as Otto continued into his elderly years, Eli never really saw him as old even on that day. What he really saw, though, was the little boy. The little boy who had comforted his sister, Hannah, in the wardrobe back in the German ghetto when the Nazis were hunting people. He saw the little boy who had reached up and touched the fur coat belonging to his mother, in an effort to comfort himself so that he could do the same for his little sister. Eli saw the little boy who listened to his mother call to her young husband when their street had become a river of blood and shattered glass. It was the boy who had been separated from Hannah and his mother at the camp, the boy, who did not know that his family was dead when still he saw Hannah and heard her voice tell him, "You have to find hope. You have to find Hope."

Eli saw the little boy who had survived dysentery, cholera, and starvation to become one of the most respected members of the American Psychiatric Association. Eli realized then that you only have a short time to decide how you will use the gift that is your life. He knew that his words could never capture the essence of his experience of this man, this mentor, who changed his life when Eli needed his life to change.

Now sitting in the truck, his eyes on the windows of the lookout tower, he could see the outline of a hand on one of the small panes of glass. His rational mind, his analytical mind, his lawyer mind, his psychotherapist mind all disagreed on what it could be. Eli often formulated two beliefs at once, one he could tell others that would make sense and one he believed deep in his heart.

He imagined reaching all the way up to the turret and placing his hand on the near side of the glass. Through so many lucid moments and epiphanies he had experienced in the last ten years, he trusted that Otto was there, assuring Eli he was only a blink away, just on the other side of the krystal. "You have healed my heart, young man. I never would have imagined that you or anyone could have taken the shards of my past, finding the missing tessera, and help me finish the mosaic that was my life on earth. Tausend dank."

Back in his truck, he placed the folder, full of good intentions, in the passenger's seat.

Shifting into reverse, he backed out of the driveway and

onto the street, a sigh escaping his heavy heart. Eli held the tiny dog on his lap for safety and comfort. He told him, "Let's go home, Pep. Home is where you feel loved and protected and I promise you that's where you are headed."

As Eli rolled down the street toward the highway, that ocean breeze whipped a wisteria branch from the clutches of the pile and sent it scrambling like a rogue tumbleweed toward the icy blue bay.

3

Piper moved through the bookstore the way one moves through a museum of their favorite sort. Her fingers trailed the spines of books that had been printed over a century ago as her eyes fell on current bestsellers. She'd been to Shakespeare's Bookstore in the 5th district a few times on her trips to Paris over the years but she preferred the older, more out of the way shops that felt more like home to her. On this particular evening, this small shop was quiet with just one other patron who was dressed for the bitter cold and seemingly in their own world. The shop owner sat behind the counter, scrolling on her phone while talking with a teen who was also scrolling on his phone.

Piper saw this as a sign of the times and felt ever more grateful these shops were not just still open but appreciated by lovers of the written word, even if on this evening it was just a small handful of people, half of whom preferred the digital version.

As she rounded the narrow aisle to start down the adjacent one, a book jacket caught her eye. She stood, for a moment feeling the pull of her mind wanting her to pay attention to another time, perhaps a memory or something else. She took in a deep breath and held it for a moment before audibly exhaling. *Not now,* she thought. Learning to center herself and stay in the moment was still a bit of work for her but now she felt it was due to getting older and not so much reliving a past life.

This life was full enough and she did not want to go backward.

She crossed her arms and bent slightly forward to look more closely at the book.

Victorious by Default
Reclaiming Your Self in Difficult Times
By Eli Cranston, J.D. Ph.D.

Piper took a picture with her phone and sent it to John, who was home holding down the farm and everything that Piper needed to get back to soon. She turned the book over and scanned the back, noticing that Eli's headshot revealed more gray than the last time she and John had visited. When she looked back at her phone, John's reply was short but excited, "Finally! We will have to pay him a visit."

When the bell over the door rang, Piper looked up and noticed the clock over the counter. *An hour! How have I been here that long?* Instantly feeling the need to hurry, another feeling that upset her to some degree, she took the book to the front counter to make her purchase. The woman looked up but seemed to look beyond Piper or through her. Piper was caught off guard and slowly looked over her shoulder to be sure there was nothing to be concerned about then felt a little embarrassed as the woman laughed and shook her head, apologizing but keeping her eyes on the man behind Piper.

Before leaving, Piper turned to look at the man who had come through the door just moments before. Red cheeks and running nose, pale complexion, coughing into a tissue. The man turned to the shop owner with pleading eyes. The woman looked surprised, hand rising to her throat. "Why does he come here! Why doesn't someone take him away so he doesn't come here!"

Then from the man, "I love you, Lena. My heart will always love yours."

Not knowing what to do, Piper slipped out of the shop and onto the street, the cold air quickly filling her nose and waking her up as only the cold can do. She looked down at her phone and back into the shop through the glass in the door, her breath fogging it slightly. She knew they didn't say those words out loud. For the first time in a long time, Piper questioned why her brain worked the way it did. Was it her brain? Was it her intuition? Was it something else entirely and if so, what was it? Peering back into the shop again she saw the man looking at a magazine and blowing his nose. The woman at the counter was scrolling on her phone again. She didn't seem bothered by the man one bit.

Piper hurried across Rue de Rosnard toward her hotel. Her flight was just fourteen hours away. She stood under the streetlight, catching her breath and looking at her phone for comfort, familiarity. *Maman, you are home! You are home!* Piper shook the memory free, to go back to the century in which it belonged. She sighed and pulled her coat around her.

In her mind's eye she was on the shore, the dunes drenched in the setting sunlight, the fog retreating. The silhouette of a young child waving to her. "Manan! Look who's here!"

Breaking into a frantic sprint toward the hotel, she knew she would feel better once she was on her way home, to this lifetime, to her grounded world with John, the farm, her clients, and bland coffee. She wondered why she had even come back to France. *You can't go back. Why do you try so hard to go back?*

4

Piper left the airport in her dented and sun-bleached work truck with a sense of familiarity and anticipation. Home is where the farm is, where John is waiting. Trying to put the week behind her and resolving to never go back to Paris again in an effort to connect with her past felt like the right thing to do.

There are wounds left by love that are just as deep and pain-filled as those left by hate and discord.

This single line from Eil's book jumped from the page to her tired eyes midway through her flight and she felt it was best to leave the rest to read at home. She felt those words described something she hadn't been able to express in all these years since Paul's death; since discovering that her entire childhood had been a coverup the mob would be impressed by, and then tracing every detail back through time to her former life in Provence and Paris; and not to mention marrying John, the once young child of the priest turned hypnotherapist who treated her as a child when her parents were terrified of the memories that bled through the decades to remind her that love never dies.

So much therapy, so many experiences, so many words written and burned. And there, on the page of her husband's friend's book, the words sat plain as day for her to find in Paris and lay her eyes on at thirty thousand feet over the Atlantic.

She changed the channel on the radio as she turned onto the pike and headed west toward the far reaches of Massachusetts. Her phone lit up with several texts and a voicemail as time caught up with her phone and for a split second she wished she could text back to the 19th century to tell Vander she needed to say good-bye one final time, that this was it. No more. No more going backwards in life, that she would block him if need be. The very thought brought tears because she knew the love they had could never be replicated. Not with Paul, and not with John even though she loved them each deeply.

Soon after she had married John, she had a session with a hypnotherapist John had known for many years, and who had her, in meditation, walking the shore backward, trying to place her feet exactly in the footsteps she had made moments before while walking forward. He implored her to see that no matter how hard she tried, she cannot walk with the same stride or ease backward as she can forward; and though she thinks she remembers her past as clearly as the edges of her footprints appear, if she looked more closely, she'd see that by walking into the past, she was not hitting the mark as perfectly as she had assumed. Her new footprints were toe to heel, not heel to toe; they didn't fit with exact precision. "This is why we need to keep moving forward," he told her. "It's actually easier to move forward but the tug of the familiarity of the past is a tough addiction."

Exit 51 glowed in her headlights and she took a breath, inhaling the future and exhaling the past. She had avoided the voicemail until now with all the tenacity of a horse avoiding being caught in the field for the farrier. Any other time, he'll gladly gallop to the gate. Somewhere, tucked away, she still had the small flip phone with the voicemail from Paul all those years ago that she could not listen to after his death. She refused to listen to it when he was alive because she knew she screwed up his big evening and was rushing from Feeding Hills to New York to get labels for the bottles the very day of the grand opening of Paul's winery. In her haste, she had ordered the wrong labels. She'd intended to order the self-stick type but had, in fact, ordered labels with no adhesive. Her previous blunder, the cocktail napkins that read Black Whores Farm instead of Black

Horse Farm had shown itself with plenty of time to correct, but the labels arrived the day before the grand opening of Paul's Winery. He was desperately trying to reach her, not knowing where she'd disappeared to. When she finally got back to the farm, he was so angry. She remembered showing him the labels and discovering they weren't self-sticking like she thought. In an effort to salvage the plans that had taken years to build, Paul drove off to find the right glue and then ....

She shook her head, wondering why all of this was flooding her now. This was all in the past. She was healed or so she was convinced. "Just rip the bandage off," she told herself aloud in the darkness of route 57 at nearly midnight. She hit the tiny arrow on the voicemail and held her breath. John's voice calmed her immediately.

"Piper, just spoke to Eli about his book. He wants to speak to you about some family stuff going on. He wants to know if you can take on an apprentice at the farm. Things have been difficult with Grace. I'll explain more later but Eli wants to find a place Hope can be free to grow.

5

Rebecca looked at Eli across the kitchen table like so many times in the past two years, wanting to speak her mind about Grace's behavior while not wanting to upset Eli. He had done so much for her, Hope, Clem, Otto, and Elise. It was his time now and he should be enjoying the rewards of all his earnest work and finally publishing his book. She wanted to say something, but it seemed her mouth knew something her heart didn't.

Eli pushed a carrot around his plate like a bully, finally stabbing it. He looked up at Rebecca then down again. Gently, placing the fork on the side of his plate was like pressing the on button, the lets-get-this-over-with button.

"What's on your mind, Becca?" Eli sat back and defensively crossed his arms over his chest, checked himself and put them back on the table.

A sigh escaped Rebecca. She never knew the right way to tell Eli that his daughter was self-destructing and that she, Hope, and Eli were collateral damage. *Doesn't he see this?* she often wondered.

"It's just," she stopped. "It's Grace. I mean, it's more than that, Eli, but it starts with her. I know you see it. She's getting worse. It's like she's regressing. She's like a ..." she stopped again, choosing words carefully for the man she loved who was just as hurt by what had happened to Grace as Grace herself was. "She's like one of your clients who needs more than—" Eli cut her off defensively, angrily, "She needs more than what?

More than I can give her? Don't you think I know this? Don't you think I have known this all along?" He could feel his blood pressure rising, his face hot, his body agitated. He closed his eyes and drew a deep breath. He realized he wasn't being fair. Rebecca had endured a lot at the hands of Grace, all while trying to protect Hope and give her what she needed for the first time in the child's life. *But neither girl was a child any longer.*

Rebecca never connected the same way with Grace, who was pregnant when she showed up in their lives. She and Eli were just starting out, a second chance at love for both of them.

"I'm sorry, " Eli looked in her eyes when he said it. She bit her bottom lip the way she did when she was nervous or scared.

"I really don't know what to do about her. She can't be on her own, Rebecca. I know you think she can but for Grayson's sake," he stopped.

Rebecca got up and began clearing the table. It was clear she did not agree with Eli.

"She's thirty-two, Eli. She is acting like an entitled seventeen-year-old. I mean, Hope is more responsible, hard-working, and appreciative and she's been Grace's punching bag for a long time. It just isn't fair."

Eli didn't want to argue. They'd gone too many rounds in the ring on this and sometimes he wished she'd just knock him out finally. It was exhausting, this dance. He held such guilt for what happened to Grace when she was a teen and such hurt from what Antigone had done as a result. In the years since, he could understand that Antigone left him from the heartbreak over Grace but he would never understand or forgive her for leaving him for his brother ,Jay. He completely overhauled his entire life to have what he knew he deserved and wanted for so long. *Sins of the father,* he thought. But he hadn't been in the wrong, not even back then. There were forces at play he had no control over. Countless nights he lay awake replaying that phone call so long ago, not knowing how it would shape his child's life in the years to come. He simply turned down a case he knew he could not win for a doctor who was clearly guilty of a crime and thought that money could solve his problem.

That one phone call resulted in Grace not having a fair trial and being incarcerated during her critical young adult years. She was angry and she wanted Eli to pay and pay handsomely, at that. Eli realized some time ago that he was willing to pay even though he would never have given that advice to his clients who carried the shackles of self-inflicted punishment like the flagellants of plague times. How was Eli to know that the phone call from a doctor who assaulted a patient as she was climbing back to consciousness in the recovery room after surgery would become the father of Eli's not yet born daughter's best friend. And even if he thought he could win the case, his father and Jay would have rejected the idea out of hand. End of story.

"You're right, Becca. It isn't fair. Hope doesn't deserve the way Grace treats her. I've tried hard to mediate between them. I've sat with them both countless times. You know this. But Grace is an adult." Eli stopped, realizing he was proving Rebecca's point. She looked at him as she put dishes into the sink.

He stood up from the table, straightened his glasses nervously, and pushed his chair in.

"I'll talk to Grace."

Eli watched as Rebecca flinched for a moment before continuing to clean the kitchen. He knew the script. He knew what she was thinking, how she was feeling, and what she wanted to say but refrained. Eli knew her heart and he knew when it was breaking. He felt stuck and unable to fix this for her, for Hope.

Rebecca did not turn in Eli's direction but instead looked out the window to the darkening landscape. "Hope is my only child. Not by birth, true. But I love her just as much as you love Grace. I won't," she stopped. Not wanting to say something she couldn't take back, she angrily flicked a tear off her cheek.

When she turned back, Eli was gone.

6

Piper sat in her loft office for the first time in almost a year; nor had she facilitated a group there in well over two years. It had once been Paul's office when they built the barn so long ago, the winery taking shape, all their dreams coming to fruition, or so they thought.

She looked at the chairs lining the perimeter and imagined all the people who had sat there over the years. Some came out of curiosity, some in need of comfort, and some to truly learn how their intuition was working in their own life and more importantly, how to hone it and use it as the tool it was meant to be. Reflecting on the tears, grieving, and healing that happened here, she wondered if it was time to begin again. There were texts, calls, emails, and interesting, seemingly random requests from people over the last couple of years and recently it had become harder to ignore them. There seemed to be a need again and some of the group members would not take no for an answer.

"Blame it on Covid," she said to the dust on her desk as she swiped at it with her fingers. She and John had adjusted to the lockdown well since they both already worked from home. No matter what is happening, people need therapy and horse people need horses. Letting go of something she had built as a way to share with others what had gotten her through her darkest days, though, was a bit of a sting. The intuition development group had begun haphazardly and not with conscious intention. In fact, she didn't have a name for it at the outset. It wasn't until a couple of years in that she read a description of a development group and realized that was what her group was.

Typically, people came for the horses either for themselves or to bring a loved one for therapeutic riding; through Piper's sessions, they gained much insight about themselves, their energy, and how it is perceived by a horse, which made them want to learn more. How did Piper know what she knows and how do horses heal the way they do?

Sitting in one of the folding chairs, feeling the cold metal through her jeans, she shivered.

She could hear the laughter and exclamations from the group and the resounding, "You can't make this stuff up!"

We never did make those t-shirts, she thought.

She breathed in the present and exhaled the past. A scuffling sound across the office caught her attention. She looked to see a field mouse, plump and scared in the corner. She took a box down from the bookcase that lined one entire wall and approached the intruder. "You're lucky the cats are sleeping."

She scooped the trembling little creature into the box and walked down the steps to the main barn and out to the chilly late winter night. She let the mouse go at the edge of the paddock and watched it run zig zag into the night.

She closed the sliding barn door and checked it, twice, as barn owners always do and walked toward the house. She could see John through the kitchen window and for just a moment wished it was Paul. It wasn't the first time but it was the first time she did not admonish herself. "Be curious," is something she told her group time and again.

"Don't think you know what you know because you're so smart. Sometimes you're receiving guidance." Lately she had decided to be curious about her own brain and how it seemed to be pulling her in different directions and wanting to go back to places and times she thought she had healed from.

She stood looking at the window. "Paul," she said to the night air, "why now?"

"Piper?"

She jumped, her hand flying to her chest in utter shock before she realized it was John.

"Jesus!"

"Haha. No, just John," he said from the edge of the driveway. "What are you doing?"

She was doubled over laughing so hard John wondered if she had taken a gummy. She hadn't used them in months to his knowledge.

"Nothing. You just scared me." She stood up straight and tried to compose herself.

"Okay, well, dinner's ready, weirdo," he tried to keep a straight face but she could hear by his voice he wasn't doing a very good job. He turned back to the house and Piper's heart leapt in her chest.

"Paul. Why is all of this coming up now? What do I need to know?" Piper waited a moment and let the energy around her settle. She learned enough since Paul's passing to know that what is meant to come to her, will and that even if she didn't understand it in the moment, she would when the time was right.

7

Hope was in the tack room, cleaning a bridle, quietly, meticulously, like she had for years at Eli's first property where Clem and Annie now lived as caretakers in return for a place to enjoy in retirement. It was a small reward for all the hard work and friendship Clem had extended to Eli when he arrived on the East Coast looking for a new beginning in life. A place to call home without the weight of the past around his neck is what he found on Mount Desert Isle, as far as possible from the firestorm that was Los Angeles and life as a defense attorney in a family of cutthroat opportunists. Clem, the confidant and friend disguised as the local handyman, became one of several way-makers during Eli's transition from the frenetic chaos he had left behind and the dream life that now seemed to be fading.

Eli stood in the doorway for a moment, a lump in his throat. Hope had been so tiny when she used to come to his house on Ogden Point Road across town. Eight years isn't a very long time, but to a nineteen-year-old it's almost half their existence. He was so proud of the young woman she'd become, almost as tall as him and with twice the character and integrity. It wasn't lost on him that his own flesh and blood was the antithesis. Before he could clear his throat she turned and stopped.

"What are you doing?" She laughed and looked at him like he was as out of place as a fisherman in a Sephora.

"Just wanted to say hi," he knew that wasn't going to land well.

She shook her head, eyes wide. "Eli, stop being so sus."

At this, Eli rolled his eyes. She had upped her sense of humor, sarcasm, and wit over the time she had lived with him. Traces of little Hope would always be there but this was no fragile, helpless, lost girl anymore. Hope had begun training horses, technically, when he met her at age eleven when she left a yellow sticky note on his door asking more than once if Eli needed help with his ponies. Boy, did he. He just didn't know it. At age sixteen she had taught herself to back the trailer and practiced taking Pirate all over the farm, then eventually trailering to other farms for shows and to haul other horses for people who needed it.

"I'm no such thing. I just wanted to talk to you. Is that a crime now?"

Hope raised one brow and tilted her head. "Okay?"

Eli swung his leg over a saddle on the wooden stand and looked around. Neat as a pin, just like at Ogden Point.

"Listen, Hope," he started but knew it was going to sound like a we-need-to-talk moment which never goes well with kids, wives, or colleagues.

Hope tossed the small round sponge into the bucket of water and placed the glycerin bar back on the shelf next to the sink and put the bridle back on the rack. She turned toward Eli, hands on hips, and waited. When Eli didn't speak immediately, she reached for the milk crate of unraveled, dirty polo wraps and began methodically picking bits of pine shavings off them, waiting.

"I want to apologize for Grace's behavior."

The statement hung in the tack room like a neon pink halter. Silly, unnecessary, and cheesy.

"Eli," she started.

"No. Hope, I mean it. I don't know what to do or how to make it better. Grace was wrong and what she's done is hurtful. I see it and I know you do, too. I have tried very hard to be a good father to both of you," his voice betrayed him, cracking, faltering. He cleared his throat and straightened his posture.

"Eli," Hope said again. "Stop. I don't even care anymore. She hates me. I know that. I'm fine with it. I don't need her. I never did. I mean, I thought it would be cool to have a sister but if that's what a sister is, I'll be fine as the only child I started out as."

"Ouch. That's hard to hear." Eli stood up and swung his leg back over the saddle.

"Sorry, but it's true. I mean she hates me, she hates Rebecca, she hates everyone except you. She wants you all to herself."

This wasn't the first time Eli had heard this theory. He paused, wondering if Rebecca shared this idea with Hope. It didn't really matter because it did appear to be the case. He just didn't know what to do about it. How was it that he could help hundreds of people heal their lives and relationships but not his own? An age-old question for healers of all kinds, he knew. *It's all part of the journey.*

"I'm leaving, Eli."

Eli's head spun. He stepped closer to Hope, his heart racing, panic trying to fill his throat.

"What? Leave? What are you talking about?"

Pirate called from his stall, breaking the tension and giving Hope an excuse to step out of the small room and into the much wider aisle of the barn. She could have run. *Run far and fast* she could hear in her mind and wanted to but where could she go? She slid into Pirate's stall, sliding the door closed behind her. She bent down and checked all four hooves for packed ice but knew they would have melted by now.

Eli waited patiently. He walked to the hay bales under the small white board in the grain room and cut open two bales. He took an armload and began tossing a couple of flakes into the first few stalls where the always hungry Ink, Smudge, and Cayenne were impatiently waiting. He went back and got more for Pirate. He slid the door open to Pirate's muzzle coming at the hay, ears back far enough to make Eli a little nervous. He wouldn't do that to Hope but then, he respected her.

"Hope? Where did you go?"

He stood with the defiant bay tearing mouthfuls of hay off his shoulder.

Eli sighed and let the still green, fragrant alfalfa fall to the pine shavings at the horse's hooves. An offering of sorts. Pirate was Hope's everything. Eli reached into his pocket, and pulled out a butterscotch from the farm store. Pirate's demeanor changed at the first crinkle of plastic wrap. Ears forward, a soft nicker. "You're a little bit obnoxious," Eli whispered to him. He got the plastic off the shiny, golden candy just as the velvet muzzle nudged his hand, stealing the treat without so much as a thank you.

Above his head, Eli could hear the soft muffled sounds of Hope crying in the loft.

Eli closed his eyes. *The more things change, the more they stay the same.*

8

Reminisce, Heavenly, Aura, Beckon.

Who comes up with these names? Piper took the box of paint cans and brushes up to her office. *What else is there to do on a cold and rainy January day in New England?* John had prepped for her by clearing out the chairs and wiping the cobwebs and dust. "Looks like you should be all set," he turned when she got to the top of the steps.

Piper looked around, remembering when John had initially brought the chairs home from a yard sale for her, encouraging her to use this bright, airy space with the beautiful light and large window overlooking the main pasture. Resistant. She remembers John asking her why she was resistant. Still learning to take a breath before speaking, responding rather than reacting, she merely smiled and thanked him for the chairs. The walls were white and the floors still plywood but it worked. The people who came to the development group looked forward to their time there with Piper and each other. She'd always thought it would look cozier painted a soft green or perhaps a deep purple but it hadn't happened.

"Today's the day," she said. "I'm really going to start again. Just like that."

John stood in the center of the room, scanning for any spots that had escaped his corn broom. "Just like that," he nodded. "Are you nervous?"

Piper unfolded the large drop cloths and pulled her graying hair into a slightly thinner ponytail than she was used to.

She looked at John, the man who had saved her life on many levels and felt immense gratitude for him and for his patience, of which she often still lacked. "Not nervous, John. I think. I think I'm. I think I'm just wondering why this is coming back around. I mean, it's been years. Do I really want to commit to having people here and spending time nurturing beginners all over again?" She knew the answer and she knew John did, too.

"Life's work," she said.

John nodded and pursed his lips. He knew she was questioning so many parts of herself lately and felt this was a way to connect all the dots, to make peace with where she was in life. And, more importantly, where she had been.

Piper poured the first color, Reminisce, into the paint tray and watched the amethyst wave expand slowly, giving the plastic an extravagant, almost royal makeover.

John stood at the top of the loft stairs watching his wife and remembering the first time they had met as children at his parents' home.

Jacks and rubber balls.

He could feel the jacks in his hand then and he recalled the severity of Piper's mother's gaze on him as Piper sat expressionless, completely still until John handed her the tiny metal pieces. She smiled at him, tentatively. Watching him bounce the ball up and down, up and down. Piper thought he must play this game every day. John grabbed the ball just before it touched the floor, never taking his eyes off her. When it was her turn, her cheeks flushed pink, the pressure to pick up the jacks while the ball was in the air and then to catch the ball, too, just seemed too great.

Vander was there though and even if her parents wanted to banish him by bringing her here to this hypnotherapist, she knew he would never leave her.

What John never told her, not then and not fifty years hence, was that he saw Vander, too.

9

Grace tossed her phone on the couch next to her and locked her gaze on Eli. He stood in front of her, calmly and as patiently as he could.

"Can you explain to me what happened with Hope? What did you say to upset her, to make her want to leave?"

Grace Cranston was a complicated woman, much like the patients Eli served.

Her eyes lit up and seemed to grow in size upon hearing Hope wanted out. Finally.

She felt a fire ignite in her chest like a match scraping a strikebox. This was what she fed on for the ten years she was in Chowchilla. The drama, the pecking order, and the survival tactics in the society of baddies, this was life for Grace.

The corner of her mouth tugged downward as her brows lifted. Eli could see the slightest hint of the little girl she once was, so gentle and kind, wanting his approval, attention, and time.

Rebecca was right, though, Eli needed to observe her without bias, not through the lens that showed his little girl but unfiltered and raw as the destructive force she had become.

"I told her the truth. That's all. Isn't that what we all want, Dad? I mean, how long did Mom keep the truth from you? How long did you keep the truth about Dr. Willaston, and how he needed your help, to yourself, and then pretending you didn't know why I wound up in prison?" Her high-pitched laugh was more than Eli could bear.

Eli recoiled. Grace was adept at slicing to the bone or warming the heart, whichever would get her what she wanted. She could also do both at once, a skill that Eli saw with border-line patients and narcissists.

"We are not talking about that right now, Grace. We are talking about what you said to hurt your sister."

"Not my sister. I don't have a sister. You know this," Grace said, eyes never leaving Eli's.

"You know, Dad, this mess you created is your karma. It has nothing to do with me."

She took her phone, slowly scrolled, got off the couch, and walked past Eli like a ghost.

He stood, still looking at the couch where the impression her body made was still visible. How could he argue with what she said? She was one hundred percent correct.

The door slamming upstairs was the punctuation to the heavy footfalls on the steps leading to the second floor of the farmhouse. Grayson yelled at his mother, "No, I'm playing my game. Stop!" The music from the video game gave way to cry-ing. Eli walked to the kitchen sink, peering out to the frozen field. He wished he could burrow like the groundhogs, fox, and rabbits deep into the ground, until better times.

10

The pale amethyst walls and crisp white bookshelves looked far better than the primed drywall ever did and yet Piper was still stunned by what the light could do to any color. The early afternoon winter glow ignited the pale purple hue into a Caribbean sunset, impossibly beautiful. The floors were scheduled to be installed in just two days, and her group was reconvening the following Thursday evening. Piper shook her head, thinking of all the people who'd signed up with just a few emails and texts.

From the closet she pulled some artwork and a few ceramic pieces to add to the shelves. They were all gifts from clients and people she had mentored over the years. She cherished them, yet still feeling the importance of starting fresh, she planned to leave the bulk of the items in storage. A pair of horse-head bookends, antique books from her travels, a copper vessel, and ceramic candle holders seemed like a good start. As she picked up a painting of the farm, which she planned to hang over the desk, and a sign that would go on the wall next to the closet door, her phone buzzed on the chair she had stood on to reach the trim earlier. Hastily she put the painting down and thought she heard the frame crack. "Damnit!" As she fumbled to pick up the phone that was dancing across the surface of the metal chair, she glanced at the sign. Don't Shoot the Messenger.

"Hi Eli! How are you?" Piper stood looking out the window at the glistening white blanket on the untouched pasture, horses in for the afternoon and snow falling at a good clip.

Eli's voice sounded drained but was still the familiar, friendly Eli she had met for the first time years before when he came to John's past life regression workshop in Boston.

"Piper, hi. I guess you could say I've been better."

Piper sat on the chair, feeling the muscles in her legs elongate, relaxing for the first time all day. "I spoke to John a couple of weeks ago about Hope. She is such a good kid and a really hard worker. I need to help her, " Eli's voice trailed off. "I need to help her reach her potential. She has no interest in college at the moment and Grace? I just don't know what to say about Grace. She's been terrible to Hope. Actually, terrible isn't a strong enough word."

Taking a breath and being sure she let Eli finish, Piper could picture in her head, Eli scribbling on a notepad as he tried to stick to the basics. She knew this had to be very difficult for him. "Yes, John mentioned something about the possibility of Hope working here for the summer. Something like that."

"She really would excel at any riding discipline and she admires you so much. She wants a career but starting out is hard and she's limited here without an indoor arena and living in a place that winter calls home most of the year."

Piper could feel a constriction in her throat. Not strong and not really hers. She knew it was what Eli was feeling. "Do you think she will want to live out here in Feeding Hills? Not much of a social scene for someone her age. Or, any age for that matter."

Eli laughed. "She only socializes with other horse people so I think that's not a big consideration. I just want her to be happy and feel comfortable in her own home and right now that isn't the case. I really never imagined any of this happening."

Piper recoiled and scrunched up her nose. Burnt hair.

She got a quick flash of heat and could see a snaking tendril of smoke. She shook her head slightly and focused on Eli's voice telling her he heard she had a copy of his book.

"Yes! I saw it in a bookstore in Paris and texted John immediately. We are both thrilled for you. Truly."

"Thank you. Life has been crazy but someone once told me

that there is no good time to have a baby, go to grad school, buy a house, or make any other big commitment. You just have to do it."

"How about you tell Hope to give me a call in the next week. I'd love to get a feel for what she wants to do and we can talk about arrangements. And maybe, Eli, things will get better."

"Sounds good, thank you. I really had hoped they would be better by now. It's been a couple of difficult years."

Piper laid the items from the closet onto the floor, knowing that dried paint didn't mean cured paint. She spoke to her newly curated office. "Well, I guess we are going to have a busy summer."

The phone again, this time a text.

Hey we met a while ago and you gave me your card. I'd like to come by and see what it's all about.

Piper looked down at her phone. No name. She wondered what people thought and if they assumed she would know their details without them offering any. She thought about responding but it was her day off and she could respond tomorrow.

Before she could put her phone in her pocket, it buzzed again.

I'd like to come Thursday. Piper went to her desk and added GUEST to her list of participants, shut the light and headed out to do evening barn chores.

11

The short book tour that Eli planned was becoming shorter; not that he didn't enjoy meeting readers and talking with groups eager to know more about his work, because he did thoroughly enjoy it. It seemed, though, that his patients needed him more. His calendar populated his schedule for him each Sunday and he received alerts throughout the week when someone tried to book but there weren't any available time slots, which meant his weekly clients weren't leaving any space for his biweekly clients who needed to check in when something threw them off, stress was too much, or they just needed to connect with someone.

He had mentioned to Rebecca that he needed to go back into his office five days again, which left only Saturday and Sunday for book events. At the outset it seemed she understood, but recently Eli was beginning to feel her acceptance was just exhaustion, a quiet quitting, that perhaps she was learning she could not depend on Eli the way she had in the beginning of their marriage.

Tonight he was heading to the Karma Connection in Brunswick, a cute little place that used to be a very well-known bakery but now focused on really good coffee, art, and flex space for creatives, including a podcast studio.

He loaded up the passenger seat of his truck with two large boxes of books, five good black gel pens, and a bag of assorted candy he knew he would probably end up eating on the ride home.

When he walked through the door underneath the red and white awning he felt a sense of anticipation. He realized that for the last decade, he had listened to hundreds of patients tell him their most intimate and awful moments of trauma and grief and most of all, utter sadness at what their lives had become. Though he was adept at separating his feelings from theirs he had recently begun to feel the toll of all that empathy. *This will be a nice change, to have people listen to me instead,* he thought.

"Hello, Dr. Cranston!" The voice from behind the counter, Eli recognized, was the one that had set up the details of this evening's event.

"Jackson, can you help our guest with his boxes?" Eli turned to see a young man coming from one of the tables with his arms out. "Thank you," Eli said as he was relieved of one of the heavy boxes. He was delighted to see a table with a sign welcoming him as the night's special guest speaker. The wall ahead was a dazzling hot pink, the one to his left, metallic gold, and the ceiling a blue that reminded him of the shutters he and Antigone had always wanted to get rid of back in the hills of Los Angeles. Here, the blue was comforting and grounding.

In front of the table were twenty chairs in three rows. He quickly scanned the cafe area to see if perhaps some of the patrons were planning to attend the signing. He had no way of knowing but had hoped they would trickle over.

As Eli opened the boxes to see his book jacket looking back over and over, he grew more excited. *Victorious by Default* was not the original title, but his publisher had a knack for capturing the essence of his authors' work. Eli gave up "Success Despite Setback" quickly when he saw the jacket mockup. He knew it was perfect.

Rebecca had laughed at how quickly a man he met once could change his mind in an instant and she had to beg him to think about what needed to be done in the house and on the farm.

As Eli stacked half a box of books on the table and placed one on the overstuffed chartreuse velvet chair that looked more like a throne from a Disney movie, he hadn't noticed that a few of the seats were filling. He checked his pockets to be sure his truck keys were somewhere close and that his phone was on silent and was caught by surprise to see an older, refined looking gentleman sitting in the front row watching him intently.

"Hi, welcome," Eli said and then noticed the others. He waved nervously and straightened his tie. It was still fifteen minutes before the presentation was set to start, but he was anxious to begin. The event manager, Darcy, brought him a bottle of water and said she would make him some tea to keep his throat comfortable during the evening. There was a part of Eli that was trying to be recognized, remembered, or uncovered. He couldn't deny he liked the attention, but wasn't sure where this was coming from. He had plenty of attention, just not always the pleasant sort.

With a few minutes left, he checked his phone and then wished he hadn't. A call from Rebecca, two from Grace and a ticker tape of texts filled with language that was on par with the color scheme of the Karma Connection.

Darcy arrived with lemon tea sweetened with honey in a cobalt blue teacup and placed it on the table as she cued Eli that she would introduce him in one minute. Eli smiled and nodded at the young woman who he felt could easily be a patient of his: green and yellow hair, nose ring, perfect makeup, and working in a place where she probably, he guessed, felt most accepted. Among the artists, the writers, the dreamers, and the healers, were some of the most talented and most traumatized of souls. Eli long ago had realized that the effervescent beauty that these people infused their art with was a direct result of the hardship and healing they had endured and struggled through. In essence, these were the people who raised the bar for society. They were the ones who posted "do better" on social media posts about children being mistreated, animals being sent to slaughter, and of course all manner of political posts. These are society's greatest allies if and when they can get their feet beneath them and speak their truth, voice shaking, thoughts racing.

"Welcome, everyone," Darcy said on the little stage with Eli's table and books. "The Karma Connection is pleased to introduce you to Dr. Elias Cranston, a psychotherapist who also happens to have his Juris Doctorate. He is the author of the new book *Victorious by Default*. Thank you for coming out tonight to support our co-op and we hope that if this is your first visit, it will be the first of many."

Eli walked across the floor toward Darcy and shook her hand. As he faced the audience and said, "Good evening. Thank you, Darcy, for the wonderful introduction. Ladies and gentlemen of the jury," he stammered, embarrassed. The people in the folding chairs laughed, thinking it was an icebreaker. Eli took a grateful breath and realized what was happening, why this attention felt so good.

He missed the courtroom.

12

The peony pink walls of the bedroom, once comforting, now seemed irritating and almost insulting to the young woman who had spent her teen years here growing, maturing, navigating what life sent her way.

Hope recalled the day she and Rebecca chose the paint from the Ace Hardware in town and transformed the oatmeal-ish guest room into a happy, delicate pink cocoon Hope could relax in, retreat to, watch Pirate in the pasture from.

Slowly, the room had become an unwilling witness to many of the atrocities committed by the woman Hope once had looked up to and wanted to view as a sister. She was not able to pinpoint the start of it all because it had started slowly. If she was honest, she didn't really mind the yelling and the drama. Afterall, Hope had raised herself in the dilapidated cabin in the woods off Ogden Point Road, that is, until Eli and Rebecca plucked her out of all that filthy fishbowl of chaos. What the mind experiences as normal remains normal unless it is shown the clean waters and healthy ecosystem of love, support, and safety. She wasn't startled by aggressive behavior or shouting matches. Her nervous system was set to HOT and though she had worked with Eli to move herself out of fight and flight, her brain had not forgotten how to flip that switch.

Running her fingers over the ribbons she had won with Pirate, Ink, Smudge, and Cayenne through the years, she fought the tears that wanted to wash away all the pain that came, not from the challenges of barn, the arena, the hot, back-breaking work that was farm life, but from the deeds done inside the home where she was promised she would always be safe. *So much for promises,* she thought as she opened the wicker fisherman's basket that adorned the back of her bedroom door. She wasn't sure why she kept them or hid them for that matter but there they were, a testament to dysfunction. Partially blackened ribbons of blue, red, yellow, and white, with mostly obliterated farm names, some with a few golden letters remaining, sat in the darkened basket like silent victims of crimes society turned a blind eye to. Crimes that most would never, so they thought, touch their lives. Grace, on a particularly hot July evening, in a fit of jealousy, doused a handful of Hope's prized ribbons with a glass of vodka and set them aflame on the wooden floorboards of the farmhouse. She laughed and mocked Hope's way of life and passion for her horses. "All those hours of mucking shit and washing horse tails for a seventy-nine-cent piece of cloth. I don't know if that's dedication or retardation!"

Frantic, Hope threw a blanket on the small fire, then screamed, realizing it might feed it, not starve it. She burst into tears and pleaded with Grace to help her. "Gracie, please! Put it out! Put it out! Help me!" Grace's expression changed, not that Hope noticed through her tears while stomping on the blanket that was indeed charred but not still burning.

Grace went from tornado to cool breeze once she got the charge she was looking for, the fear in the teen's voice, the fuel she was hungry for. Satisfied for the time being like a barn cat after devouring a mole, she stepped into the hall. "Rebecca! I smell smoke! Rebecca! I think Hope is smoking or something! Rebecca!"

13

As Darcy, Jackson, and Eli packed up the handful of books that hadn't sold, the older gentleman who had arrived early to hear Eli, remained, his notebook open and pen working methodically on what Eli assumed to be notes. Jackson asked, "Dr. Cranston, are you taking new patients? I think you could really help my mom. She says she can't find the right therapist."

Before Eli could answer, Darcy chimed in, "I was going to ask the same thing. I have a whole list of people who could use your help."

"I'll leave some cards for you. I have a pretty full docket, uh, I mean schedule, but I am adding some additional openings soon." Eli said this and wondered why it was his knee jerk reaction to accommodate, knowing he was already overbooked and adding a day as it was. He knew he needed to work on his own boundaries.

The elderly gentleman closed his notebook, tucked his pen into his tweed coat pocket, and put his flat cap on his head. Darcy noticed his scarf had fallen to the floor. "Sir, your scarf. Let me get it for you." She had already scooped it up before she finished her sentence.

"Thank you, young lady," he said, his white mustache curling slightly, hinting at a smile.

He turned to face Eli as he approached. The man extended his hand toward Eli and said, "And to you sir, thank you for an enlightened evening. It is really good to make your acquaintance." Eli shook the man's hand firmly and looked into his smokey green eyes. "My pleasure, truly. Thank you for coming." The man nodded, reaching for his signed copy, notebook, and car keys. Straightening his back and nodding to Darcy and Jackson who both bid him a good evening, he stood a moment longer and seemed to want to say something more to Eli who waited. The phone at the cafe rang and seemed to animate everyone, perhaps reminding them it was closing time and they had obligations to meet. Always somewhere, someone needed attention, dog food, Motrin, or to be tucked in.

The man turned to leave, tugging at his coat to button it before heading out into the cold. Eli stopped him. "Sir, I didn't catch your name."

The man turned back for a moment and replied, "Let's say it's best if you just call me Sir."

14

Piper was in the grain room, measuring supplements and mixing them with grain for the evening, her breath visible in the chilly morning air. It was easier to get as much done right after feeding in the morning because on a farm, one never knows what might happen. Having a routine and as foolproof of a plan as you can muster each day is always a good idea. And of course, always expect the unexpected.

She glanced in the industrial wheeled laundry cart and was happy to see only three completely mud-covered blankets. By Thursdays it was usually overflowing, but this winter had been cold. The only two things that are good about cold on a horse farm are less mud and fewer flies. She grabbed the broom from the wall and swept, walking backward up the ramp to the barn aisle. Her phone buzzed and stopped as if it knew she would ignore it, then decided it would try again. No luck. She knew it wasn't a barn emergency since she was standing in it. She wasn't expecting any clients for another three hours and John was in the house still asleep. She walked to the end of the barn aisle, glanced out at the pasture to see that the blanket-destroying culprit was the newest therapy horse, Oliver, a dappled grey mud-loving fiend. "This is why I have never bought white horses," she said to Chloe the barn cat who sat on a clean blanket hanging on a stall door. Piper spun on her heel, sensing someone behind her. Nothing. She shook her head, "Hello?" Her voice echoed slightly down the one hundred ten-foot aisle. She waited. Nothing.

Chloe stood up, back arched, eyes scanning behind Piper. There were footfalls coming from the ell midway down the aisle where the arena was attached to the barn. "Hello?"

Piper didn't recognize the voice that returned her cold greeting or appreciate people coming to the farm unannounced, then remembered she had ignored her phone. Around the corner came a man dressed in navy blue coveralls and matching down jacket. "Hi. I tried to call a few minutes ago. I'm Slade."

Piper stood for a moment trying to recall if she'd taken a call or made an appointment she was forgetting. He didn't look like he was ready to ride so she didn't think so. "I'm sorry. Do I know you?" She tried to sound friendly but knew she didn't. The man shook his head. "I texted you last week about coming by."

Piper, still confused, raised her brows and tilted her head slightly as if the information she needed would just tumble out for her to see.

"Sorry, I really am at a loss." The man turned to look over his shoulder, suddenly wondering if there was another farm on the same road. "Uh, I texted this number," he said as he pulled out his phone and recited Piper's number. He read the text to her, "Hey you gave me your card a while ago. I'd like to come see what it's all about."

"Oh! Yes. Sorry. I do remember now. I thought you were coming tonight, for class."

Slade laughed, "I'm confused. I worked on your truck about eight months ago. I was having a shitty day and you were really patient. I felt bad. I thought you were mad but you weren't. You gave me a tip and your card."

Recognition lit up Piper's face. "Yes, yes. I totally remember that day. I was preparing for a class when you texted last week and assumed you were coming to the class," she stopped. "Anyway, yes. I remember you and I'm glad you reached out. I just didn't know who was texting." She walked toward Slade, removing her glove to shake his cold hand. "I'm Piper. It's nice to see you again." Slade smiled with half of his mouth. Piper remembered the scar on his left cheek and had wondered how it happened. She focused on not looking at his scar. "So now that I know who you are, the next question is what would you like to know about?" Slade's shoulders dropped. A sign of relaxation. Or defeat. "I don't really know. I guess by your business card, you help people with issues and stuff."

Piper knew that most people did not come for therapeutic riding on their own but rather as a referral, especially adults. "Yes, that's what we do here. My husband is a hypnotherapist and I run the riding program. Most people are referred to us by a therapist or doctor." She waited to see if this resonated with him but could see the look of resignation instead on his face, as if he was realizing he was, in fact, in the wrong place.

"Oh, okay. I'm not sure what I'm doing, really. I just thought maybe you knew something the therapists and doctors didn't. I mean I guess that's why they refer people? I don't really know how it works. Therapy has never helped. Doctors can only do so much and usually just prescribe a pill you'll eventually get addicted to, then they take it away and you're on your own."

This wasn't the first time Piper had heard this story; in fact, it was quite common. "I see," she said. "Have you ever ridden a horse?"

The man shifted his weight from foot to foot. "Do iron horses count?"

Piper smiled, relaxed now. "No, although I have heard that can be a form of therapy, too."

Something caught Slade's attention in the pasture and the look of concern caught Piper by surprise. She turned to see Oliver on the ground, rolling in the pasture, blanket and all. "Oh, Oliver," she said.

Slade, surprised at how calm she was asked, "Is he okay? I didn't know horses did that. Is he hurt?"

Piper laughed but appreciated his concern. It was a good sign. Empathy.

"Horses roll—in grass, ponds, shavings, sand, and this guy, mud. Thankfully it's frozen over today."

Slade's withdrawn demeanor changed in an instant when

he saw Oliver get his legs beneath him and stand, shaking the snow from the blanket which was now torn at the shoulder, a small bit of blue plaid waving in the winter breeze.

Slade looked relieved. "I want to start. Whatever this is, this therapy. I want to start."

15

Early spring in Maine is a little like arriving early at Thanksgiving dinner. You're hungry, but the turkey isn't finished cooking and it seems no one knows when it might actually be done. If it comes out too soon, everyone could get sick; it stays in too long and there's not enough gravy in the world to make it palatable. So you arrive early, hope for the best, and try not to fill up on mixed nuts and cheese.

Twenty degrees one day, the next you could be in a t-shirt swatting black flies, but Hope had only known Maine. It was home and she had never wanted to leave before now.

She left the farm store after baking the thirty custard cups, two sheets of brownies, and seven apple pies Rebecca had on the list of must haves for the next two days. She took the apple peels and eggshells with her, heading up the hill to the barn. Monday was the only day the farm store was closed. Hope enjoyed working in the kitchen when there were no customers and she could play her music as loud as she wanted. She crushed the egg shells as she walked and sprinkled them on the flower beds that lined the driveway, excited to see the first signs of life poking through the soil, still partially covered with snow. The warmth of the sun on the top of her head felt good in a way that a beanie never could, her heart glad to have some quiet now that Grace was back in California.

She brushed the remaining bits of shell off her hands and plopped the plastic container of apple peels on the tack trunk in front of Ink and Smudge's stall. She wondered if she had time for a quick ride before meeting Eli and Rebecca at Rosalie's Pizza for lunch. She decided she would wait and ride longer later. After her barn chores, she stepped into the grain room. As she distributed the apple peels among the five buckets that stood lined up in front of the grain bin, she heard a car pull up to the store. The sign at the end of the drive clearly stated that the store was closed on Mondays until June first, but inevitably there were at least two or three cars that pulled in each week anyway. She peered down the hill to see a woman get out of the car and try the door handle, stand back, hands on hips. She tried the door a second time before retreating to her car and pulling away, hitting the gas unnecessarily hard. Hope shook her head. She really didn't understand people. And mostly, they disappointed her on a regular basis. Taking her phone out of her jacket pocket to check the time, she saw something she never imagined seeing a simple text asking, "Can I see you?"

Her breath quickening, she put the phone back in her pocket and wanted nothing more than to be sitting opposite Eli and next to Rebecca at the restaurant. She hurried down the hill, glancing at the field to see the two horses, two ponies, and one donkey enjoying the sun. Getting into her truck without her keys, she admonished herself, ran into the house to get them and stopped. Why was she so anxious? She wasn't even sure who the number belonged to. There had been times in the past when she had received a text from an unknown number more than once, leaving her to guess who it might be, never considering texting back to ask. She then assigned the contact a name: sometimes a former classmate, horse owner, or other acquaintance. As time passed, she learned she was right about eighty percent of the time. Grace once called her Hopeless for doing this, but Grace didn't live the life Hope did. It was one of quiet protection against the sting of disappointment. She learned not to share anything with Grace except what she absolutely had to: Eli, Rebecca, and the upstairs bathroom.

Calmly, she took her keys from the entryway table and walked back to her truck. She pulled out her phone while she waited for the diesel engine to warm up. She opened the text and assigned the name **Mom?** before heading into town to have a conversation that was about to change her life.

16

Rebecca waited for Eli at Rosalie's. He was coming from his office and had texted he was running late. Looking over the menu she knew by heart, Rebecca had rehearsed what she needed to say to Eli and Hope over and over a thousand times. She wrote it out, recorded it, listened back, and edited where necessary.

Eli surprised her with a kiss from behind the booth, startling her. "Hey Becca. Sorry, on hold with a new insurance company." She nodded as he sat across from her, loosening his tie. "Is Hope on her way?"

Rebecca looked at him as if for the first time. What was happening with him? Antsy, rushing, late. "I think so. She texted when she was finished baking and was going up to the barn for chores but she should be on her way." Before Eli could reply, he saw Hope parallel park her Silverado like a pro. He couldn't take credit for her parking prowess. That was all Rebecca's and Clem's doing. She trotted across Cottage Street, dark ponytail swinging side to side. She slid into the booth beside Becca who put her hand on her back, something she always did when the only child she had ever loved like her own was near. "Hungry?" Rebecca asked Hope but was looking at Eli who was looking at his phone. "Starving," he said. Hope looked up. "Eli."

Eli blinked and put his phone down. "Oh hey, Kiddo. How did baking go this morning?"

"It was fine," she said. Sensing tension between Rebecca and Eli, she picked up a menu and scanned her favorites:

pepperoni pizza, chicken fingers, veal parm.

Her phone buzzed but she was too anxious to check it in case it was from the same number as earlier.

Eli asked if they were ready to order and they both told him they would get their usual, which he knew. If Eli had a superpower it was remembering details with laser accuracy. His phone buzzed on the table. Rebecca glanced and saw **Darcy** on the screen. *Hi Eli! Call me. I have something to tell you.* Eli stood and made his way to the counter to order drinks in the busy lunch rush.

Hope's eyes were on Rebecca. She wanted to ask why it felt like all the sap had run out of all the maple trees too soon. Why the geese were flying south instead of north, why the fawns didn't stay put when their mothers were feeding. Instead she said, "I made two extra apple pies. I had the apples and they were starting to get soft." Becca winked at her.

"All set, Ladies. Fifteen minutes," Eli said as he brought two glasses of water and a Coke back to the table.

He settled back into his side of the booth and looked at Rebecca, who did not meet his gaze. His phone lit up with a reminder about the text from Darcy. His brows raised and he put his phone in his coat pocket.

He listened as Becca and Hope talked about the upcoming spring rush that hits the store in the run up to Easter and their plan to try to attend some markets if time permitted. The farm store and cafe had been a lot of work, a true labor of love, but it was something Rebecca had planned to create with Grace and Hope as a family enterprise. It was something she had wanted to build and eventually leave to the girls when she and Eli retired and traveled. What she hadn't foreseen was Hope's green thumb. Alone, she cultivated several large beds behind the store for cut flowers, which are always in demand at markets, not to mention the store. Grace was nowhere to be found concerning the store, the farm, or anything that required work, responsibility, or accountability. Rebecca had begun to realize that everything with her was an uphill battle she wanted nothing to do with. On the other hand, Rebecca adored Grayson and wished she could take him away from Grace, though she would never intimate this thought to Eli. How could such a sweet and kind boy have come from someone so devoid of values and stability?

Hope took a sip of her Coke and said, "Okay so ..." She looked at Eli, assuming he was the one who wanted them to meet for lunch to discuss something important. Eli waited to hear the rest of her thought. It didn't come. She looked at Rebecca who noticed their order was heading to the table, and felt relieved.

Eli thanked the boy who delivered the order as he grabbed a fry off the tray. Hope rolled her eyes. Hope anxiously looked at the mound of food on the table and estimated it would take at least twenty minutes to eat it all. She couldn't wait that long. "Becca, why are we here?"

Becca looked at Eli and then Hope and said, "It can wait. Let's eat first." Eli looked uneasy. He thought they were just meeting for lunch since they had a day off and Eli no longer had a day off during the week to spend with them helping in the store. He shifted his weight in the cushioned booth. "What's going on, Becca? Let's hear it. What's on your mind?"

Rebecca took a sip of water and sat back, turning slightly in the booth to face both of them.

She took a deep breath but before she could speak, Hope blurted, "My mom wants to see me."

17

Sitting with her feet flat on the new wood floors of her renovated office, Piper was anticipating the development group participants arriving. Some always came early, hoping to catch up or dig for insight on a subject. Piper enjoyed everyone who had been in the group prior to the pandemic and saw most of them on her list for tonight. A few new names had trickled in as late as that morning. Eleven in all. She thought that was a good number.

The table in the center of the circle held a jar filled with slips of paper and pens, a small decorative box and a battery-operated candle. No open flames in a barn. Number one rule on any farm.

A knock at the door startled her. She hurried to the door to greet her guests only to find John standing in the doorway with a bouquet of pale pink roses and baby's breath. He kissed her forehead, wished her luck, and trotted down the steps.

A single tear slid down Piper's cheek. To have someone's support, someone to pick up the slack so she could create, study, or work was a true gift and she knew she was blessed to have John as that partner.

She placed the roses on her desk, sliding one out of the vase and placing it in the box on the table. *This is the perfect item for the treasure box!*

Piper sat in the chair that had once been Paul's and closed her eyes, asking for guidance for the group. Letting the gentle music pull her into her mind's eye, she felt the familiar pull of her own higher self, wanting to show her what she needed to know.

The cry of seagulls as they swarmed the fishing boats, the fishermen tossing them scraps they'd rather not clean up. Piper turned away from the sea then, toward the dunes. The sand beneath her sore feet gave way as she stepped carefully, avoiding shells and stones. "Maman!" Her heart surged to hear the sweet call. "Maman!" Fog rolled in from the sea as it often does, unapologetically fast. The vague outline of a child sat atop the dune, waving to her. "Maman! I am here. I am here!"

Giggling jolted Piper back into her office. *No. I want to see!*

Footsteps on the stairs was a familiar sound, pulling Piper fully back into the moment. Breathing deeply, centering herself, she waited.

Camille and Trish were the first to arrive, gushing as they entered. "Piper! Oh my gosh. Look at this place! It's so beautiful."

Piper hugged them both and welcomed them back to the new and improved office. They each had a small gift for her, but told her to wait until after class to open them. *More items for my shelves,* she thought.

The others arrived in much the same manner, all happy to be reunited, and though life had changed some of their circumstances, they were committed to gathering and to continue their work. The new participants entered quietly, introducing themselves, and sitting nervously on the folded chairs, not sure what to think. Piper busied herself at her desk and changed the music as people shared pictures and stories of their kids, new houses and in some cases, ex-husbands. As much as Piper felt time was short and that each minute of the group's time was precious, she had learned to allow the socializing. For some, it was the only social interactions they had all week and this group hadn't been in the same space together for two years.

Gently, Piper directed them to write their intentions on slips of paper and place them in the crystal prayer bowl. The room became hushed as people fell right back into the rhythm of the circle. Jamie, a new member, asked for clarification and apologized. The woman next to her explained how to write the intention and that she shouldn't be sorry. "Say everything." The room erupted in laughter. Piper smiled. *They remembered!*

Listening to the wisdom the original members shared with the new ones was heartwarming. She hadn't really thought the impact to her group would have really lasted; listening to them each share how their intuition shaped the decisions they made, the choices they knew were right for them, truly made her heart full. She wondered now why she hadn't gotten them together again once life went back to somewhat normal post pandemic.

The hour went by quickly as it always had and the room was buzzing with excitement as the members made connections with what they were writing in their journals and what others were saying. "You can't make this stuff up," Trish said. "Wait! Do we have time for the box!?"

Another new member, Claire, sheepishly asked, "The box?"

Piper nodded. "Yes. The box. Before class, I place an item in the box on the table." She pointed and all eyes went to the box. Some of the women began jotting things down in their journals. Claire watched them, then focused on Piper.

"Your intuition is instant. It doesn't need time to think. Just focus on what's in the box and whatever comes to your mind—shape, color, consistency, etc., just write it down. Don't judge what you've written. Trust yourself."

Piper shivered then. Claire laughed, thinking it was exaggerated but it was not.

Claire began to write in her journal along with the others, listening to the music and feeling that perhaps she had found people who would understand her. Maybe.

"Okay. Let's see how we did after all this time," Piper said, breaking the concentration that she could see had replaced the instantaneous reactions. There was a collective, audible sigh from the group. "Who remembers when there were yaks on a winter journey in the box?" Anne who had been quiet most of class, was now feeling relaxed. She looked at Piper to be sure it was okay to say that. More laughter and quizzical expressions on the new members' faces. Piper winked at her. She certainly remembered the yaks on a winter journey. It was Anne's vivid way of describing the items in the box. She was always traveling through the galaxies during meditations and having fascinating experiences in her dream life as well. Working in healthcare, she dealt with a lot of people, a lot of personalities, and a lot of problem solving throughout her week. Coming to class allowed her to connect with herself, her own spirit. And what it showed her was the beauty and infinite possibilities outside of her everyday life. This is exactly why Piper cultivated this group, even if she hadn't realized that was what was happening when she began. As she reflected back on it all, she realized that listening to her intuition was the bravest thing she'd ever done.

One by one, the women described what they intuited to be in the box.

Laughter was the energy of the evening and as the women shared their answers, realizing they were wildly different from each other, with some crossover details, that excited them; Piper could feel the energy in the room, dancing like a candle flame.

Claire sat, perplexed. She was the last to go and though she wanted to bolt from the room, she knew she had to share. All eyes were on her, something she was never comfortable with. What she had written wasn't anything close to what the others had said. Piper asked her, "Claire, would you like to share?"

Nervously, she nodded slightly as she looked directly at Piper across the office from where she sat. She could feel the color flush her cheeks but reminded herself that coming here was a commitment to herself. To her own journey. "I really, I um, really didn't get anything," she said, looking at the floor.

"That's fine. No pressure. This activity isn't everyone's favorite," Piper said with a giggle. Trish added, "Did you have anything pop into your head tonight that didn't really fit with what we were talking about?"

Claire shook her head no. "I think I'm just drawing a blank."

Piper said, "Happens all the time. That's why we practice. Trish, can you open the box?"

Trish leaned forward and took the lid off the box to peer in. "Yaks!" Silence was quickly replaced with surprised laughter. Reaching inside and drawing out the rose had everyone looking at their answers to see how it could have related to what they wrote. Many voices at once, "I said pale. I wrote delicate. Oh, summertime. I said love. Well, I guess silky white scarf doesn't fit. I was way off!"

Claire sat, in disbelief as she looked at the words she had written:

Petal, soft, blush, pinchy, gift, love, plant, perfume, Auntie.

A single tear escaped down her pink cheek.

She looked at Piper and smiled.

18

"But how do you know he's not going to kill me? Or you? I mean, like how do you know?" Piper wasn't completely surprised by the question. Afterall, plenty of people have been killed by horses, mostly by accident. What made her hesitate for a moment before answering was the look in Slade's eye. He wasn't scared. He was curious.

"Well, the first thing to know about horses is that you can expect the unexpected. They spook easily, have strength they are generally unaware of and those hooves ... yes they can kill you. Or me. But generally, we don't believe it'll happen. Why? Well, training, connection with your horse, groundwork and," she paused, "and trust. Just plain trust. That's what we are going to work on today. Okay?"

Slade reached up and gently put his hand on Oliver's poll, slowly stroking his neck while the horse bobbed his head up and down. "Why is he doing that?" He looked over his shoulder at Piper.

"Ask him," she said.

He laughed. "Ask him?" Piper didn't answer. Instead, she walked down the aisle toward the ell. "And when you get his answer, you can lead him into the arena."

Slade looked at her as if she were joking but when she turned and put her hands in her coat pockets and disappeared, he realized she was not. He ducked under the cross tie so he could be closer to Oliver's face. The horse stood still now, looking out to the pasture where he planned to demolish what was left of his blanket when this nonsense was over. Slade looked up into the horse's dark eye and was surprised he could see his reflection in it. He waited, not sure if Piper was coming back. "Okay, so ... why were you bobbing your head like that, pal?" He shifted his weight. No answer. "What the hell am I doing here?" he said under his breath. He shrugged and turned to look out at what Oliver was looking at: the last of the spring snow mixed with mud, a water trough, two of Piper's horses that were semi-retired hay burners who had been used in her program for more than ten years, the woods lining the pasture, one crooked fence post looking like a tooth knocked askew perhaps in a drunken brawl. Slade put his hand in his pocket to check his phone. As he pulled it out, the sound of the peppermint wrapper elicited a sharp whinny from Oliver. Slade immediately stepped back, eyes wide, scared. Oliver looked at him then and bobbed his head up and down. Slade looked down the aisle to see if that would make Piper reappear. It didn't.

He slowly took out the candy Piper had handed him upon his arrival and watched as Oliver stepped to the side and craned his neck, nostrils flared, his lip moving side to side. "This is what you want, pal?" He had watched Piper feed peppermints to a couple of the horses at his first session but turned down the offer to do it himself. Now, here he was faced with the challenge of doing it alone. "Trust," he said to himself. He carefully unwrapped the mint as the distinguished dappled gray nickered softly this time, his forelock neatly covering the scar on his forehead. Slade held the peppermint out to Oliver, wondering how badly a bite would feel. What he wasn't expecting was the fuzzy muzzle of the horse to find the candy and swipe it, no teeth involved. He watched as the horse's jaw moved side to side as he chewed, sending the scent of peppermint out into the frosted air. He reached up and felt the soft velvet of Oliver's pink nose. He hadn't realized how delicate an animal this size could be, or how intimidating.

"Okay, pal. So bobbing your head means you like something?" Oliver didn't answer. "We have to go but I don't really know what I'm doing so, umm. So, work with me, okay?" Oliver was looking for another peppermint, which made Slade laugh. Oliver tossed his head up, gently as if to say, "I know there's more." Slade looked at the clip on the end of the crosstie. He hadn't paid attention when Piper took him from his stall and positioned him in the aisle but the clip looked just like the type on a dog leash, just bigger. He gently unclipped one side and let it go, not sure what to do with it. It landed against the stall making a soft thud. Then he unclipped the other side and realized the horse was free. "Uh, wait." He looked around hoping to see Piper. "What am I supposed to do?" Oliver stepped backward, then to the side, making Slade nervous. "Dude, c'mon." He reached up and took the horse by the halter and imagined Oliver would flip his head again, ripping Slade's shoulder out its socket for a third time in his life. He braced himself. Instead, Oliver lowered his head and turned his body completely around in the aisle. "Three-point turn, nice," Slade said and noticed the size of the horse's hooves. He wondered how they supported such a large beast. He took a step forward, assuming he would need to tug the horse down the aisle like an unwilling puppy but was surprised that Oliver walked calmly by his side. He stopped and was again surprised when the horse stopped next to him. Slade wasn't registering the satisfaction he was feeling. He did realize, though, that he was communicating with this animal; but he had no idea how he was doing it. When they reached the ell, they turned and walked a few strides before entering the softly lit indoor arena. Piper stood in the middle and smiled at them.

"I see you two had a talk."

19

Hope sat in the train station, nervous, excited, and a little scared. It had been seven years since she had seen her mother. So much had happened since the day she had visited Missy in rehab, hoping to find out when she would be returning home only to hear that her mother was not, in fact, coming home. She looked up at the screen over the counter to see if the train had arrived yet, though she knew it hadn't. Hope was early for everything from dentist appointments to invitations to a movie, lunch, a date. She thought she was being responsible and wondered why other people weren't as conscientious about arriving when they said they would. Never had it occurred to her that she learned this behavior very young. Early meant that she wouldn't miss something important like eating, finding a safe place to hide, or an open classroom door where she could get homework done before school started. Early was survival.

The hand on the back of her shoulder startled her. She jumped, her hand instinctively going to her chest. She spun around, knowing who she'd see but not exactly what she'd see. Her eyes wide, scanning back and forth at the face in front of her.

Missy Barlow's face was a roadmap of wrinkles and scars, eyes dull yet somehow alert and something Hope couldn't quite put her finger on, but it made her shoulder blade twitch though she had no idea the two were related.

"Mom!" Hope stood still, stunned to see her mother was a little shorter than her. How could that be?

Missy threw her arms around the young woman she remembered as the quiet little peanut who was able to raise herself without much help from anyone. Hope reached around her thin mother and breathed in the scent of her clean hair, noticing she was wearing earrings. Eli often explained to her how the mind notices things that are different, new, dangerous, interesting, unusual. She could feel her mother's heart beating as she clung to her, not knowing how much she had missed her until that moment. "Mom," she repeated as hot tears blurred the white walls of the station and the people who were glancing at two women who they might assume were sisters or friends visiting before heading off to college or meeting up for vacation.

Missy stood back, keeping her hands on Hope's shoulders. She looked at the eyes that once pled for her to stop using, eyes that steeled themselves when Missy would ask her to sneak money out of Stan's wallet. Eyes that held secrets about who she was and where she came from. Though Missy wanted her baby, she knew somehow, there was nothing about her that deserved any part of Hope.

"How've you been, Honey?" Missy's voice was gravel and salt, sharp enough to cut you if you weren't careful. Hope could smell the cigarette smoke in her clothes. She wasn't aware of all the things her mind was reading from this woman who she once depended on but it was being received on some level. Sorrow, guilt, neediness, desperation, love. It was a powerful mix and it pulled at Hope who suddenly felt ten years old again and in need of digging her toes into the sand to anchor herself from the riptide that was Melissa E. Barlow.

"I'm good," she said more loudly than necessary, as though that would make it truer than true.

"That's it? You're good? I figyah'd you'd be fuckin' fabulous living with the Cranstons, all high and mighty, those two."

Hope flinched, not realizing her eyes betrayed her. Was it too much to ask to have five minutes of normalcy with this woman?

"Sorry, Honey. I didn't mean nothin' by that. They fed ya when I couldn't. I really should send them somethin', ya know. Like one of those fancy fruit baskets at Christmas. That's what I'll do."

Hope bit her lip, wondering what weird carnival ride it was she had just stepped on. *Was this a mistake? Was Rebecca right? No. Rebecca was not right. This is my mother. I love her. I have to be- cause ... because she is my mother.* Tilt-a-whirl it was.

"Hey, wait right here, Hope. I'll be right back. I see an old friend ah mine. Let me just say hi and then we can get outta this place."

Standing alone once again in the station, Hope watched now through the eyes of an adult and the perspective seven years provided as her mother handed a young man some money and then tucked something into the pocket of her jeans.

A woman who had stepped off the train with Missy was there, her two young kids squabbling over who was going to be the first one in the pool at the hotel. The woman looked at Hope with kindness or maybe it was pity, Hope didn't know. Hope missed the smile that conveyed, *I know. But you'll be okay.*

Hope averted her eyes and pretended to be enthralled with the poster that showed the Downeaster route and all the fun stops in Portland, Old Orchard Beach, Boston.

When she looked back, the lady was walking toward the station door, wheeling a large piece of luggage and holding the younger child's hand. For a moment Hope wished she could be that little girl who was well dressed, clean, and carefree. A flash of anger and jealousy lit up her heart. *Why did that child get that mother and why did I get mine?*

She looked nervously around to see if anyone else was watching her or Missy. She didn't think anyone else had.

Missy came back as if nothing was out of the ordinary. In reality, to Missy, nothing was.

"Let's go. C'mon. I'm stahvin." She walked past Hope and for a moment Hope wanted to run to the window and buy a ticket to somewhere. Anywhere would be fine. She wished she hadn't responded to the text from her mother the week before.

If Eli or Rebecca had seen what the text read, they would have changed Hope's phone number and sent a few frantic texts of their own.

20

"Hi Darcy—It's Eli Cranston. We've been playing phone tag. What's up?"

Darcy asked Eli to hold on as she started an espresso for a customer. Eli looked out the window to see Rebecca loading the van with baked goods and her famous coffee blends. She had branched out the year they were married and was stocking a handful of stores in the area with her signature recipes. Part of Eli was a bit jealous that she found pleasure in work that was as old as time. Baking, creating, and feeding people will never not be a commodity. He also admired how she could stick to a plan and see it through. Eli was much more of the mindset to let the work lead him.

"Sorry, Eli! It's been busy here. How are you?" Darcy's voice was cheerful. Eli wondered if she had changed her hair color or if it was still reminiscent of fruit punch.

"Doing well, thanks! I am curious to hear what you know about 'Just call me Sir.'"

Darcy laughed a hearty, deep laugh that surprised Eli.

"I have been dying to hear this," Eli continued.

Darcy told Jackson to cover the register for her and walked to the storage room for privacy.

"Well, he came in the day I texted you. I almost didn't recognize him. He was wearing super casual clothes. Like jeans and a polo shirt. He just ordered a cappuccino and sat by the window. I'm pretty sure I had never seen him before your book signing so seeing him again was a surprise."

Eli wondered if there was more to this story or if she was just letting him know the mysterious Sir had come back to the cafe.

"So he's drinking his cappuccino and I hear him on the phone. He says, 'I'm still looking at Cranston. I think he checks out.'"

Eli said, "Looking at me? For what?"

Darcy giggled this time and said, "That's what I was hoping to find out! I hung out near the cooler behind his chair but he was mostly listening to the person on the other end."

"Hmm, Sir is even more mysterious than I thought," Eli said.

"I know. So listen to this. When he got up to leave, he brought his mug back to the counter and told me the cappuccino was delicious. I thanked him and asked if he was at the book signing event we had. He just picked his chin up a little, you know like when someone is ..." she searched for the word.

"Defensive," Eli said.

"Yes, defensive! It was so weird. Anyway, he said he was at the signing but he goes to a lot of them and couldn't remember which author was at this location."

Eli held his cellphone in front of his face now, incredulous. "What? Seriously?"

Darcy said, "Yup and I knew it was bull because he took notes the entire time you were talking."

"So then what?" Eli was getting impatient.

"He left a card, you know a business card, on the counter. I'll send you a picture, hold on."

Eli could feel that old familiar hunger that only detectives and lawyers seem to be able to enjoy. He waited, watching for the text that seemed to be taking the scenic route to his phone by way of a satellite. Then it was there. Eli didn't hear what Darcy said.

His heartbeat was in his ears now.

Patrick Neeland, Psy.D
American Psychological Association
Ethics Committee President

21

Clem sat on the bench on the porch of the house at 9 Ogden Point Road waiting for Eli. The crocuses were still coming up early here, under the dryer vent. Clem remembered when his friends the McCabes lived here. "A lifetime ago, it seems," Clem said to the bluebird at the feeder. Annie bought mealworms at the feed store for them, her favorite birds. "Bluebird of happiness," she always announced. It reminded Clem of the way his mother would make the sign of the cross when she passed a church. A ritual of sorts.

He reflected on Charlie planting those crocus bulbs for Louise so they would come up earlier than usual since he didn't know how much time she had left, and if there was one thing Louise loved as much as Charlie, it was her flowers. She planted spring bulbs in the autumn, summer bulbs in the spring, and her dahlias. Oh boy, did Clem remember the dahlias, a forest of gorgeous pom poms, stars and firecracker-looking blooms. He couldn't believe how she got them to grow any more than he could imagine the trouble she'd put Charlie through, checking the forecast, throwing a tarp over them when early spring frosts or rains threatened to freeze or rot the delicate tubers. She would send him out in the summer nights, too, with a flashlight and a bucket to pick off the slugs and earwigs. Charlie told Clem, "I asked only once why I couldn't do it during the day." Clem laughed and scared the bluebird away, remembering his friend relaying the argument he had then had with

Louise. "I made a blundah one night, jeezum crow, Clem. I was trying to get at why Lu was so outta sahts. She was crying 'bout these friggin' flowahs like they were children. And I says to 'er, You goin' through the change ah somethin?" Clem laughed again remembering the look on Charlie's face. He had been bewildered. Charlie told him, "I'm tellin' ya, hard tellin' not knowin'. I just went down cellah for a bit while she slammed the doors and called me every name in the book!"

Clem's sight was blurry then, tears teetering on the rims of his eyes as he remembered his own confusion when Annie started to go through some of the same changes that made life less than pleasant for them both. A tear slid down his cheek for the shame he remembered feeling when using that as an excuse for his drinking. "Ah, buggah," he said when he heard Eli's truck approaching. He wiped his eyes, cleared his throat and stood up, creaking, from the bench.

Eli honked and smiled at the role reversal that had occurred since Clem and Annie moved into the house that Eli had lived in upon his arrival on the East Coast so long ago. Buying the house at auction, knowing nothing about the condition of the interior was a risk but Eli was drawn to it and never looked back. It was the house that introduced him to Clem, the most honest man Eli would ever meet. The house being sold due to Charlie being in a nursing home and Louise passing away, didn't mean Clem was erasing all the history he and his friend shared. As Eli was fond of saying, "My house came with a handyman."

"Hey Clem, how's it going?" Eli stepped out of the truck and saw that the early spring grass was as bright as it was at the farm. He never had the lawn looking this good when he lived here.

"Well, I could complain, but what good would it do?" Clem straightened his back and winced. "What's got yer panties in a bunch, pal?"

Eli laughed though his answer wasn't a particularly comical one.

He stood in the dooryard and looked at the now elderly man who had become an instant friend and handyman extraordinaire when Eli first purchased the McCabe's home.

"Well, uh. I think we have a problem but am not sure."

Clem's hand went into his pocket as his thick brows went up a notch. "Trouble brewin', Pal?"

Eli's shoulders went up, hands in his pockets, too, a defensive gesture.

"Melissa Barlow is back in town and she has Hope thinking she's here for a reunion but I have a feeling it's more than that."

Clem opened the door to the house and gestured for Eli to come along inside.

"Well ain't that pissah."

22

Oliver shifted his weight in anticipation of Slade asking him to lift his hoof, with no more than Slade's shoulder slightly leaning on his. Slade held the hoof with one hand and used the hoof pick to clean out the packed mud and manure, taking pride in how clean he could get it before gently guiding the horse's pastern down toward the cement aisle. Immediately, Oliver shifted again, anticipating his hindleg was next. Slade whistled as he groomed Oliver, bringing his own peppermints now. "Two bags for a buck at the dollar store, pal." He was instructed to only give him one or two each visit. Slade's word to do so was good, though Oliver was pretty persuasive and might have begged an extra one here and there.

The saddle, as light as it was, presented a challenge for Slade. His injuries were old but plentiful. He worked, not disabled in the sense that he couldn't do physical labor, but by the VA's definition he was in fact a DAV. He took the saddle by the pommel and with his right hand lifted it up above the horse's back. Seventeen hands was no small pony but Slade was a bit above six feet so he could easily manage. He gently lowered the Wintec onto the saddle pad over the horse's withers and slid it back an inch, settling it into the correct spot.

He stopped for a moment as Oliver's ears shot forward, head high, nostrils flared.

Slade put his hand on the horse's neck and looked out the barn door. He didn't see anything at first, but knew there had to be something as agitated hooves crossed over one another and back again. Movement caught Slade's eye. He petted Oliver, to reassure him. "It's a rabbit." Before he got the three words out, Oliver blew frosty breath through his nose which reminded Slade of a diesel engine. He followed the horse's eyes and was shocked to see a fox snap the rabbit up and somersault as the rabbit kicked and to Slade's horror, screamed.

Slade reached outside the barn and slid the heavy door closed on the long metal runner. The temperature difference was immediate as the sunlight and violence was blocked from the barn. Oliver's head lowered, eyes softened, long lashes allowed to do their job once again. The sense of protection Slade felt for Oliver was one he could never have explained to anyone, including himself.

More than once he'd heard himself say, "It's just a dog, for God's sake," when a friend would mourn for months over a lost pet, but now he understood.

He warmed the snaffle bit with his hands and his own breath until it didn't feel frigid any longer, then slid it into the horse's mouth, waiting for Oliver to position it in his mouth before guiding the headstall over his ears and fastening the noseband and throatlatch.

He led Oliver to the arena where Piper was talking on her phone. She smiled and pointed to the rail, reminding Slade to walk Oliver a bit before mounting up.

"Eli, let me call you back this afternoon, when my sessions are done. I'll talk to John at lunchtime and we can come up with something."

She turned to see where Slade and Oliver had ended up and to her surprise, she saw that Oliver was standing with his head over Slade's shoulder, gently chewing his jacket.

She recognized that her younger self would have admonished both horse and human but the wiser version of her understood that Oliver was in fact grooming his new family member, comforting him in return for his not so hard-won leadership.

23

The sound of the lighter and the smell of tobacco brought Hope back to the rundown cabin in the woods she had called home for eleven years. It was woven into her childhood like peanut butter and jelly, cartoons, rubber rain boots, and pushing past empty beer cans to find her baby doll. She watched as her mother took a long drag from the cigarette and held it out to Hope.

"Uh, no. No thanks," Hope said as she started her truck. "I don't smoke."

Missy didn't seem to mind either way. She ran her hand over the dashboard and turned to Hope. "This is Cranston's truck?"

Hope's head, on a swivel now, looked at her mother then back to center and stared out through the windshield hoping to find a sign that read, "Exit Here, Hope."

"No, it's mine. I bought it," Hope answered, cautiously.

Missy's head leaned back and softly bounced off the headrest. "No shit. You really bought this ride?"

Hope put the truck in drive and nodded.

"So yah workin' at the fahm?" Missy blew smoke in Hope's direction, laughing at the way Hope ducked to avoid the cloud.

"I've been working since I was ten, Mom. You know that."

"Yah, you always liked counting yah money, Ha! I used to watch ya. You were like a little squirrel hiding acorns all ovah the place. You were good! Afta a while, I couldn't find it any moah!" The congested laughter-turned-cough made Hope wince. *This isn't the Tilt a Whirl. This is the Scrambler.* She had thrown up at Palace Playland more than once on that ride.

"Let's get somethin' ta eat, Honey. I have some money."

"Okay, where do you want to go?" Hope was the farthest thing from hungry but the longer they stayed away from Full Circle Farm, the better. Now she wondered if in fact Rebecca was right. This was a bad idea.

Missy was searching her phone. "The Social Goose. Let's try that one."

She read directions to Hope, "Union ta Pleasant ta Main Street."

Hope hopped out of her truck and looked around, hoping the restaurant wasn't open so they could just get on the road back to the farm, deciding that was the only place she wanted to be. It was a two-hour drive as it was.

Missy swung the door open and held it for Hope to walk through, then went straight to the bar, pulling out a barstool for her daughter. Hope's green eyes grew wider as she looked at her mother, wondering if she remembered that Hope was only eighteen.

"Sit," Melissa said.

Hope pulled the stool out further and timidly took a seat. The bartender glanced over and smiled. Hope ran her hand over the smooth bar and realized that no matter how many bars she'd been in as a child, she'd never seen a bar top.

"Hi, Ladies." The bartender was young but still had at least five years on Hope.

"What can I get ya?" Hope looked at Missy, apprehensive and a bit curious.

"Gin n tonic," Missy said and picked up a menu.

The bartender looked at Hope who was nervously looking at all the bottles lining the bar. "I'll just have a Coke, please."

The young woman behind the bar leaned closer and said, "As long as you guys are outta here by two when the boss comes in, you can sit there but I'm guessing you're not twenty-one."

Hope jumped off the stool. "We can sit at a table. Mom, c'mon."

Missy laughed, a throaty, sarcastic, and cruel laugh that made Hope feel the need to get to a restroom. Her eyes darted toward the bartender who looked just as surprised as Hope.

In the bathroom, Hope waited in the stall until what was left of her breakfast came up. She wiped her mouth and waited. The bathroom door opened and closed but she didn't hear footsteps. She breathed as best she could as she stared at the mostly clean toilet. When she was fairly confident that she was finished, she straightened her long legs and wiped at her mouth again with the back of her hand.

Settling into the booth across from her mother, she felt physically better but imagined what would happen if she just took her keys and drove off, never to speak to this woman again.

"Whatcha gonna get, Hon? They got a BLT special. You always liked them."

Hope looked out the window and wondered if she had ever eaten a BLT in her life or if this woman had another child somewhere she was remembering.

"I'm not that hungry, the Coke is fine."

Missy put the specials menu down and leaned forward. "What's wrong with ya? You pregnant or somethin'?" The laugh again, sent shivers through Hope. Now she was wishing not to just leave but to go back in time and block the number that came through as "Mom" just six days ago.

"I'm just bustin' ya balls. Get a sandwich, c'mon."

Hope agreed to a fish sandwich with fries. Her phone buzzed, startling her already-aroused nervous system. She jumped as it buzzed in her back pocket. It was Rebecca. *Thank God.*

Hi Sweetie - Guest room is made up for your mom. Let me know your ETA. Hoping everything is going well.

A sense of complete relief washed through Hope's veins. So much so, a tear threatened to roll down her cheek, but thankfully her Coke arrived.

Missy was busy texting, laughing, and making comments under her breath that Hope didn't understand. She watched her mother, knowing she was locked into whomever it was she was texting. Her mother's once smooth skin was now showing wrinkles on her forehead and around her eyes, and there were small scars above one eyebrow and her upper lip. She wondered, but did not want to know, how they got there.

The bartender came with their order and as she placed Hope's plate in front of her, she admired the woman's tattoos. A complicated-looking compass, a symbol she didn't recognize and a Pegasus. Hope pointed to the winged horse and said, "I like that one."

The bartender took a bottle of house-made ketchup from her apron and placed it in front of Hope and said, "Thanks! It reminds me that one day we will all have wings to get us outta this place." She giggled, lightheartedly.

Hope looked at her, feeling that the tattoo meant something more but knew not to ask.

Lunch was, for the most part, silent. Missy ate her meatball sandwich and fries quickly and ordered a second drink. Hope watched as she threw it back in one gulp.

"Want some fries, Mom?" Hope was surprised at her own voice.

"Nah. We should hit the road, dontcha think?"

Hope put the rest of her sandwich down and wiped her mouth with her napkin, nodding.

The bartender came with the bill and told them to take their time.

Missy thanked her and waited for the woman to get back to the customers at the bar. She put a $10 bill on the table, put the check over it and grabbed Hope's hand.

"C'mon. Time to go."

24

The pieces of paper, some folded once, some twice, and some twisted tightly into a tiny ball all sat in the prayer bowl in the center of the table. The women sat, looking at their journals, deciding what to make of the drawing Piper had asked them to create. The elements were all very common things but they knew there must be a reason and explanation coming.

"Okay! You can put those aside for now. I'm going to have you work with each other. This is the fun part." Piper looked around at the varying reactions: excitement, fear, trepidation, surprise.

"Everyone will work with a partner. Trish and Camille ..." She stopped as the room erupted in giggles. "You two can't work together, pair up with someone you don't know that well." Camille feigned a sad face, complete with a pouty lower lip. Trish jumped up and grabbed Claire's hand. "You're working with me!"

Claire's face flushed pink, feeling accepted and a little bit pressured.

Piper placed some essential oil bottles on the table, instructing the group to take one that they were drawn to without looking at the label, and to use it if they were feeling nervous or on edge as they worked on their assignment.

"Okay, now take an item of yours: a pen, lip gloss, keys, anything that belongs to you and hand it to your partner. Sit with them as you hold their item and just let yourself write down or if it's easier to just say it, tell them what comes to you about them. Don't overthink, just write or speak."

Immediately, Trish's hand went up. "Wait."
Piper, calmly yet sternly answered, "No waiting."

She sat at her desk and flipped the calendar from April to May. She wondered how it was spring already. *Time marches on, but why do we follow?*

Piper felt a shiver that wanted to course through her body but she had long ago learned that she could override her nervous system and if need be, outsmart it. She shook her foot instead, letting off that energy surge the way she chose to.

The excited giggles and hushed discussion happening had her smiling. She walked quietly throughout her office, which was dimly lit and smelling of sage, lemon, verbena, as people wafted the essential oils and wrote as they held onto a ring, a pillbox, a handful of keys.

Below her she could hear one of the horses lean on his stall door, making it squeak.

She began to go through her mental list of things to order in the morning: hay, sweet feed, beet pulp, shavings, and Cosequin for her older, creaky gentleman equines. She walked among the participants who had scooted chairs to the corners of the room; some sat criss-cross applesauce on the floor, shoes off, completely at ease. She smiled to think that these women, earlier in the day were running a pharmacy, holding stake-holder meetings, drawing blood, and suturing wounds. Here though, they were pure spirit. The human stuff fallen away.

"Piper! You're not going to believe this," said Anne, who was more of an observer than anything.

"Oh, I'll believe it," she replied.

More giggles. The women who had been coming regularly before the pandemic knew all the Piperisms: "Say everything. You can't make this sh** up! I believed it a long time ago, it was you who needed to catch up. Just start, Spirit will take it from there but you have to start." Piper listened as their conversations unfolded, revealing bits of intuited information to each other.

When twenty minutes had passed, Piper called the group to get back to their seats.

One by one they shared with the group the information they had gotten while using psychometry. Anne, with a sudden animated expression said, "Oh! This is why I have anxiety in antique shops! It's all the energy that's still in all that stuff? Really?"

Piper had learned to facilitate rather than always teach. She let them share their experiences, not so different from one another.

Piper looked up at the clock on her desk. "Okay so we only have time for either the treasure box or a name."

Claire's eyes went around the circle to see if anyone was going to make a motion or protest in any way. This was only her fourth meeting and she had come to look forward to the treasure box. Trish spoke up, "Name!"

Camille said, "No torture box tonight! Haha, whew!"

Claire sat quietly, disappointed but also curious what the name activity would be.

Piper had written the same name on eight slips of paper, each folded twice, and then placed them in a pale blue Harney and Sons tea tin. She walked around the circle and had each person pull a slip of paper. The women assumed they all received a different name.

Piper dimmed the lights a little and put on some soft music and encouraged the women to just relax and ask their own higher self to help them write any impressions they got about the person on the paper. She added, "Oh, and this person is alive but that's all I'll say. Okay, go ahead."

Around the circle, each woman unfolded their paper.

Hope, Hope, Hope, Hope, Hope, Hope, Hope, Hope.

25

Eastern daybreak on Mount Desert Isle is not something you can ignore easily, especially if you are from away, meaning you weren't born there. The light, saturated and muted paint strokes of pink, coral, and gold, blends with whatever it touches, warming, slowly, the landscape and if you're conscious of it, the heart.

Rebecca sat on the edge of Hope's bed and cradled her, just like she had done when Hope was eleven and first moved into the spacious bedroom at Full Circle Farm. She and Eli had prepared the room the way a couple does when expecting a baby: with love, consideration, and anticipation. It was eight months before they could get Hope to sleep anywhere but the couch in the parlor downstairs. In the Barlow cabin, there was one bedroom and it was not for Hope. The couch was hers and it's where she was comfortable. Rebecca spent more than a handful of nights curled up in the occasional chair in the corner of this bedroom when she was finally able to convince Hope to try sleeping in the queen-sized bed complete with linens and pillows from Pottery Barn.

"I don't know why she wanted to come back here," Hope said. Her voice, interrupted by sobs and sniffles, was as heartbreaking as it was healing. She was no longer a child. The disappointment Rebecca heard wasn't pure sadness. There was a healthy dose of anger below the obvious pain.

She was comforted by Rebecca's soft voice. "Have you asked why she wanted to come back?"

Hope sat up then, wiping at her face and pulling her hair up to make a ponytail. Rebecca reached out for the hair elastic on the nightstand but Hope was faster. Rebecca watched the magic that happens when a woman is intent on getting something worked out, fixed, finished, or finagled. The young woman who had overcome so much in life and deserved the chance to be happy and free from her past hopped off the bed then, her lanky frame straightening, casting off the despair that had come in like the tide overnight. "I don't even know where she is. I've texted her so many times and she won't text me back. I called. Nothing."

A soft knock on the bedroom door came and startled her. "Mom? Is that you?" She reached out and swung the door open as she let out a heavy sigh.

Eli stood with his fist still in the air. His eyes surveyed the room and landed on Rebecca's drawn face.

"Sorry, Honey. It's just me," Eli almost whispered.

"Don't be sorry. I shouldn't have agreed to meet with her. I just thought," her voice trailed off and then roared back like a lioness. "I just thought she wanted to see me but I was wrong. I'm so stupid!" She brushed past Eli and trotted down the walnut staircase. Rebecca shrugged her shoulders while Eli stood still in the doorway, holding his breath.

The back door opened and slammed closed as Hope headed to the barn to feed the horses.

"What do we do, Eli?" Rebecca stood and watched out the window as Hope approached the barn, her ponytail swaying back and forth like a rudder working hard to keep her on track.

Eli sat on the edge of the bed the way he did when Gracie was little. His tall frame out of sync with the delicate looking furniture and hushed tones of the feminine space.

"I don't know, Becca. I mean, Melissa is up to no good. We both know it. I mean, the timing—it seems obvious what this is about. She isn't interested in Hope's life. She's looking for money."

Rebecca turned back toward Eli and for the first time in a very long time, she felt compassion for the burdens he carried. Grace had disappointed him greatly and he blamed himself for all that she doled out. Eli shook his head. "I'm just glad Grace and Grayson are back in California." Rebecca knew not to agree or add or even acknowledge. Grace was the mistress of drama, whipping herself up like a batch of burnt sugar, encasing anyone in her vicinity in utter sticky chaos.

"I just want to protect Hope from whatever it is Missy thinks she has to gain from coming back here. She doesn't deserve any of that bullshit and Missy doesn't deserve Hope."

Eli stood up then. He knew Rebecca was right but also didn't have the bandwidth to get into an argument about any of it. His wife's intuition was on point and he long ago resolved to be a partner in whatever ways she needed him to be. He wasn't always successful but he did make the effort. Rebecca wasn't Antigone and she wasn't Grace. He reminded himself on a regular basis that Rebecca took on a lot when she took on Eli Cranston.

The sound of tires on the gravel driveway was as normal as any when the store was open but Rebecca moved quickly out of the bedroom toward the hallway window. "Eli. It's her. Go! It's Missy."

Eli ran his fingers through his mostly gray hair and made his way down the curved staircase, not sure of what he was about to say.

Rebecca wasn't far behind him but she was more than sure about what she was going to say.

They waited for the door to open and when it did, they were both speechless.

26

John was comfortable in the barn but it wasn't where he would choose to spend his free time. Work kept him busy and he found a bit of distance to be essential to a husband and wife who both worked from home. Springtime chores on the farm, though, called for all hands on deck.

Piper printed several copies of her list of chores and pinned them up in the tack room, grain room, at the arena entrance, and staircase to the loft. Her two boarders and all clients were invited to help out in exchange for a discount during the month of May. If horse people were anything, they were tough as nails, gentle as angels, and always, always in need of a discount.

John walked down the aisle with an armful of clean horse blankets, some in need of stitching and some just of folding before being stored for the summer. He dumped them on the table set up in the tack room, groans coming from the preteens who, despite being clients, took pride in the running of the farm.

"More to come. The dryer is working overtime," he told the kids. They got right to work, smoothing out the giant polyester and nylon blankets, folding the leg straps, tail flaps, straightening the surcingles to lie flat, a contest to see who could get it done the quickest. "Geez, I'll bring out our laundry, too, if you guys get bored." John missed having children around. He and Kayla had had dreams of their own but life didn't always go to plan. He thought then how life can bring the unexpected, both tragic and sweet. Finding Piper again as an adult after Kayla's passing, to him, seemed like a true miracle.

He walked down to the end of the aisle, knowing Piper had planned to scrub the water trough in the pasture. Before he got there, he heard a man's voice, not as common in the barn unless it was the farrier.

"Hey, you must be Piper's husband." Slade stepped out of a stall and wiped his hands on his jeans before reaching out for John's hand. "I'm Slade."

John looked up at the slightly taller man, trying to place him. "Hi, Slade. Nice to meet ya. Are you the new boarder?"

Slade was surprised but wasn't sure why he was. "No, no. I've been taking lessons for a couple of months."

John was confused but hid it well. "Piper's got you on cobweb duty, I see?"

Slade took a step out of the stall and winced. "Yea, she does. I don't mind it. I like the barn and the horses. It's a whole new world for me." He reached down and rubbed the side of his knee.

"You okay?" John asked, genuinely concerned.

"Oh yah, my knee swells when the weather changes. It's all good."

John looked over his shoulder knowing it was his wife entering the barn. The horses 275 didn't call like that to just anyone.

"I see you've met Slade," Piper said as she reached up and put her hand on John's arm. "He's been in the program for a couple of months."

"Oh, the program, okay. So therapeutic riding." John looked at Slade with a little more understanding as the gears in his head seemed to come together now. He turned to Piper. "What's next? Or dare I ask?"

Piper pulled out a copy of her list and demonstratively unfolded it. "Choose your own adventure, sweetheart." John looked at the list and decided that sweeping the hayloft and picking up baling twine was the easier and least messy item left on the list.

"Hayloft, my dear," he said.

"Hey, Slade. Nice to meet you. I look forward to seeing you again. Take it easy on that knee."

Slade shook John's hand again. " Yes sir. Roger that."

Piper walked toward the tack room, stopping to call up the steps to John, who was halfway up them, "Hey, we need to talk about Hope later. I think she will be here before summer. I just spoke to Becca."

"Our home is hers. Just let me know when I should paint that room. And for god's sake, pick a color."

Piper smiled up at him. For a split second, she saw Paul. Her heart wanted to run down that neural pathway, kicking up the dust of the past. The love, heartache, guilt. Her heart was stubborn but it knew those pathways didn't lead anywhere anymore. John had taken care of that with hypnosis, time, and a boatload of love. John lowered his voice and took two steps down toward his wife. "That guy. He's a vet?"

Piper nodded. "I'll tell you more later."

27

The quiet of Eli's new office was a welcome reprieve from the busyness of the farm and all the events that had unfolded in previous months. He looked out on Cottage Street from his second story vantage point, squinting at the strong light that spoke of spring.

His phone buzzed. His 11:30 client would be five-ish minutes late which he knew meant ten-ish to twelve-ish minutes late.

He pulled out the legal folder he hadn't had time to go through since he brought it to town, feeling it was safer there than at home.

He ran his fingers over the gold lettering and opened the navy-blue cover as he pulled it from the file drawer. Otto and Elise's will was not very thick. It had been amended over the years as is often the case when people live as long as they did. Eli, of course, had offered to scour it in addition to meeting with their real estate attorney, but he wasn't needed. "You've done enough, my friend. You've done more than enough," Otto told him.

He started at the last page, a habit he picked up in graduate school, recognizing it was his impatience and his misguided thinking that a doctorate in clinical psychology would be a breeze in comparison to law school.

His phone buzzed again. Piper, not urgent.

He flipped through the pages, not for the first time, but with a feeling of apprehension nonetheless. Had anything been overlooked? Was there something the Gunther's lawyer had missed?

Footsteps on the stairs, a quick glance at the clock on the wall. Only seven-ish minutes late.

In rushed Lois, his 11:37 appointment.

"Dr. Cranston." she huffed. " I'm so sorry. I left on time but my kids. Augh, kids. I do everything for them. Why can't they let me have just one hour to myself, for me? For therapy, for God's sake!"

Eli slid the folder back into the drawer.

"Lois, that is a great question. Let's start there. Why don't your kids let you have an hour to yourself? They are young adults now."

Lois, a newer client who Eli enjoyed working with, sat in the nautical-themed chair across from Eli's desk. She smoothed her blouse and skirt as she settled into the sea blue fabric. Eli took a seat in the matching chair and mirrored Lois's posture, legs crossed, hands folded.

"I know, but kids today aren't adults now until they are at least thirty. I mean, when I got married and started having kids, I was twenty-one! These kids are still trying to figure out what they want to do for work, they can't afford rent, student loans are ridiculous, and their maturity level. Ha! My God, I had a twelve-year-old by the time I was my son's age. A twelve-year-old and he sleeps until noon, can't find a job, plays video games 'til the sun goes down then goes out with his girlfriend. And she's just as bad but at least she makes money. Granted it's on-line but still, she has a job."

Eli waited, taking deep breaths and nodding until she came up for air.

"You're not the first to describe an adult child that way. I have several clients who did all the right things for their kids, gave them all the opportunities they didn't have growing up, and yet their kids just aren't motivated to get their life in gear." Eli knew he had hit a hot button and it wasn't by accident.

"Well, I mean," Lois started, "he is motivated. He has been applying for jobs. There isn't a lot out there and I do think he's depressed. We've talked about that. I want him to feel better and take his time, not just take any job."

Eli nodded. It was natural for a mother to defend her child but Eli wanted her to see she was part of the equation, making it too easy for her adult son to live the lifestyle he was living.

Eli nodded and waited. He knew there had to be more. Lois worked two jobs and didn't get much support from her ex-husband who moved down to Portland to be with his girlfriend who was just a few years older than their daughter. Lois was not unique in the sense that a lot of women were playing the role of mother, father, breadwinner, homeowner, and ring leader. They are worker bees and they do not ask for help. They double down, smile, and post on social media about how beautiful their family is, the sourdough they baked, and inspirational quotes to make other people feel good about the world. Eli devoted a chapter to them in his book. It was titled "An Absolute Shame."

Lois's lip quivered as her hands smoothed the hem of her charcoal knee-length skirt.

"Sometimes I wish," she stopped. Eli held out the tissue box to her. "Sometimes I wish I didn't care so much. I mean, it would be so much easier if I could be like those parents you hear about. They give their kids eighteen years and then they cut them off, toss them out of the house to figure it out on their own. And, my God—they do!"

Eli smiled and nodded, waiting. Lois dabbed at her eyes, careful to catch the tears before they could scurry away, making tracks through her makeup. Her blunt blonde haircut and immaculately manicured nails completed the picture that Eli estimated would be looked back at decades from now as a hallmark of the mid 2020's era woman: highly educated, burnt to a crisp, still trying to do it all, have it all, and figure it out alone because somehow society told them they were boss bitches and this was par for the course. Some received no child support and some even paid alimony to the man they once entrusted as a partner. What Eli found distressing was that they truly thought it had to be that way, that they couldn't change their circumstances. It was always, "My retirement, my plan, my career, the knot at the end of my rope."

Lois unfolded the tissue and folded it back up, concentrating on keeping her voice from shaking. She looked up at Eli through fresh tears and said, "Oh. I don't mean that. I can't imagine a mother ever doing that and being able to live with herself."

28

Melissa stood in the doorway of the farmhouse, her red top torn off her shoulders, hanging down around her waist. Her makeup smeared over her pale complexion, one eye swollen almost completely shut, she looked like she had lived a lifetime in the seventy-plus hours she'd been away from the house. Ashes fell from the half smoked, lipstick-stained cigarette in her mouth onto her Coach bag. Rebecca thought later how odd it was that she noticed, from all the details that were on display, that Missy had a tattoo under her left breast. "S" was all that she could make out, the rest of the letters covered by a bent underwire. She guessed it must have read Stan. She thought, *Who still wears underwire bras?*

Eli put up his hands like a scarecrow might when it saw a tornado blowing through, useless and almost comical if it were not for the absolute decimation. "Wait. Melissa. You can't," was all he could get out before she was shuffling past him to the kitchen.

"Mahnin'. I just need some coffee. No breakfast for me."

Rebecca blinked several times and chuffed. "Eli, what the hell?" He looked at her as helplessly as he once had looked at Antigone when Gracie spiked her first fever and vomited on his freshly cleaned suit a half hour before work. He froze.

Rebecca walked past Eli into the one place she felt she had complete control, be it in the house or in the farm store. The kitchen was Rebecca's domain.

"Excuse me, Melissa, uh. Are you? Are you okay? Do you need a ride to urgent care or?"

Melissa poured coffee from the carafe, pushed her hair back with a shaking hand and asked, "Where's my kid?"

Eli's eyes widened. He felt rage surge from his legs up into his solar plexus and out toward the woman who had done so much damage to Hope and was evidently bent on continuing down the same path of destruction.

He jumped out of his skin when he heard Rebecca shout for only the second time since he'd known her, "She is not your kid anymore! She is ours! You have no right to do this to her. Hope is the strongest and most loving young woman despite the shit you and Stan put her through! We saved her. Don't you forget that! We loved her through all that trauma when you walked out of her life and we are not going to stand by quietly while you crush her again!"

Melissa slurped her coffee, unfazed. She waved Rebecca's words away like a fly at a picnic.

She scratched her head and looked somewhat disappointed, as if Rebecca was off to a good start but needed to keep dancing, entertaining, fanning Melissa's flames. It wasn't lost on Eli that Grace was of the same caliber.

Rebecca's eyes were wildly fierce. Eli would think back to this moment years hence and realize that a woman did not need to give birth to a child to possess all the wisdom, instinct, and downright blood boiling rage it sometimes required to keep one safe. It would be a very long time before he would string the appropriate words together to capture the respect he had felt for her in that moment.

Melissa's phone buzzed in her bag. The tossing of lipstick, wallet, and lighter onto the counter was a scene from a movie, Eli was sure. One of those 90s drug-fueled and violent ones you could watch for free now on a streaming service; there were several. They never seemed plausible when you were in college, eating popcorn, and your smuggled Mike and Ike's on a Saturday night, trying to escape the pressures of final exams. And yet, here he was on his midlife career change trajectory, in his second wife's kitchen with his adopted daughter's biological mother playing the role. In the flesh. To a T. She swiped her phone open.

"Hey. Give me a sec. I just gotta wash up and then ... no, like ten minutes, Dude. C'mon." Missy walked past the stunned Cranstons and down the hall toward the stairway. They looked at each other in disbelief as she giggled, promising to make Dude's patience pay off.

Behind them, the back door that attached the main house to the back house and farm store opened. Hope kicked off her boots, her cheeks pink from the chilly morning air.

"My mom texted. She'll be here soon."

29

The smell of the fly spray caught Slade by surprise. His first thought was Brake Kleen but then it hit him. DoD-issue insect repellent. He never thought he'd smell that again. He stepped back from Oliver's side and felt that familiar rub on his knee that meant one thing. He tried to ignore it but it played in the background like the annoying music every company chooses to assault your senses with when you're on hold, just trying to pay a bill or refill a prescription.

The sounds of late spring were a welcome change from just a month ago when Maine was still teetering between slumbering and fully awake . The warblers and thrushes singing their way into the fabric of the farm was not lost on Slade. Birdsong was soothing and he had learned to appreciate it when he returned from overseas. The therapist at the VA hospital explained to him that humans evolved to relax in the presence of birdsong because it meant there was no danger in the environment. It was when birds suddenly stopped that you could be certain there was a predator nearby. She had even suggested he listen to meditations that incorporated birdsong when he had trouble sleeping. At that time in his life he wondered if that young chick knew he was always about five minutes from using a bullet to solve his problems. He figured she didn't.

Slade led Oliver into the arena and walked him, painfully, to the mounting block. He couldn't walk around the arena before mounting this time. Piper called down from her office, "I'll be down in two minutes!"

Oliver bobbed his head once and Slade laughed. "She sure does have everyone in her sites all the time, doesn't she, pal?"

Slade stepped from the mounting block into the stirrup and swung his throbbing knee over the saddle, Oliver stepping off a moment later. "Hey, hold up," he said and gently leaned back, careful not to pull on the reins.

"Good job," Piper said as she entered the arena. It was the first time Slade had seen her dressed in anything less than Carhartt coveralls, fleece headband, and Nordic sweater.

Today she stood at the X position in the center of the arena in jeans and a pink hoodie.

"You and Ollie are a good team, Slade. You take good care of him."

Slade shifted his weight to the inside of the arena, his left. Oliver veered off the rail toward the center. Piper quipped, "Oh. I spoke too soon."

Slade laughed. "Sorry, my leg is killing me." He shifted his weight back and Oliver followed back to the rail.

Piper asked, "Want to stop? It's fine. You can come back another day this week."

"Nah. I'm good to go."

He relaxed into the rhythmic walk his 16.2-hand friend settled into. A barn swallow suddenly swooped down from a rafter and caught Slade by surprise, one arm flying up instinctively. Oliver stopped abruptly, nostrils flared, head high.

"Let him know, he's okay. Give him a squeeze. Remember, he needs you to be his leader even when you're on his back. Horses are prey animals and they need their leader to keep them safe."

Slade, slightly embarrassed, apologized to Oliver and stroked his neck. "Sorry, pal. It's okay." Oliver stomped one hoof and stood firm. Slade was unsure what to do and felt nervous.

Piper was as calm as they come, which helped, although Slade hadn't the faintest idea that she sounded the same way when horses bolted with children aloft.

"Just breathe. He will feel you calm down. He's honed in on

how you are feeling, that's all. He wonders what the fuss is about. Now give him a squeeze."

Slade squeezed his legs and winced at the pain in his right knee. He knew it was infected. *Dammit* he thought.

Oliver moved forward then, head lowered and back to his relaxed self.

"See that? When you relax, he will. He needs to know you'll keep him out of trouble. I'm telling you. That is the beginning and end of horsemanship. You have to be dependable and he will come through. Ten outta ten."

As they walked around Piper for the third time, John ducked under the rope in the open doorway of the arena that faced the back of the house. Piper seemed surprised to see him and when John turned his back to Slade to speak in a low voice to Piper, Slade felt like he was intruding in some way. Without trying he could hear bits of the conversation, thanks to the fantastic acoustics of the arena "Oh. Geez. That's not good. Yes, tell them to send her. We've been waiting."

He kept his eyes forward and asked Oliver for a twenty-meter circle to see if he was paying attention.

"Nice job," John said. Slade turned to look at him.

"Hey, John. Thanks."

He leaned back to stop Oliver in front of John who reached up and rubbed the tall Iberian horse's slightly concave forehead. "How's that knee, Slade?"

"Oh, not too bad," he lied. "Good days and bad but it is what it is."

John looked up at the man and could see he was uncomfortable. "Well, don't push yourself. My wife will have people riding with pneumonia, dysentery. The plague!"

Slade smiled and relaxed as Piper, shouted. "O-U-T!"

John jogged out of the arena and back toward the house. Piper was intent on texting Rebecca and Eli that Hope's room was ready for her. It was painted a pale aqua called Tranquility. Rebecca responded with, **Perfect. That's exactly what she needs.**

When the session was over, Slade told Piper he didn't think he could slide off the saddle and land on his right foot without consequence.

"No worries," she said and walked Oliver toward the mounting block. "Just like mounting up but in reverse."

Slade wasn't sure he could execute that, since mounting took months to perfect but he surprised himself. He also hadn't seen Piper working with clients with cerebral palsy, multiple sclerosis, and other physical limitations. This is what she had dedicated her life to and had trained many years for.

Piper moved Oliver away from the block and held her arm out to Slade to help him down from the three small steps he stood atop.

Slade was uncomfortable and not wanting to rely on a woman to help him, despite all the nurses, doctors, and therapists at the VA who happened to all be women.

He stood for a moment on this little island in the sand arena, unable to shit or get off the pot. He looked at Piper and said, "I just realized I wore the wrong leg today."

30

The golden light streaming through the western-facing window of Piper's office warmed the chairs as the women entered, chatting and exclaiming how nice it was to be there before the sun faded. Excited chatter about the evening, and how hard it was to wait two whole weeks before sharing what they had meditated on the last time they met, filled the warm room. Piper adjusted the music volume as she greeted the group. They had fallen into a nice rhythm with eight consistent people every other week, tonight being the first class with a person missing. Soon they would realize that not only did they learn more than they were previously aware of, but that the group's energy was different without all its members; the delicate balance could easily degrade the integrity of what they'd begun to build.

Piper waited while the women placed all the written intentions into the bowl before asking them if they'd like to share any experiences or dreams they'd had in the last couple of weeks. No one was surprised that Trish spoke up immediately. She was brimming with enough energy to replace her friend Camille's absence.

"I had a dream that you and John had a child," Trish said provocatively. The silence that settled into all the available spaces of the office could be felt. Piper nodded, "Go on."

Trish said, "I mean not a baby, obviously, but that you had a child and for some reason he had to go away."

Anne watched the micro-expressions on Piper's face from

her vantage point two seats away. She could feel Piper's unease. Trish continued, "I didn't get a clear sense about why he was away but it seemed deeply upsetting. Then the scene changed and I woke up in a cold sweat. I really wanted to go back to sleep and see if I could somehow help. You know, I have been astral projecting for a long time and I can change things in the dream that really help people." Then, as quickly as Trish's energy bubbled up, it now receded. Piper looked around, "Anyone else?" Anne wanted to ask Trish at least thirty-seven questions but held her tongue. She tolerated Trish's need for attention and approval and she believed others felt the same way, but she kept her opinions to herself. What she had a hard time swallowing, though, was Trish's ability to make people nervous by throwing out little barbs like this and then going quiet.

Piper shifted in her chair, opened her journal to the page where she had taken notes from last class. "Oh, right. We need to go over what everyone got from the names they drew at the end of last class."

Immediately, journal pages turned, pens clicked, and Piper could feel the energy of the group ratchet up with intention and nervous anticipation. Claire sat, hands smoothing both pages of her open journal, not yet aware that she sometimes depended on her sense of touch to access her intuition in some cases. Her eyes went around the circle and landed on the women who had been in the group prior to the pandemic and tried hard not to compare herself. She might be new here, but she was proving to herself that she was progressing quickly, even if there were days she doubted herself.

Piper took a breath and slowly exhaled. "Okay. So, we will go one by one around the circle and I want you to read what you got from the name I gave you but don't say the name. Okay?" She looked around at the women, nodding. "Okay, so let's start on my left. Remember, no name, just go."

Sherry, who was even quieter than Claire, crossed her legs at her ankles, turned her journal page, turned it back again, adjusted her glasses, cleared her throat, and began.

Everyone knew it was difficult being the first to go. "Okay, so I feel like I didn't get a lot that night, but the next day I wrote more. Is that okay?" She looked at Piper for a brief moment and looked away as if Piper held some sort of power and that perhaps Sherry had done something wrong. Piper smiled wide. "That's exactly what you should do! I've been telling people for years: most of the valuable work you'll do is between classes. Good job!"

Sherry visibly relaxed, sat up a little straighter, and started again. "Okay, so what I got was that this person is struggling. I'm not sure with what, exactly, but I heard, 'She's in the wrong place right now? That she needs to follow the arrows?' I don't know what that means." Sherry looked at Piper to gauge if she was correct or not. Piper stared straight ahead and people laughed. "Piper has the best poker face," Trish said.

"Well, I felt like this person was planning to move but I think it might be temporary, not sure. She is definitely an animal lover. I think she's an only child but again, not sure."

She closed her journal softly and didn't look up. "That's all I got."

Trish was already speaking before Sherry finished her last sentence.

"Well, all week, I have been going back and writing more and more."

Piper's eyelid began to twitch, her chin moving slightly forward. Anne noticed, confirming her own feeling that Trish was embellishing or simply lying.

"So this person is female, on the shorter side, a little bit thick through the middle, is mid-40s, married, has two children, both boys but not twins, wants a divorce, and is possibly involved with someone else, but no one knows yet. She works a high-level management job and is hungry for something more: attention, accolades, and recognition. She also has amethyst crystals on her work desk and carries obsidian in her purse. I feel like she has some childhood trauma, maybe also some past life stuff going on."

Anne wanted to blurt out, "That's you, Trish!" but she would never. She let people be who they are, but she didn't have to like it. She understood now that Trish's friend Camille actually balanced her in a way, keeping her more likeable somehow and in Camille's absence, they were seeing Trish, un-filtered.

Several others read their list, including Anne. There were some similar details like hair color and other characteristics but mostly there were lots of random bits of details. Piper felt they had done an exceptional job but definitely needed to work on honing the details further. Piper looked to her right, at Claire, who sat patiently, confidently. She cleared her throat and read her list.

"Dark hair, ponytail, sad but not always. She has been through a lot of family changes but rolls with it, until now anyway. She's—" She stopped and tilted her head. "I'm getting something but it doesn't make sense. I'll see if it comes back later. Anyway, she is missing someone terribly, maybe a parent? But really, she's disappointed in her parents, both of them. In spite of their faults, she's grown into a capable (that's the word I heard) young adult. I see her on a horse. At first, I thought it was my imagination since we are sitting in a hayloft above horses but no, it was clear. She was on a horse and this was the thing that made her most happy. I also got that she will soon be really disappointed in someone, maybe the parent she is miss-ing? Not sure but that would actually be a blessing in disguise."

Piper quickly jumped in, "Why?"

Claire didn't look up. "Because it will make her so uncom-fortable, she will have to keep moving."

Piper asked, "What else?"

Trish interrupted, "I actually feel that's not at all correct, sorry." Anne wanted to throw her pen across the circle at Trish for how rude she was being. Trish was incorrectly reading Piper's inquiry as impatience for Claire when in fact it was quite the opposite.

Ignoring Trish, Piper urged Claire, "Tell me more about her." Claire looked up and shrugged. "That's all I got when I did it. " She closed her journal to make her point: she did not want to continue with Trish acting like a pariah. Piper said, "Okay but what about now. Remember, you can tap in now. This person is alive, she is living her life right now." Claire sheepishly bit her lip. Anne quietly said, "You can do it. You're doing a great job." Piper winked at Anne. Sherry added, "Say everything, Claire!"

Claire took a deep breath and said, "She's about to find out something really important about her father. Something that will change her life in a big way. Not a bad way, just something she had no idea about and," she stopped. "And she will also be traveling. She's quite independent and capable. And, something about," she stopped, squinting her eyes in concentration, "something about a round metal instrument. It's lost but not for long."

A flash of knowing lit up Claire's eyes. The soft hush of the other women was reassuring: "Wow, she got a lot. Amazing, She's so good. I wish I got that much!"

Trish said, "Sounds like she just added a couple things to what everyone else got, which is weird because we all got different people. I mean, it does happen, you'll figure it out." She stared at Claire from across the circle.

The tension in the room had enveloped and then snuffed out the pleasant energy like a jar candle cover starves the flame inside.

Piper adjusted the music again and planned to adjust this group if Trish continued to contaminate it.

"Okay, let's do our meditation now. Feet flat on the floor, we can ground ourselves and just ..." She stopped as Trish interrupted, "Wait! That's it? Aren't you going to tell us who is right? I mean what's the point of the exercise if you don't tell us if we are right or not?" Piper's face remained expressionless as she explained, "In time, Trish. You all got some important details."

Trish's attitude would not be squashed. She refused to feel embarrassed and demanded in some way to be compensated. "Well can we at least share the names so we can have some homework?"

Piper shrugged, not impressed but also not wanting to

admonish Trish in front of the others.

"Sure. Let's go around the circle and everyone can read the name they got."

Piper watched as Trish stared at her feet, wanting to disappear into the floorboards as everyone went around the room, "Hope, Hope, Hope, and when it was Claire's turn, she said, "Hope is rising."

31

Slade got to the shop before it reached its frenzied, noisy fever pitch. The days leading up to Memorial Day weekend had everyone suddenly needing oil changes and tire rotation. He sipped his coffee at his desk, which was hopelessly covered in invoices, bills, and parts orders.

He cleared a small space for his laptop and opened it. He reached down to rub his knee and stopped himself. The less he touched it, the better. He searched his inbox for a response from his doctor but didn't see anything. He needed to get his knee figured out soon.

A honk in front of the first bay reminded him that customers knew his vehicle and that he was there even before the 7:00 am start time. He looked out the side window of the shop and recognized his boss's daughter's car. Normally he would open the door for an early customer but didn't want Bill's daughter there without Bill. She could wait.

He searched online for a prosthetist outside of the Veterans Administration network. He had to do something.

Another honk, longer this time. He looked at his watch. 6:58. He knew Bill would be there any minute so against his better judgement, he hit the button to open the door and before it reached the top of the track, the Mini Cooper was rolling in. He waved at the young woman behind the wheel. She opened her window and yelled, "Air. Tires." Slade grabbed the hose and hit the compressor switch. Anissa swung the door open and almost hit Slade when she did. "Oh sorry. Can you wash my windshield, too? These bugs are in-*sane*." He nodded, smiled. Slade knew she could be trouble and he couldn't afford to lose his job. He planned to retire just as soon as he could but that was several years away. He had seen more than one guy fired because of her.

"So Dad said you've been learning to ride." Slade stared at the tire in front of him wondering why his boss would tell his kid about that.

He looked over his shoulder at her. "Yea."

"I used to ride. Thoroughbreds, mostly. And Warmbloods. Dad always promised me a barn but that's never gonna happen. He's too busy with his slut girlfriend and her ugly kids."

Slade was relieved to hear Bill's truck pull into the lot. He finished adding air to her tires and went to grab the squeegee for her windshield. She got out of the car, her shorts shorter than Slade expected, a tight tank top and flip flops. Bill walked in and immediately said, "Nissa, put some friggin' clothes on. Where are you going?" She looked at him, still angry about their argument the night before. Who was he to tell her how much pot she can smoke? He was the biggest pothead she'd ever seen. "I was just talking to Slade about how you never built me that barn."

"Oh, Jesus Christ, Anissa. Really? You want a barn? Okay, then all the vacations, toys, and money are going away. You can have a barn. Who's gonna clean all the shit and feed them 'cuz we know it's not gonna be you and I sure as hell ain't doing it. Time you grew up a little. Maybe get a job."

Slade busied himself with an arriving parts order in the parking lot while the hothead he worked for and his equally hotheaded kid exchanged words.

He walked back into the shop, limping now. Anissa noticed and asked, in a soothing voice, "Oh, Slade. What happened. Are you okay?"

Billy slammed his work bag on his desk. "Oh, for fuck's sake," he said under his breath.

Slade nodded. "Yea, I'm fine. Tires and windshield are all set. Want me to back it out for ya?"

"No, I got it. Thanks. Hey, where is the barn you ride at?" she said as she stared at the back of her father's head. "I'll have to check it out."

Before Slade could think of something to divert his attention, Bill jumped into the tiny car and backed it out of the shop, turned it around, got out, leaving the door open. "Have a fun day with the girls or whoever you're going to the beach with," he said and pointed for her to get into the car.

"Who said I'm going to the beach? You're so lame," she said and slammed her door.

When she was gone and Billy was making orders for tires, Slade made a phone call to the VA.

"Yea, I need to make an appointment for my leg. Yea, it's definitely infected and I also wanna talk about something to help me sleep. Yea, nightmares. I mean no different than usual but more often. Okay, yea. Sooner than later."

He rolled up his right pant leg and popped off the prosthetic, removed the neoprene liner and took a picture of the angry raw skin with his phone. The VA wasn't known for efficiency but at least if he added a picture to his online chart, he might get some attention.

32

The text from Eli's agent both motivated and scared him a little. He had gotten a sizeable advance for his manuscript but without his promotion, the book wouldn't likely be a huge success. In other words, he needed sales. Of course, Rebecca reminded him, the agent only got paid when books sell and that the agent should be doing more to promote Eli and his work. In any event, having been invited to speak about his work would provide him a chance to make a shameless plug for the book.

The conference room at the Portsmouth Hilton was bustling with therapists, psychologists, a few medical doctors, psych nurses, as well as a handful of law enforcement, school superintendents, and to his surprise, some media personnel. He opened an email in the parking lot to read that the keynote speaker had changed at the last minute but the program still had the original person's name. Eli shrugged, just glad he had arrived early so he could calm his nerves and have a cup of coffee. He had always felt that restaurant and hotel coffee mugs were too thick and too small. He was not a sipper. He liked his caffeine in one fast dose.

A few participants had settled at the large round table, looking over their welcome packets and sticking their "HELLO my name is" sticker on their shoulder or lapel. Eli looked over his notes, checking to be sure he not only had bookmarked his reading selection but also had taken pictures of the paragraphs he would be reading just in case he needed backup. It was not

lost on Eli Cranston that if his professional acuity had trans-
ferred to his personal life, he'd be living a perfect life. He knew
what Otto would have to say about that. One thought about
that man who taught him so much in the handful of years he'd
known him could put Eli back to rights in an instant. He fiddled
with his tie, looked at the room filling up with men and women
who were on the frontlines, helping those in need. He never
really liked the saying, *It takes a village,* but the longer he worked
in the mental health field the more he realized the weight of
those words and how true they rang.

A woman named Lucile, dressed in business attire, stepped
up to the podium to introduce herself as the organizer and to
let participants know the wifi password could be found in the
program, that the keynote had yet to arrive but should be there
shortly, and that in fact lunch would have a vegan option, and
apologized that it had been mistyped as vegetarian. Someone
in the back corner clapped. Eli's eyes widened as he stared at
the screen behind the woman. He wished he had poured himself a second cup of coffee before now. He looked at his watch
and decided it was worth the chance he wouldn't be back in
time for the start. He meandered his way around the large
tables, clad in white tablecloths with pitchers of water, a glass
for each participant.

Out in the carpeted foyer there was still plenty of fruit,
muffins, and orange juice. He grabbed a banana nut muffin
and filled his coffee cup to the top. *No allergen signs?* He thought.
He had learned through many, many years of working as a therapist that not everything was his job, duty, and responsibility.
As a former lawyer, though, he knew the consequences the
hotel could face if someone accidentally ingested something
they shouldn't. *Keep moving,* he thought to himself and made
his way back to the table near the podium.

His eyes landed on a man speaking to Lucille. He froze, almost missing the chair he was attempting to sit in. Mid sit, his
coffee spilled. *Dammit* he thought. Two women immediately
jumped up and blotted the spill with napkins, letting him
know he was fine. They were mothers and this was a knee jerk

reaction. They couldn't help themselves. He laughed, embarrassed. *Who was that man?* His mind worked on it like the raccoons trying to breach the grain bin in the barn. He couldn't let it go but he knew this would distract him if he didn't figure out how he knew that man.

Much to his surprise, the man followed Lucille back to the podium. She introduced him as Dr. Patrick Neeland of the American Psychological Association.

Eli's mind raced. *That name, how did I know that name?*

Dr. Neeland thanked the woman and apologized for being a bit late. "As you know, I was not the first choice to speak to you today and only got word last night I would be doing so." Laughter erupted around the room. "I suppose it is still an honor to be here and I do hope Dr. Harris enjoys the golf course today." Eli relaxed at this and laughed along with the crowd.

Eli listened to the speech with half an ear as he went over his notes and tried to read Rebecca's texts without emotion. It wasn't easy. **Have a great day. I'm so proud of you. Just a reminder that Hope agreed to see Melissa tonight. I'm nervous. Please try to get home by dinner. Love you.**

He texted back a heartfelt promise and shut his phone off, something out of the ordinary for him. He was nervous and needed to concentrate. Eli turned quickly when he heard his name. The man had just mentioned his name but it wasn't his turn to speak yet. Flustered, Eli smiled and hoped he could catch on to what was happening. Luckily Dr. Neeland realized Eli hadn't a clue what was happening. He reiterated, "I'll say again, that I am honored to introduce to you this year's winner of the American Psychological Foundation's Gold Medal Award for Impact in Psychology, which recognizes the work of a psychologist that is impactful and transformational. Dr. Cranston's groundbreaking work in the area of forward life progression has proven time and again to help people from all backgrounds move forward into the life they want without decades of talk therapy. His new book, *Victorious by Default, Reclaiming Your Self in Difficult Times* captures the importance of his work. Eli's mind spun. *What is happening right now?* As Dr. Neeland waved Eli to the podium, he looked at his green eyes and finely waxed mustache and suddenly the memory slammed into him. He smiled and shook the man's hand. "Thank you, Sir, uh, doctor." He laughed nervously, "Thank you, doctor."

Neeland looked at Eli in jest and, still at the microphone, asked, "Now do you remember me?" Eli's laugh was genuine, his cheeks blushed as he said, "I do. Yes, I do now. Wow."

Dr. Neeland stepped away and began to clap as the audience joined in. Eli was stunned to see hotel staff wheeling carts of his book around to the tables for each participant to take.

Suddenly all the stress of the previous months faded and Eli was standing, not in a courtroom where he thought he would live out his entire career, but here at a psychology conference in New Hampshire, receiving an award for the work that grew out of his thesis in graduate school. Forward Life Progression had helped many hundreds of his own patients over the years but it wasn't until he began teaching online at Stanford that he got to see the foothold the work had taken and how it rippled throughout many therapists with practices all over the country and in parts of Europe. For a moment he realized that he hadn't given himself enough credit.

"To say that I am shocked and ill-prepared would be an understatement," Eli said as he loosened his tie the slightest bit. "I had no idea this was happening. I thought I was going to be speaking about my work and maybe get in a word edgewise about my book." He looked nervously at Lucille. "Am I still speaking about my book?" The laughter from colleagues was an instant comfort. The woman nodded emphatically. "Yes, Dr. Cranston. That's still one of the reasons you are here. The first is the award." She paused. "Which is the reason we asked you to speak about your book." Now it was Eli's turn to laugh. His emotions were high and he was suddenly feeling the double shot of caffeine now. He nervously turned to the passage in his book he had planned to finish with but felt it was appropriate to open with now.

"When one reaches a point in their life when they have tried all the tools in the toolbox, so to speak, and nothing has worked, not talk therapy, not medication, hospitalization, or major life change, that's the very time that Forward Life Progression works best. As odd as it seemed to me in the early years, it often wasn't as transformative when utilized prior to other modalities nor was it as effective alongside them." He surfaced for air and looked around the room at people taking notes, listening, flipping through his book.

He looked back at the highlighted paragraph. "It seems that FLP works best when people have reached their lowest. It's as if, for those willing to try, they have nothing left to lose and I do believe that is a key component to any type of therapy working on a substantially deep enough level to be of great benefit. The person has to suspend all belief, all expectation, all judgement. What I have been deeply moved by as a therapist, a husband, and father is that even in that state, the one quality that all clients who benefit from FLP is that they still hold onto hope."

Eli was stunned to feel his throat tightening, eyes welling up, thinking about Hope and how he felt he had failed her, just like he felt he failed Grace. Was he failing Rebecca, too? How could he help so many people, receive this award, write this book. and accomplish these goals when he was letting down the very people he loved the most? He suddenly felt like an imposter. He cleared his throat and continued.

"In closing, I would like to thank the foundation once again for this award and all of you for doing the work you do." He contemplated ending there but continued. "I know it is not easy work, nor does it get easier. The more you help, the more there seems a need to help. I will leave you with this thought. When you care for yourself enough to treat yourself with all the dignity and respect you treat your clients, you will become the best version of yourself. Not only that, you will give the gift of time, love, and patience to those who mean the most to you. Don't let this career run you down. Let it build you up. Thank you.

And to you, Dr. Neeland, Sir. I know a certain barista who will absolutely love this story." Dr. Neeland leaned back and laughed. "Dr. Cranston, you are funny. I can assure you, she already knows."

33

The flour-covered, stainless steel table was the canvas on which Hope tossed small balls of dough. She enjoyed most of the farm kitchen chores but this one was a favorite. As she rolled out the balls into perfect 12" circles for the chicken pot pie crusts, her arms seemed to work on their own as her mind had its own job to do. It had been two weeks since her mother disappeared to who knows where and now she was back again and wanting to take Hope to dinner.

Rebecca knew about it but she wasn't sure if Eli did. Becca was the one helping her work out this mess with her mother. Growing up with an addict and trying to keep her alive when you were only eight or nine years old was hard enough. Then to have a seven-year reprieve, only to be confronted with the mess again was hard to take. Rebecca had told her, "You do not owe your mother anything. She is an adult and so are you." Hope knew Becca was right but she felt such a strong pull to see her mother again despite her ways. There was always the chance that she could change.

Jack came by the table, rolling a large cart covered with the pie plates full of chicken, carrots, peas, and gravy. He wiped his hands on his Full Circle Farm Apron and began placing the round discs of fresh dough onto the pies. Hope reached into the utensil drawer and pulled out a fork. She laughed as Jack grabbed one, too, and used it like a sword to poke at her with it. Together, they docked each of the ten pie crusts with holes for steam to escape. As Jack began to roll them toward the walk-in freezer, he said, "Next up, baked beans."

Hope sighed. Another project she enjoyed but a longer one.

"Hey Jack!" She waited, knowing you can't hear much when inside the frozen tundra. When Jack reappeared, his glasses were frosted over and his arms were covered in gooseflesh. He shivered and laughed. Hope said, "Jack, I have to leave at 5:00 today."

She bit her lip, a habit of which she was consciously trying to break herself.

She continued, "Becca knows already."

Jack, who had worked on the farm since Rebecca first opened the store, was a few years Hope's senior and knew the operation of the farm kitchen inside and out, backwards and blindfolded.

"It's only going to take us an hour to prep, twenty minutes to clean up, and I'll put them in the oven. You can leave whenever. You're the boss's daughter anyway. Why are you telling me?" Hope giggled. He was right but she never wanted to feel she was taking advantage. She clocked in and out just like Jack and the other employees.

Her phone buzzed. *Hey! I'll meet you at Galyn's at 5:30, k?*

Hope's stomach churned. Why Galyn's? The food would be more expensive and after what Missy pulled at that spot down in Brunswick, Hope didn't want to chance her stiffing a local establishment. She texted back, hands shaking, *Can we just go to Rosalie's?*

Each baked bean pot was the same: brown on the top, white on the bottom and marked with a blue crown, a number 3 inside, signifying the number of quarts it held. Durgin Park, Boston was stamped on the opposite side of each.

She carefully took these down from the pot rack above the largest steel work table and placed them in rows of three, each four deep for a total of twelve. When she first began working in the kitchen, shortly after coming to live with the newlywed Cranstons, she asked Rebecca why she didn't buy more pots so they could double the amount of beans they cook at once since it was such a popular item. She giggled when she remembered

Eli interjecting with, "Too much methane gas over Bar Harbor, that's why. The EPA would shut us down."

Truth was, Becca had just the one oven for all the items that needed cooking and it only fit twelve bean pots which needed to sit in the oven overnight. She asked Rebecca why she didn't just buy another stove. Becca, quick on her feet said, "Well, we have some bills coming up that have to be taken care of first."

Hope would never, as long as she lived, know how much they spent on the process of fighting for her, adopting her, and keeping her safe from Stan's and Missy's antics.

Jack drained the large kettle of navy beans, which soaked for several hours prior to being cooked. The steam was earthy, thick, and quickly fogged up his glasses. He took them off and wiped them with his apron. Hope said, "Why don't you just get contact lenses?" Not a moment later, a rag wrapped itself around the back of her head unexpectedly and made her laugh. "Jerk," she said.

She measured and placed all the ingredients except the pork fat into the bottoms of all the pots: dry mustard, brown sugar, ketchup, chopped onions, maple syrup, molasses, a tiny bit of red pepper flakes, and some smoked paprika. Jack hefted two strainers full of beans, handing one to Hope. They carefully emptied them into the pots, going back to the kettle to retrieve more beans until they were all carefully assigned to a pot. "Now the fun part," Hope said, grabbing a large, long-handled spoon. Jack rolled his eyes and teased, "Nerd."

She mixed each pot, bringing up the ingredients from the bottom, careful not to lose a single bean, while Jack added chunks of pork fat to the top. When they were satisfied, they poured in some of the water the beans had cooked in. "Right to the tippity top," Jack instructed. "That's a scientific term ya know." Hope ignored him as she carefully began to transfer the pots from the table to the oven. Jack followed until all twelve were neatly arranged inside. Hope set the oven to 200° as Jack wished the pots a good night and closed the oven door.

Jack could see Hope was distracted by her phone. He didn't have a lot of details, but he had gathered from Rebecca that

Hope's mother was on the loose and causing trouble. She told Jack that if anyone could keep things on a positive note in the kitchen, it was him.

Hope left the kitchen with her dirty apron still on. She texted her mother: **See you at Rosalie's soon. My treat tonight.**

34

Morning barn chores were more than a necessity to most people who were in the habit of starting their day that way. It was somewhat of a meditative practice. Some would call it spiritual, some would call it a pain in the ass; but all knew the unspoken connection with animals while the sun rose was a privilege. The feed room was prepped the evening before with supplements scooped and placed in clean feed buckets. On the mornings Piper fed grain, it would be added to all the buckets and feeding time was a lot quicker. This morning was a beet pulp morning which meant loading a five-gallon bucket with enough beet pulp for all seven horses and soaking it with warm water from the faucet. Long gone were the days of using cold water from the hose the night before and hoping it didn't freeze overnight waiting for it to be soaked well enough to feed the next morning.

The calls from the horses ranged from soft nickers of, *"We are hungry. We want breakfast,"* to wild screams of, *"We are dying. We are starving. We are literally fading away!"*

Piper cut open two bales of hay that sat in the aisle. Taking two flakes to each stall and tossing them in, sliding the doors open and closing them back up, Piper's routine was the same as it was when this barn was built as she and Paul were just starting their lives together. The protesting of the famished horses transitioned from dire admonishment to stomping and finally chewing. Piper reached for the broom when her phone buzzed. She ignored it. A second buzz. Then it rang. She sighed, meditative flow meets concrete dam.

She pulled her phone from her hoodie pocket as it continued to buzz, ring, and buzz again. *Might be time for a new phone,* she thought. Her brow furrowed as she realized her phone wasn't malfunctioning.

Trish missed call (3).

Trish texts (6).

And they continued. She sighed and waited.

Not answering

Back in the grain room she took the small sand shovel used only for mixing beet pulp or bran mash and churned the muddy brown slop, mixing it well, and dividing it among the waiting grain buckets. She drizzled molasses over the top and mixed again. Tossing the vibrating phone onto the pile of neatly folded clean fly sheets, she went to each stall, doling out the main course. She was greeted again, this time with softer, calmer calls.

Piper knew that her email to Trish would not go unanswered. It was brief and to the point, something that would not satisfy Trish, but Piper wasn't out to please her.

Hi Trish—Just a quick note to remind you of the expectations and behaviors for members in the development group. Please see the attachment that I provided to everyone years ago and also recently when we started up again.

I do hope you can understand why I am sending this. If the behavior you showed last night continues, I will have to ask you to remove yourself. The group is meant to be supportive and kind. No one above or below, that's why we sit in a circle.

Piper

Updating the white board at the entrance to the barn with information for the day's lessons and client sessions, and adding a note to boarders about purchasing their own Ivermectin within the next week and scrubbing water buckets, Piper wondered if she had time for breakfast before her first client arrived. Her phone screen was lit up when she returned to the feed room but she planned to ignore Trish's haranguing attempts for attention. Her most recent text was concise: **Please. I'm sorry.** Piper's shoulders dropped as she took a deep breath. *Later. I don't have time for this, sh*e thought. When she looked up, Trish was standing in the doorway of the feed room.

Piper, startled but not showing any signs of the like, stood with her phone in one hand and the stack of seven now empty grain buckets she was hugging.

"Trish," she said and instinctively placed the buckets between them.

Trish looked the part of lost puppy. It wasn't a new act. She leaned forward onto her toes and back again, the buckets an obvious barrier.

"Piper, I tried calling and texting. I was so worried," she paused. "I felt a *sudden* urgency I needed to come here."

The hair on Piper's arms stood at attention, her shoulder blades twitched. *Marek*, she thought. Why would she be thinking of him? Why was she still able to recall these memories of another time, another place. She'd been having what John called breakthrough memories, starting on her most recent trip to Paris. He suggested they do a few hypnosis sessions. They hadn't gotten around to it. Truth be told, since Piper started the development group again, her intuition seemed to come roaring back to life. It was something she counted on; a part of her she loved.

Trish knew what the rest of the group knew about Piper; what Piper allowed them to know. She knew Piper's husband Paul had died and that Piper married a hypnotherapist named John, that the farm's original name had changed from Black Horse Farm and Winery to All in Time Farm, and that Piper had no children. It was what she didn't know about Piper that she mistakenly forgot to take into account.

Piper stared at Trish, waiting her out. She knew her well enough to know there had to be more and it would be drama soaked.

This woman who had been coming to her home for years, playing the part of interested student, had always plucked at the edges of Piper's tolerance but never in a hair-raising way until now.

Trish's hands began to move then, in a way that reminded Piper of snakes, a bit fluid, not to be trusted. She said, "I really feel like you're in danger, Piper." Her hands fluttering near her chest and throat. "I don't know what it is but I had the *strong* sense that I needed to tell you this and not in front of the group."

Piper feigned a smile and nodded, knowing that arguing or asking questions would just put a spotlight on this act. Either Trish was having a mental health crisis or she was going to great lengths to be able to stay in the group, which Piper found odd. She waited. There had to be more. She felt it in her bones. A flash of charred ember, a blanket draped over a small boy, fresh soil, and despair so deep it left her unable to take a breath. She coughed, her eyes watering. *Just a reflex. It's okay.*

Trish looked up at the rafters of the barn and sighed, slowly walking in a small circle. "This was such a beautiful barn. You had a great run here, Piper. John and the horses, uh. The horses! I just ... I just can't!"

She covered her eyes as she cried that social-media-tear-less-cry.

In what looked like a choreographed succession of moves, Piper kicked the buckets clear of the feed room door, swung it shut, narrowly missing Trish's, toes, face, and fingers, and dialed 9-1-1.

35

Rosalie's Pizzeria was a place Hope couldn't remember her first time visiting. It was the pizza place any kid in any town might have visited a hundred times before graduating high school. The warmth from the ovens, the unmistakable aroma of garlic, onions, sausage, and pizza sauce, the sizzling of the grill, and squeaking of the pizza oven door, a phone ringing, people talking as they enjoyed dinner, the music playing in the dining room.

Looking around and not seeing her mother, Hope relaxed, exhaled, and looked up at the menu she knew by heart. She missed seeing Annie here and having lunch with Clem and Eli. She was too young then to understand how fortunate she was to have these salt-of-the-earth adults in her life protecting and comforting her. The door opened behind her and before she could turn, she heard her mother, "There she is! That's my beautiful kid." Hope turned to see her mother's hair now had heavy highlights. Missy's eye had healed, Hope was happy to see. Overall, her mother looked like herself.

The smell of tobacco and something else, burnt, is all Hope could think to call it, was in many ways the way Hope would always remember as her mother's signature scent. Missy hugged Hope tightly. In that moment they were just two souls who belonged to each other for whatever reason God chose for the lessons they needed to learn.

"Hi, Mom. I've missed you," Hope said and felt the tears come. Missy pulled back and waved her hand at the tears. "Oh stahp it, ya gonna make me cry." Hope laughed, "Sorry. Don't cry." Missy was already moving toward a booth at the back of the dining room. Hope smiled at the girl at the register. "One minute. I'll just see what she wants to order."

Hope sat across from her mother and just let her eyes take in all that was in front of her. Missy's green t-shirt was wrinkled, but not dirty. Her hair looked clean but smelled of smoke. Her face was haggard but her lipstick was pretty. It would be many years before Hope would realize she could make the best of any situation and that, in some cases, it was the saddest and most desperate coping mechanism a young woman could cultivate.

"Are you ready to order, Mom?" Hope watched as Missy texted, smiling at her phone like a kid who had won a seventeen-foot strip of tickets at the arcade, enough to get a Twizzler and a Pokemon card. She put the phone down and smiled at Hope. "What did ya say, Hon?" Hope smiled. "I asked if you are ready to order. Dinner. Order dinner." She didn't know what more to say to engage her mother's expression.

The light was gone.

It hit her like a branch in the face when she rode the trails too fast, not ducking in time. The realization shot through her and seemed to exit her feet. Her own eyes scanned back and forth, searching for that glimmer, the one that meant her mother was clean and sober.

"Nah, I'm not wicked hungry yet. I thought we could talk for a few minutes. Catch up ya know."

"Sure." Hope was concerned but smiled. "What do you want to talk about?" She wasn't sure she was ready to hear what her mother had to say, but it was better than worrying about her and where she was and who she was with. She sat on her hands just like she did the day she and Eli met the Gunthers here: the very day she learned they were her great-grandparents, the hamsa necklace she wore confirming it.

"Well, Honey, we need to talk facts." Hope wanted to laugh about her mother sounding like a teenager but she realized then for the first time that she didn't need to laugh to make someone else comfortable or to cover her own true feelings. She had a right to be embarrassed. Part of Hope had always longed for parents who were good to each other, who didn't swear and scream in public. She wanted to be a normal kid who didn't need to be sent on an errand at school every May when the rest of her class made Mother's Day cards.

"Okay. What do you mean? What facts?" Anxiety tried hard to take control but she used the trick Eli had taught her many years before. She reached for the extra hair tie around her wrist and snapped it, hard. It stung but it kept her in the moment.

"Well, Honey. I want to talk about you and me."

Hope swallowed involuntarily, her mouth wide open.

"You don't remembah when you were real young, probably not, but we used to dream up a place we were gonna live someday. Me and you." Missy's eyes were dull but there were tears that gave Hope the sense that this wasn't going to just be dinner at the pizza place tonight.

Hope sat looking at the woman she called Mom and wondered how she had survived what she did and also how on earth had Hope herself survived? *Who took care of me?* she wondered.

"We used to take walks and talk about all the things we wanted our house to have like a big yard and a dog. That's what you wanted and ah coss, a pony." Missy's wistful smile made Hope's heart melt a little.

"And I," Missy stammered, "well, I wanted a nice playroom for you, near the kitchen. I wanted a big, sunny kitchen where you and me could cook and bake cakes and have tea pahties. Do you remember that, Hon?"

Hope squinted her eyes, a flash of green grass and a statue. She did remember. "Maybe? Were we in a park or something?"

Missy clapped like a sea lion at the Portland Aquarium. "Yes! You do remember!"

Hope smiled. She was stunned to be sitting here having this conversation. Eli had worked with her on these memories and helped her piece together the reality and flesh out the little girl perception.

"Were we having a picnic? I remember sitting on the grass." The words escaped Hope's mouth before she realized what she was doing.

Missy flinched. "Yah. Somethin' like that. A picnic." She nodded.

Gooseflesh arose on Hope's arms. She wasn't sure why. Her stomach growled, having not eaten that afternoon in anticipation of dinner with her mom.

Missy continued, "So ya know we never got that house, me and you. And I know yah fatha wasn't the best and I had my own stuff goin' on but you had a good childhood. Right, I mean. I always loved ya, Kid. You know that."

Hope felt the tear drop onto her arm and immediately brushed it away. She didn't want to cry nor did she want to feel bad for the woman who was supposed to keep her safe. Her eyes scanned Missy as she held onto the memory of being in the park. *We weren't having a picnic!*

She saw, in her mind's eye, her mother carrying a sign and people hurling angry words at her as they pointed to Hope, dancing on the grass and chasing pigeons.

Hope stood. "Mom, I'm going to order. What do you want?" She was agitated. "Pizza? Or do you want a sandwich and fries? Mom?"

Missy was emptying her purse, softly telling herself she knows there's one left. *Just one.*

Hope shouted, "Mom!" Missy stopped, mouth agape.

Hope, finding her voice and her limit, asked, "Am I ordering for you or am I ordering takeout and leaving?"

Missy's energy shifted. She pouted and put her hand softly on her heart. "Oh, Hope. I am sorry. Of course we are going to break bread, that was the plan."

Hope waited near the lobby while their order was being prepared. She held back tears and decided she would look online for a new pair of stirrup leathers for her saddle to keep her distracted.

When their food was ready, she sat in the booth across from

her mother who now seemed more alert and ready to eat. Hope figured she must have found the pill she was searching for.

Missy took a bite of her fish sandwich and rolled her eyes. "So freakin' good, right?" Hope smiled, a bit embarrassed to hear her mother sound like a teen. *I've already surpassed my mother's maturity level.*

"Well, Honey, I think it's time."

Hope took a sip of her Coke and waited, nervously. "Time for what?"

Missy sneered then. Whether it was intentional or not, Hope couldn't be sure, but it disgusted her either way.

"Time for you ta get ahold of my grandparent's money. What did ya think, I came back here fah a fuckin' vacation?"

She knew this conversation well. She'd danced this floor before. It was slippery and uneven. If you weren't careful you'd trip and wake the bear.

She waited like a child waits for the sting of the vaccine at the dreaded doctor appointment. No promise of a lollipop could erase the sheer terror of that piece of shiny metal puncturing your skin, the obnoxious smell of alcohol announcing its approach.

"The Cranstons. They have to have money in that house."

So here it was, the cold needle breaching her pristine skin.

"There's stuff in there I need. I have *rights.* I have rights to what my grandparents left and so do you. We are blood. The Cranstons are not. If you love me, Hope. You'll do this fah me."

Her arms crossed over her chest as she pressed her back into the booth, willing herself to find her way to Narnia or Mars or anywhere far from where she sat.

"Mom, I have to get back to feed the horses. I'll text you later." She grabbed her keys, scooting out of the booth when she felt a boot against her shin. She tried to pull her leg free.

"Hey, Frankie! Let 'er go. Don't trip her, Jesus Christ, that's my goddamn kid."

The foul-smelling man who sat next to her mother stared at Hope's body, shaking his head and smiling, revealing at least two gaps in his revolting smile.

"I don't care about ya fuckin' kid. Let's get this done. *Now.*"

For the first time since Hope was about eight years old, she wished her father Stan would appear, to grab Missy and force her into the green Corolla and take her home. He was good at scooping her up before she completely self-destructed.

36

Slade carefully slid out of his truck, landing on his left foot, trying to keep his right knee as stable as possible until he saw the new prosthetist at the end of the week. He woke early and decided he probably wouldn't make it to his session at the farm; however, after meticulously washing his knee, taking some Motrin and wrapping his stump before sliding into the prosthetic, he reconsidered. He didn't want to miss Oliver and, if he was honest with himself, he didn't want Oliver to miss him. Only two weeks previous he had asked Piper if anyone else rode "his" horse. Piper had laughed and shook her head no but he wasn't sure if he believed her.

He reached back into his truck and tucked the bag of peppermints into his coat pocket. He stood, weight equally on both feet and decided he could do this.

He looked over to the house to see if John might be on the patio. He remembered Piper saying John slept through morning barn chores but in exchange did the cooking and laundry. She admitted it was more than a good deal.

He jumped when he heard what he thought was a horse kicking stall boards. He walked toward the opening of the barn and with the morning sun streaming in from the door at the far end, he made out who he thought was Piper. He waved. Stopping at the whiteboard to read notes that usually included saddle/horse assignments, chores to be done, and horse health updates, he got the sense something was amiss. Then he heard Piper's muffled voice. His brain wasn't working it out fast enough so he turned only to see a blonde woman in what could only be described as the Starbucks run outfit. Definitely not Piper. His eyes adjusted to the light now that he was inside the barn. *What the hell?*

The woman lunged at the feed room door, shaking the handle and stomping her feet like a toddler.

There are some people who think, some people who react, and then there are things Marines do. Slade's training, no matter how many years had passed, was just beneath the surface; his PTSD, however, was always on the surface. From behind this unhinged woman, he restrained her, tackled her, and put her on the ground before he could wonder who she was or what she was doing in a barn dressed in a white jogging suit and camel-colored coat. The sound she made as she hit the ground was not that of pain but anger. It was deep. Guttural.

Piper, knowing it could not have been the police unless they were camped out in her yard when she dialed, peered, terrified through the glass on the feed room door.

The boot attached to a leg that was not attached to a body about seven feet from the writhing woman kept Piper's attention longer than she'd have liked.

"Slade," she said quietly, then louder, "Slade!"

Slade rolled to his side, holding his knee. Trish was on her feet and full of adrenaline. Oliver struck the bars of his stall door with his teeth, the whites of his eyes glowing in the dark of his stall. Fear is contagious and spread like fire through the barn. Kicking boards, pressing against the bars, squealing, and rearing. They were under attack. Oliver told them so.

Piper knew retreating to the feed room could be a dangerous move but before she needed to decide, the shouts of, "Police!" echoed down the aisle. Oliver's dragon roar answered back, "This is my herd. Go away!"

"On the ground! On the ground! Let me see your hands! Hands! Let me see your hands! Hands behind your head, now!"

Piper placed her hands over her head.

Trish ran toward the back door of the barn, screaming,

"Keep him away from me!"

Slade held his hands over his ears, face down on the concrete and cried , "Moose! Help me! Moose! My leg."

37

The traffic on 95 was a mix of long stretches of go-as-fast-as-you-want to parking lot. Eli looked at the time: 4:58 with still at least an hour to go. He quickly texted Becca to update her. He knew she would still be in the farm store but would see her soon enough. Reflecting on his incredible day, he began thinking of next steps. His mind was wanting to take him in several different directions. Another book, a lecture series, A TED Talk, find a position, and teach full time. He'd had several universities reach out to him in recent years. *But I love my clients*, he thought. *Keep moving* had taken on a new feeling for him. It wasn't so much a reminder to not wallow as it was becoming a promise that there was more to find, create, share, and explore. He also recognized that he and Becca hadn't been on a real vacation since their honeymoon. That was it. When he got home, he would talk to her about where she might want to go.

His phone buzzed . Darcy! He answered. "Hello there!" Darcy was laughing. "Hi, Dr. Cranston. I hope you're aren't too mad at me." Eli laughed, "Yes. I am so angry, young lady. How could you keep this from me?" She explained that the day she called him, she swore she knew nothing about the award. When Sir came back in with his wife for coffee, that's when he confided in her that Eli was in the running for a prestigious award and though it wasn't top secret, he would like it to be a surprise. "Surprise? I was completely shocked," he told her. He could hear that Darcy was at the cafe. The whirring of the milk frother and the clanking of coffee mugs on the countertop were a give-away.

"You should think about having another book signing here. You had a great turnout! Also, I wanted to tell you something." Eli was surprised but again, people told him everything. Clients anyway. "Shoot," he said.

"I've decided to go back to college. I'm going to study psychology. You really inspired me."

Eli stared at the license plate in front of him, OG444. His eyes welled up. "Otto," he whispered. "What's that?" Darcy asked. Eli cleared his throat. "Oh nothing, I am just absolutely and incredibly happy to hear this. I think you are going to love the coursework. And when it's time to do some of the many hours of internship work, I want you to call me first. "You could spend a whole summer up here. I'd be happy to supervise."

Eli wasn't sure if the call dropped but then he could hear someone at the register and the jingle of the bell over the door. Darcy's voice cracked then, "You don't know how much that means to me."

Eli thought of Otto and John and all the other inspiring people he'd worked with in the field and how much they had helped shape his work.

"Hmm, I might have some idea."

38

The officer spoke quietly to Slade. "Sir, we're here to help. You're going to be okay. You're safe. We have an ambulance on the way. You're Slade, right? I'm Officer DeSantos. I was in the sandbox, too, 1st Marine Division, two tours."

John was squatting next to Slade, hand on his shoulder, speaking quietly about how this was all going to pass and he would be back to riding and work and life soon enough. "Oh, and thank you for being in the right place at the right time. Who knows what that woman might have done to my wife."

Slade didn't hear any of this in a meaningful way. He was in crisis. The officer asked if Slade wanted some water. It was all Slade could do to keep breathing and it was his breathing that John was concerned about. "Hey Slade, try to breathe into your belly, slowly if you can. Hold it for a second, then exhale. Watch me. He snapped his fingers, the way he did with clients. Slade's eyes shot over to John's fingers, which he brought closer to his face, hoping Slade's attention would follow. He modeled the exaggerated breathing in the hope Slade would follow suit. Slade's pupils were dilated, only a hint of the icy blue iris still visible. His breath rapid, sweat rolling off his brow, he tried to break free of the officer who sat quietly back-to-back with him, arms locked. The officer, a veteran slightly younger than Slade recognized him from various events at the VFW and knew his story. He said, "I got you, brotha. You're okay. You're okay. No enemy here. This ain't the sandbox. I got you."

Slade, crying, asked if he was going home. "Moose. Am I goin' home? Did you find my leg?"

Piper turned then, shaken. The sirens were getting closer. She moved to Oliver's stall to try to calm him. He was frenzied, calling to the other horses and to Slade. He weaved like a stalled racehorse, back and forth, making a ditch at the front of his stall, rearing and kicking at the metal bars. She was afraid he'd hurt himself.

Instinctively, she opened his stall door to let him out to the pasture but he immediately rushed the aisle, ears pinned. Piper gave him space. He immediately lowered his head, snorting like the dragon he was. Approaching Slade, John, and the officer all huddled on the concrete aisle. One glance at Piper had John wondering if she felt it was the wrong move.

Piper had been in the equine therapy business for many years and she was respected in her field. Often she witnessed the incredible healing that happens when a horse knows its person is in distress. She had heard nonverbal children speak their first words in the presence of her horses. She watched teens abused beyond comprehension become loving, trusting, and compassionate when caring for the ponies.

She also knew an out-of-control horse when she saw one.

"Hey, Ollie. Good boy," John said in a sing-song voice. The officer held his breath, pulling his legs up as far as he could to avoid a groin injury. He would not abandon a Marine in distress.

Oliver lowered his muzzle on the top of Slade's head, his lip nuzzling Slade's hair, grooming him, letting him know he was safe.

As surprised as everyone was at the show of protection and camaraderie, no one expected Oliver to pilfer the bag of peppermints from inside Slade's coat pocket.

39

The hush in the farmhouse was not unusual in the early evening but to Eli it proved to be a bit disappointing; anticlimactic after the high of this morning's conference.

Peppercorn stiffly greeted Eli halfway down the hall. "Hey, Pep," he said softly. He knew the dog could no longer hear him but felt it odd not to say hello. "I knew I could count on you." He scooped up the fragile dog and nuzzled his soft ear then looked for a note on the kitchen counter but there wasn't one.

Eli looked at his phone as it buzzed. **I'll be done in a half hour.** He texted back. **Okay! Have you heard from Hope yet?** He looked in the fridge. Slim pickings. He grabbed an apple out of the fruit bowl instead and intended to head out to the farm store but a soft shuffling above his head made him pull up. Bending down to let Pep onto the ground, he waited, petting the dog's head. The sound came again. His phone buzzed with a text from Becca: **Not yet.**

Walking back toward the staircase, he peered out the window to see if he had missed Hope's truck or if it might be parked up at the barn. *Hmm,* he thought.

He climbed the stairs as quietly as he could. *Have you seen Grace? Grace Cranston. She's my daughter, 5"6", brunette.* He shuddered at the memory of that fateful night that change the course of so many lives. Eli shook his head, reminding himself that he wasn't in Los Angeles and his life, though different, was so much more the life he wanted to live. He grabbed the banister and took the rest of the steps by twos. Hope's bedroom door was open. Eli's heart, a jack-in-the-box ready to burst, wanted him to run. He poked his head in the doorway, knowing she wasn't there. The room Grace and Grayson stayed in when they were visiting was empty. He waited; the faint calls of the horses could be heard. Afterall, it was feeding time.

He knew the places the floorboards creaked, in fact he had come to know and love all the quirks in the old house. His path down the hall tonight though made him look as if he'd lost all sense of balance and wits, back against the wall, high stepping like a Hackney Pony but sideways, avoiding as many of the groaning spots on the old pumpkin pine boards as possible.

He peered into the bedroom he and Rebecca had painted a beautiful ethereal blue that caught the golden western light so beautifully. More than a handful of times he had seen Becca lying on her back on the bed, eyes wide, soaking up the warmth of the slanted rays which lit her hair up like embers. Many times Peppercorn was curled up next to her, drinking in Becca's warm energy.

A soft rustling reminded him why he was creeping down his own hallway. Stepping into the room, the sound stopped. Waiting patiently, holding his breath. Nothing. Exhale. Nothing.

Suddenly the back door of the kitchen opened directly below and Becca, in her sing-song way said, "Eli! I'm done! Let's get cooking!"

40

"I just think he could benefit from a few hypnosis sessions, that's all," John said. He was still looking out the window at the fox with a kit in her mouth, bringing it back to the safety of the den.

Piper was at the kitchen table, pouring more coffee from the carafe. "I mean, we can ask Slade when he gets released. It's going to be up to his psychiatrist though, not us."

In the reflection of the glass, John saw the woman he loved deeply. She was the only woman he had ever truly loved and also the most stubborn human he'd ever chosen to deal with. After a few tense moments Piper responded, "I wonder if maybe they will recommend that he stop the program, until his leg heals anyway."

John wondered if Piper was doubting herself and instantly felt bad for thinking her stubborn. He walked to the sink and placed his coffee mug in it.

"Do you want to talk about Trish?" He waited, knowing that keeping his back to her was not rude as some might view it. It kept Piper calm, feeling less pressured, less scrutinized.

She shook her head. "There's nothing more to say. It's a legal matter now. I have my group this week and I'll do what I can to keep it professional."

John was disappointed at her avoidance. He knew she was scared and probably in some way felt responsible for Trish's breakdown. "Well, let me know if I can help," John offered.

Piper got up from her seat and walked to the mudroom.

"I'll be in the barn."

John followed her and watched as she pulled on her field boots instead of her Muck boots.

"Riding today?" He knew she was not in the habit of answering rhetorical questions or of being watched.

She gave him a quick kiss on the cheek and headed out to the late morning sun and all that brought her solace.

41

Missy waited in her daughter's truck a half mile from the farmhouse, tucked onto a trailhead. She lit a Winston while she talked the phone to the menace who had in some ways freed Hope from the conversation at the diner with her mother she hadn't wanted to continue.

Missy pulled the visor down and looked in the mirror. "Blonde? You think I'd look bettah blonde, huh? Aren't you chahmin. My old man was a tool but this might take the cake.

"Shit, dude. I'm just bustin' ya balls. Calm down. Yah wicked pissin' me off. No, I don't have his name inked on my tit. You're freakin' somethin' else. No, it's not his name. His name is Stan and even though he is a goddam tool he's twice the man you ah. Do you even know what ya sayin't to me right now? I'm not telling you whose name that is. None ah ya business."

She turned the key in the ignition and turned up the radio to drown out the voice she had only known since a couple of days after arriving back in town. *They are all the same.*

"Yah. I told you, I already saw a lawyer. He says I could have contested it but I didn't even know they died for a year and a half aftah the fact." She exhaled smoke and watched it hit the windshield and careen here, there, and everywhere. "Oh yea? You know a law-yah? Doesn't everyone?" She watched in the mirror as she rolled her eyes. *What even is happenin' right now?*

"I gotta go. My kid's back." She hung up before he could protest.

Hope opened the door of the truck and climbed in. Eyes straight ahead, she turned the engine over and pulled her seatbelt across her chest. "Where am I driving you?"

Missy tossed her half-smoked cigarette out the window, turned to her daughter, and waited for Hope to look at her.

She didn't.

"Mom. Where. Am. I. Driving. You?"

Missy asked, "What did you find? Did you get the safe open? Where's the paperwork? My Oma's jewelry in there? Tell me!"

Hope got out of the truck, walked around to the passenger side and looked in the grass until she located the lit cigarette. She crushed it on the heel of her shoe.

Missy sneered at her now. "Ain't you the most responsible little thing? You're just like my motha and fatha. Makes me sick. None ah ya know how to really live. Ya know? Always so worried about rules and shit. You should be worried about ya blood! I'm ya mothah, for God's sake! You wouldn't be here without me. Who the hell do you think you are, anyway?" She laughed in the sickening way people do when they are unwell. Like cattle going to slaughter, wailing, screaming, knowing.

Hope pulled herself back into the truck and slowly buckled her seatbelt, buying a few moments to think. She wasn't sure how to keep her mother from boiling over. She felt the old familiar energy. It was hot, desperate and intrusive.

Then, without further warning, Missy slithered like a fisher, over the console and leaned into the bucket seat, leaving Hope. With no room, no choice.

The only odor Hope could compare to the rotting mouth her mother spoke from was a hoof infected with thrush. Mixed with the smell of fried fish and chips, Hope was suddenly nauseated.

Some wild combination of chaos rose up in Hope's body. Almost nineteen years' worth: anxiety, anger, defeat, dread, disgust, and possibly hatred.

She had to acknowledge that if there was one time her mother ever made any sense, it was tonight. Who *was* Hope and why was she bent on being so good? A rule follower. With all the energy she had, she furiously shoved the wiry body of the woman who gave birth to her and sent her as hard as she could back into the passenger seat.

Breath coming hard and fast, she unbuckled her seatbelt, not sure if she'd need to run.

Missy sat, cockeyed against the passenger door like a soldier whose Humvee landed in a ditch and abruptly halted, brain bouncing in its bucket. She stared, mouth open wide, crop top askew, partially revealing the tattoo in question, under her breast. The lower half of the S and A visible. She looked at the little girl who used to fetch quite a day's pay in the park from tourists who felt bad for the mom down on her luck, a sick husband at home.

"I hate you."

42

The tourists had been back, trickling to downtown Bar Harbor since Memorial Day, but with greater regularity now. Eli was happy to see families strolling down Cottage and Main, relaxed, seemingly happy. From the vantage point of his office window, he could glimpse a snapshot of what a happy family looked like, at least to a stranger's eyes.

Daddy, watch me! Are you watching, Daddy? Daddy! Are you coming to my recital?

Grace was on Eli's mind again. He hadn't heard from her since she left after Christmas, promising to call, to come visit. He looked at his watch just as the door at the bottom of the stairs opened. *Daddy! Are you coming home?!* Eli shook the memories right back to the ethers from where they seemed to originate.

Teresa came in, quietly as ever. "Good morning, Dr. Cranston."

Eli smiled at her, a client he only saw once per month now, a far cry from the weekly sessions for two years during the pandemic. Teresa broke his heart.

"Good morning is right. It's beautiful out there. How are you?" Eli sat across from his first client of the day and mirrored her posture.

"I'm well, thanks."

Eli kept his eyes on her face but was able to notice that she had gained some weight. *Yes!*

"I feel like I ask you the same question at the start of every session so I won't start that way, fair?" he asked.

Teresa, thirty-seven years old, had what she had considered a pretty normal life before the pandemic but six months in and her life was no longer recognizable. Her husband was drinking again, not taking lockdown seriously and mocking her for doing so. As with so many others, Teresa was forced to take an accounting of the relationship and all of its fatal flaws. She asked for a divorce and moved across town. This was not an uncommon story, Eli knew, and from emerging research since, was able to confirm that the Covid years changed the courses of lives, careers, and marriages. And, more so, it was still happening. *Why can't we all reset ourselves?*

Teresa, in a pale green spring maxi dress and light sweater, seemed lost at the idea she wouldn't begin the session with her progress update.

Eli challenged her to tell him what she wanted to work on. Teresa shrugged, comically.

"Um, I don't know, really. I have been going to the gym more, work has been its normal stressful mess, and I might have a date Friday night? So, I don't know what I want to work on. Maybe all of those things?"

Eli's smile took over his face, crow's feet spreading like exclamation marks around his kind eyes. "A date! Do tell!"

Blushed cheeks and all, Teresa was the embodiment of survival. To hear that she was open to a date was tremendous growth. Eli felt proud, though he knew all the work was done by Teresa. *I only facilitate.*

"Well, I joined the gym so that I can start to feel more in charge of my health, my body, if that makes sense. Also, to get out of the house after work. If I don't have a reason to go out, I just don't."

Eli watched her facial muscles work out how she felt about that. She folded her hands and sat back a little deeper into the chair.

"I mean, I run errands after work and I do meet friends for a drink now and again, but for the most part I just enjoy being home."

Eli nodded, encouraging her to continue.

"So if I pay for a gym membership, then I have to go out."

"Well, some people buy a membership but they never go. So give yourself credit there," Eli added.

Teresa pulled a long sable-colored hair off her skirt and let it fall to the ground, the sun catching its descent. Eli looked up at her and asked, "The date. I want to know about this date. Who is this person and how did you meet?"

Teresa giggled, her hand over her mouth like a young teen. "Well, I hit him with my car by accident."

Eli was astonished, not sure how to react. "You what?"

"I mean, I hit his car," she laughed. "I know it's not funny but at the time it was so ridiculous. Anyway, he was so nice. I was a mess and really upset, even though it didn't do any damage. I asked him if he wanted my insurance information."

Eli was nodding, waiting, even though he had seventy questions he would like answered. "So he asked instead of the insurance info, could he have my phone number."

Eli nodded at this. "Meeting people in the wild is not easy today, from what I hear,"

"The wild! Oh my God, that's funny. Yes, I guess that's a good way to put it. And no, it isn't very easy. My parents tell me that people meet in the grocery store, but that does not happen today. Everyone is staring at their phone. Well, I did hit his car in Hannaford's parking lot, so maybe they were right, sort of."

"Are you looking forward to the date?" Eli pressed. Teresa took a deep breath and shrugged. "I think so. I'm nervous. It's been a long time and I'm used to being alone so I don't know. What if he's allergic to my cat or he uses drugs or doesn't have a job?"

Eli waited and wrote on his notepad that he needed to pick up paper towels and dog food which was true but the reason for writing was to distract his gaze so she would feel free to say what was rising to the surface. When she stopped, he challenged her.

"What if he isn't allergic to your cat?"

Teresa looked at her feet for a moment, then up at Eli. Her

lips wanted to betray her thoughts but she stopped them from such an atrocity.

"What if he has a great job and takes care of himself? What then?"

The cogs on the wheels in Teresa's head seized. Eli could see it. Freeze.

Patiently, he added to his list: frozen pizza, beer, flowers for Becca, birthday cake for Clem.

Then came the frightened voice that Eli hadn't heard since the pandemic.

"What if I can't swallow food again?"

43

Oliver rolled completely over on the ground; the mud felt good and would keep the bugs off of him. He groaned as he pulled himself up and shook from head to tail, like a dog straight from the tub.

Piper stood in the barn and watched the gray horse undo the bath she had given him an hour before. She wanted him to look good for Slade when he arrived the next day. "Well, now we wait for the mud to dry and vacuum him. Damn white horses."

Piper had considered pushing off her development group but the women had been calling and texting their support and she felt that holding the session was the right thing to do.

She tossed hay into each stall, quietly poured grain into the feed buckets so as not to cause a frenzy, although horses are timekeepers so they would be expecting to be fed soon enough. One of her boarders would turn them in from the pasture soon.

Up in her office, she opened the windows to let the warm early summer air into the space that hadn't been used recently. She looked around, counted the chairs and checked her emails. She removed one chair, Trish's, from the circle and placed it in the closet.

She took an item from her pocket and tucked it into the treasure box and cut up more intention slips, added a few new pens from her desk to the Ball jar on the table. She loved her space and the women who gathered here, including Trish, for all the lessons they had taught one another.

The early evening summer breeze sent the curtains dancing, twirling, billowing. Piper closed her eyes, feeling the warm sun on her face. *The compass,* she thought. Opening her eyes, she scanned the room. *What compass?* She waited to see if there was anything else but for now it was just a repeat. *The compass.* She knew enough about her intuition to know that when the time was right, she would understand.

A soft knock at the door made her jump. "Oh, Claire!" she said as she exhaled.

Claire looked startled. "I'm so sorry! I just wanted to see if you wanted help setting up."

Piper waved her in and held her arms out. Claire smiled wide and rushed into her embrace. Piper inhaled the lavender scent of Claire's perfume and closed her eyes. My God, it's all right at the surface. *Maman! How I miss you! Maman, you make everyone shine so bright. Maman, we are here."*

"Thank you, Claire. I'd love some help." Claire looked at the table and asked if she could put the decks of cards out. Piper nodded and sat at her desk, glad to have someone to talk to before the rest of the group arrived.

"How have you been," Claire paused. "I mean with everything that happened. I mean, if you don't want to talk about it, I totally understand,"

Piper shook her head. "No, it's fine, really. I'm sure everyone has questions and I plan to address it tonight but really I'm fine. It was a shock but it's over and my client will be okay, too. He's coming back this week and is looking forward to seeing Oliver who, by the way has been moping and really sad without him."

Claire said, "I've only seen him once but he sort of seems familiar. I'm not sure why."

Piper raised her brows and said, "He's a mechanic, works across town. He's lived here most of his life." Claire nodded. "Okay, the decks are all set. Is there anything else I can do?" Piper pointed to the electric kettle. "You can start the water for anyone who wants tea."

The sound of the women coming into the barn reached the loft office easily, the new security system chiming to alert her, nonetheless. One by one they came through the door, with smiles and cards, a bouquet and cupcakes. They lined up, taking turns to hug Piper and thank her for not canceling the group altogether.

"I thought about it!" She laughed with them as they all settled down and thanked Claire for offering tea. Piper watched as they all embraced Claire, too. *That's why this group is so important,* she thought. A headcount showed only six guests. Camille was missing, not surprisingly.

The collective sighs, smiles, and demonstrations of gratitude, undoubtedly aided by the warm early summer weather and the fact that they had been a full month apart, was an indicator that Piper had made the right decision to continue the group.

As the women were busy writing intentions and drawing cards, recording them in their journals, the sound of footsteps on the stairs made Piper tense. Without moving, she felt into the energy and knew it was Camille. Putting herself in Camille's shoes, she felt trepidation and a hint of embarrassment. It was Camille who had introduced Trish to the group. Piper walked to the door and peered out. Camille stood on the top step and looked like a child who wasn't sure if she was about to be run off the porch or be invited in while selling Girl Scout cookies. "Hi Camille, good to see you. We just got started." Piper stood back to make way for her to enter the office.

The group looked up with smiles and waves. Camille handed a small gift-wrapped box to Piper. "For you," she said. Piper was surprised that her eyes welled up, glinting, full of emotion.

Camille joined the group. Anne patted her arm and handed her a pen and slip of paper. Camille dabbed at her tears, relieved.

An hour always seemed to evaporate in this room, the women having so much to offer each other, all tiptoeing, however, around the Trish incident. They looked at Piper, the way they do when they are hoping she has just one more activity or name for them to work with. She felt all the energy seeping into hers and instinctively crossed her legs and arms, then uncrossed her arms and began. "So, I know you all have questions about Trish and what really happened. I know the news has a way of embellishing things." There was a collective exhale. Claire, confidently flipped her journal page and began to read, "Jealousy, unhealed anger, discontent, coyote totem, cunning, has a plan to take over the group. Has been trying to make appointments with John. Wants to be Piper."

Silence.

"I wrote that during the second class I attended. I didn't think any of it was true. I'm sorry. I should have said everything."

44

WELCOME BACK SLADE! The banner on Oliver's stall was hung with pride. It was a collective effort by clients, boarders, and the women in Piper's development group. Attached to it were cards, a pair of riding gloves, a Dunkin' Donuts gift card, and of course a few peppermints. The kids drew hearts, horses, and what looked like a rough interpretation of Slade's Dodge Ram pickup.

Astonished, he stood before the stall and inhaled deeply. "Well what do ya know," he whispered to himself.

Oliver was in the pasture grazing on deep green grass with a not-so-clean flysheet on, tail swatting at flies. It was summer.

Slade walked to the end of the aisle, his new prosthetic, made specifically for riding, was a bit heavier than the one made for walking, the one made for working, and the one made for cycling.

One of the girls who helped with stalls and turnout was in the pasture scrubbing the water trough. When she saw Slade she waved and said, "Ollie is gonna be so happy to see you!" She turned to Oliver who was at the fence line and called him. Nothing. She tried again and got the same result. She trotted off with a lead rope in hand.

Piper walked in from the arena and was surprised that Slade was there as early as he was. "Hey, Slade. Welcome back! I know a certain gray who will be beside himself when he sees you." Slade hugged her and pointed at the banner. "That's somethin'." His voice cracked and he turned back to the open door to see the girl leading Oliver to the gate.

Piper knew this would be overwhelming for Slade but she trusted he was ready.

"Hey, Buddy," he said as Oliver entered the barn. The horse's head shot up, nostrils flared as he sent out a high pitched hello. The girl tossed the lead rope onto his neck and let him continue without her as Ollie trotted to Slade, nickering, snorting, and as Piper had predicted, beside himself. Oliver sniffed him all over, two parts emotion and one part treat seeking.

John came down the aisle and waved. "Good to see you, Slade. How's it going?"

Slade, more comfortable now, put Oliver on the cross ties and shook John's hand. "Doin' okay, all things considered." John put his arm around Piper's shoulders as they listened to Slade describe the last month, his treatment, his new leg.

Slade popped a peppermint off the banner and gave it to Oliver and all at once, everything seemed right again.

"So we are going to have a new instructor joining the farm. Did I tell you that on the phone?"

Slade shook his head as he began to groom Oliver. "Please tell me it's not that Trish woman."

45

The violence of the spade slicing through the hydrangea roots was awful, primal. Hope loved it. "I've done this before. It'll be fine." She raised the spade higher and higher each time, slowly separating the cyan-come-sapphire beauty from the soil that had nurtured it for the last seven summers. As she worked her way around the floppy, lacey mops, they shuddered. What had they done to deserve this butchering, this chaos?

She told them, "You can't stay here. I can't stay here. We're going. Together. Now, come on!"

One last hack with the shovel and suddenly the fibrous root ball was free, unencumbered, tilting slightly southwest and looking every bit as haggard as the young woman who had attacked it.

Hauling it up from the earth and onto the waiting burlap, would take some effort especially in the sudden intense heat of early July, but Hope had planned to be on the road by now. If she was nothing else at all, Hope Cranston was the entire sea in a Dixie cup. Collecting all the soil she could and mounding it onto the fabric, sweat threatening to drip into her eyes, she stopped.

"Hey! What are you doing?"

That voice! It went through Hope's body like a shockwave, leaving her off balance. *How could my mother be so cruel? Had she never loved me? Was I not right in choosing to do the right thing? I'm not seven years old anymore,* she thought and closed her eyes as she breathed in the humidity that defines coastal New England in the short summer months. She waited, undeterred and unbothered, mostly. This wasn't a new feeling, nor was it unexpected. It's like the fever and chills that come with illness; you just have to ride it out. "Ouch! " She swatted the colossal horsefly to the ground and split it in two with her spade. Disgust and satisfaction co-mingled amongst so much disappointment. She could see the use in being angry now. Now she understood why Eli coached her all those years to challenge Grace's behavior, to deter her attacks.

"Hope! What are you takin' *now*? Do the Cranstons know about this? I'm calling them right now. That poor ..." Missy gestured to the drooping hydrangea as if it could help her with its name. "That plant!" Missy's fiery eyes and unwashed hair spat at Hope and wanted to burn her but Hope deflected it all. She had lived this way for over a decade before the Cranstons plucked her from the despair into which she was born. She was tired but she was not a victim. Hope would never be a victim.

The sound of the burlap bundle hitting the metal floor inside the front of the horse trailer was a relief even if it sounded like a body being tossed into a trunk like in the movies she secretly loved. The cramped space looked like a traveling circus. Two saddles, three bridles, halters of all colors, a manure fork, broom, and all manner of boots—more than Hope could ever wear out—tossed haphazardly among buckets of phlox, iris, coneflower, hollyhocks, dahlias, and bee balm, all in varying states of bloom and rest, waiting to be transported. Transplanted. Emancipated.

Missy came closer, anger flashing on her face. "You better not come back here. I swear to God, if you do, this entire town will know exactly why you're leaving right now and they will make your life miserable." Under her breath she said, "They don't even know what you came from. Goddamn townies. I'm not even from this place! I came from money. My parents and my grandparents could buy this whole back-wood swamp!"

Hope knew how to maneuver, dodge, weave, duck. She learned early and fast, long before Grace showed up and put her through her paces. Hope rolled her eyes now at the thought of all Grace had done to make her miserable and how she had stuffed it all down, just taking it. She slammed the trailer door thinking about how she just had to wait it out, Grace eventually going back to California. *I love Eli and Rebecca. They're still mine,* she thought.

"I earned them," she said.

Missy recoiled and screwed up her face, eyes rolling. "What? You earned what? The plants? God, you are so lame! Rebecca will plant more. You know she will. Once you're gone, it'll be like you were never here. All the Barlows finally gone!" She spun on her heel, hair like Medusa, catching up to her hot head as she walked away just like she had done seven years before.

Hope calmly walked in the direction of the barn, the place she loved most in the world. *Barlow.* No one used that name anymore. She never *felt* like a Barlow.

One big stride and she was in the cavernous old barn, greeted by the sharp call that sent lightning through her blood. Pirate.

Standing in his cool stall, legs wrapped, flysheet on, eyes dark as night. "C'mon, Pi. Let's go while we can, Buddy." She went to Ink and Smudge's stall and told them she would be back. "I don't know when, boys, but I will." Tears dripped onto their crazy forelocks as she cuddled their tiny faces. *Why does anyone have to leave someone they love?*

The sound of steel shoes on concrete echoed in the giant space of the old dairy barn as she led Pirate out to the trailer. This wasn't the end. Hope knew that, rationally, but there was something inside her that wanted to scream, "Don't look back. Just don't look back, ever!"

The squeaky ramp of the trailer, tightened down, water bucket and hay net filled, every detail haphazardly came together. It was time. Hope pulled herself into her Silverado, turned the key, checked her mirrors, shifted into gear and slowly started down the gravel drive, checking her brakes just once, rolling past the Full Circle Farm sign that swayed gently in the summer heat toward freedom. Whatever that meant.

46

Missy Barlow walked down Centre Street with a pocket-book, a pack of Winstons, and a plan. She whined like a starving mosquito into her phone. "Give me a call, Honey. I am so sorry. I just haven't been right since I last saw you. I need you to call me. Love yah." She rolled her eyes at her own acting job and tried another dealer. No luck. *They love me when I have cash but otherwise, I don't exist.* She'd lived more than half her life as an addict and she always found a way.

The sun had felt nice when she left the Amtrak station but now it was oppressive. Her sandals, several seasons old, were too thin to support her feet but thick enough to keep the pavement from burning her skin. To someone who had never met her, they might think her at least fifty years old. At almost thirty-six she knew she was pushing the envelope uphill both ways in a snowstorm. *Everyone betrays me. My dealer, my lawyer, my kid.*

She stopped outside of Mae's Bakery, downtown Bath, and looked inside her pocketbook. The last of the money Hope had given to her amounted to a handful of singles and some change. She lit a cigarette and looked through the window of the shop. A family of five was packaging their leftovers into takeout containers, kids already fussing to leave. *You can always count on kids.* She waited until the door opened before slipping inside, the mom holding the door for her, then recoiling at the odor. Missy went to the counter and stood in line, watching from behind her sunglasses to see how distracted the waitstaff was at the

height of breakfast. Pulling out her phone and answering the
non-call, she casually sat at the newly vacant table. "Oh sure. I
can get that done today. Yes, not a problem. I really appreciate
yah business. Talk soon, now."

Back out on the sidewalk, Missy was forty-eight dollars
richer and still having her non-conversation.

She approached Front Street not expecting to have feelings,
but if she wasn't on something consistently, Missy had all sorts
of feelings she'd rather ignore. She stopped for a moment and
peered down the long road, knowing she couldn't see the old
house because it was at least a half mile away but she looked
anyway.

The car horn, angry and close, swerved, missing her by just
a couple of feet. "Asshole!" Missy would have smashed the
windshield if she had been closer. Her heartbeat couldn't decide if it needed to speed up or slow down so it tried both.
Sweat started to feel uncomfortable all over her body. *I'll never
forgive my kid for leaving me stranded like this. Ever.*

If ever there was a person who shunned every opportunity,
God-given talent, and blessings bestowed on her just for the
blood in her veins, it was Missy. Some people are their own
lesson, burden, and obstacle.

She turned back on Centre and marched right past the
breakfast place she had just robbed and followed the turn onto
Draydon Road, tears coming now, mixing with sweat and
makeup from days previous, how many she didn't know.

Slowing halfway up the concrete walkway to the post WWI
brick building, she wiped her face on her t-shirt, smoothed her
hair as best she could and approached the door. She could feel
the blood draining from her head as she swayed. *No. I can do
this.* She leaned against the brick, thankful it was shaded simply
due to the time of day. Knocking, she prayed, "Please God. I will
fix this mess, just let—"

The door opened but the tunnel vision was closing fast. She
couldn't see him but she heard Stan say, "My God. You're still
alive?"

47

Hope turned down Farm Road and felt the heaviness in her arms lighten and hoped the same would happen in her chest soon. Her GPS informed her that her destination was a quarter mile ahead on her right. *Thank God. Not quite dark yet.* She had stopped just twice on the seven-hour drive to let Pirate stretch his legs and to fill her tank. Hungry, tired, and feeling far away from everything she knew, she pulled into the driveway. Piper had told her it was just before the gray Cape. Uneasy about having to back down a narrow drive in the dark if she made a mistake , she felt her stomach lurch. *You're fine! Just keep moving. That's what Eli always says. Just keep moving.*

Exhaling at the sight of two trailers, a pickup, and tractor, she knew she was in the right place and spotted a place to park.

As soon as she cut her engine, she hopped out onto the gravel drive and hurried around to the other side of her truck to the side door of the trailer. Pirate immediately greeted her with a sharp call as if to say, "Where are we and when is dinner?" Relief was something Hope welcomed but knew not to get comfortable in. She unlatched the ramp on both sides and lowered it, eager to get Pirate out. He knew the drill and waited for her to untie the lead rope and guide him out tail first. The horses in the barn were still calling back to him when he placed his last hoof on the gravel. Hope circled him and felt his chest temperature under the flysheet. She let him graze on the thin strip of grass between the drive and the barn.

Piper came from the house, flashlight swinging as she approached.

"You made it!" The excitement in Piper's voice surprised Hope. She wasn't sure how to feel about any of this.

"We made it, yea," she paused. "Sorry it took longer than I thought it would."

Piper ignored the apology and gently smoothed Pirate's mane. "Let's get him into a stall."

She flipped the lights on, revealing an aisle as clean as the one Hope kept at home.

The things horse people notice are lost on non-horse people but they were more than okay with that.

"Here, let's put him in this one so he isn't next to anyone. They can all meet in the morning." Piper slid the door on the track so Hope could lead him in. The light in the stall came on. Fresh shavings, full water bucket and hay in the corner feeder. Perfect.

Hope worked to remove his shipping boots while Piper watched. She knew well the sense of urgency the young woman was feeling after a long haul alone with her horse.

Hope turned, arms full of nylon and velcro. Suddenly she was able to focus and noticed Piper had on a Bar Harbor sweatshirt. With a hint of a smile she said, "Thank you for letting me come here."

Not sure how to respond, Piper was relieved that John was calling. "Let Hope know dinner is on the stove, her room is ready, and there's a stubborn cat who won't get off her bed." Hope found her way to the tack room and tucked the boots aside, thinking that John sounded a bit like Eli.

Oliver called down the aisle demanding to know who had entered his barn. Piper threw him some hay and a handful of sweet feed. A small condolence but Oliver seemed to accept it.

"I'll leave the flashlight here for you. Come up when you're ready. Just shut the lights here on the panel."

Hope promised to be in soon.

She watched Pirate through the metal bars, eating and relaxed as if he were at home across from Ink and Smudge, next
to Cayenne. She slipped back into the stall and checked his
temperature again. Cool as a cucumber. As comforted by that
as she was, it meant she had no reason to linger here. Hope was
the one who needed to acclimate. Again.

48

Rebecca pulled into the parking lot at the old mill building and looked for the directory. Dentists, a bakery, spa, trampoline park. *I wish I had left earlier,* she thought and put her truck in park. *I'll find it.* She looked at her phone. Texts from Jack about the broaster machine delivery, from the feed store about a refund on the moldy grain they sold her, from Hope to say she left a day early because her mother was unhinged *(oh God, she left early?)*; and not one from her husband. She was gone for two days without much explanation and it didn't seem to faze anyone. *Well, I suppose that makes this a little easier, then.*

No matter how much updating and renovating old buildings undergo, they retain a certain aura. Rebecca walked through the seemingly endless hallway, reaching out to touch the old chestnut posts and feel the contours that had long ago been chiseled by men who hadn't been alive in well over a hundred years now.

Suite 348. She took a breath and felt panic rise in her chest. *What am I doing?* She turned to go back the way she came. She took out her phone and dialed Eli. Nervously she walked to the large floor-to-ceiling window that overlooked the Androscoggin River. Her breath was choppy, seemingly tripping over her tonsils on its way out. *If he picks up, I'll.* She stopped. She didn't know what she'd say. *And if he doesn't then—*she still didn't know what that would mean for her.

The door to Suite 348 opened behind her just as Eli's voicemail picked up. She slipped her phone into her purse and thanked the man who held the door for her as he exited.

She stared at the woman behind the plexiglass and wondered if perhaps she had a fulfilling life. Answering phones and preparing paperwork, copies, schedules, and she guessed, attitudes. The woman hung up the phone and asked Rebecca her name and nodded. "You can have a seat and someone will be right with you. If you'd like coffee or tea, it's through that door behind you. Help yourself."

Becca looked at her phone again. Nothing.

Tea sounded good but she was too nervous and didn't want the caffeine. Two sleepless nights was enough. She planned to sleep like a baby tonight.

"Mrs. Cranston? Come with me." The woman behind the desk showed her where the restroom key was if she needed it and walked her into the large office with windows that were so clean it seemed there couldn't possibly be glass in them.

Rebecca sat in the buttery soft leather chair in front of the immaculate walnut desk and thanked the woman. She looked around at the diplomas and framed articles on the walls and tapped her foot, waiting.

"Mrs. Cranston? Mike MacLean, nice to meet you." Rebecca turned to greet the man she had imagined would be older. He shook her hand and smiled, asking her if she'd like water or coffee. She shook her head no, suddenly feeling she was in the wrong place and wanted to excuse herself and run to her truck.

The man took a seat in the executive chair on his side of the desk and adjusted his tie. "So tell me what brings you in today? How can we help?"

Rebecca looked at her naked hands. They were hardworking and bore all the signs to prove it. Wrinkled. Sure. Tiny scars from burns, cuts, bites, and old fence wire, a cracked nail she kept applying bag balm to in order to keep it soft, hoping it would grow out if she'd somehow manage to keep from smashing it again. Suddenly she wished she had applied some makeup or at least lip gloss. Working on the farm daily for over fifteen years was not congruent with her former way of life.

Manicures, pedicures, tanning beds, hair color every five weeks, massage every month. Corporate America was a ruthless place and she played the part. And to play, you had to look the part. Her wedding was the last time she'd had any of those services performed.

"Well," she started. "Well, I am not sure exactly, " she said, still looking at the top of MacLean's desk, avoiding his gaze. "I have a situation that I don't even know what to think about but it feels like I needed to come here, to just. To just see."

MacLean leaned back in his chair. This was easy, no heavy lifting. Consults usually were. He was waiting, hoping to be out soon enough, grab drinks with his grad school friend who was in town.

"Sure. Take your time. What can you tell me about the situation? What made you reach out to us?"

Rebecca heard her phone buzz. *Oh God. What if it's Eli. Is this perfect timing or is this a sign?*

"Do you need to take that? I can step out for a moment. No rush." He meant it but at the same time, wanted to be out by 5:30. He glanced at the clock on his wall. *Plenty of time.*

Rebecca looked up at him then, her blue eyes searching his much darker ones. "No. It's fine. I'm probably overreacting. It's just. It's my husband."

Maclean nodded. "Okay. Tell me. What about your husband?"

Rebecca had texted everything to Christine and Rhea back in Boston but she hadn't uttered anything out loud. That would make it too real.

"My husband used to be a lawyer," she blurted out as if that would mean something to this man.

"Oh, okay and he's retired?" MacLean was as confused as the woman in front of him seemed to be.

"Yes. Well, no. He left his practice a long time ago. He's a therapist now."

The laughter from MacLean shocked Rebecca, though she used to get a kick out of that idea, too.

Sleep deprived, hungry, and heavy hearted, Rebecca's floodwaters breached the dam that had been weakening for, if she was honest, a few years now.

"My husband is planning something. I'm not sure what. I own a farm and a business. I mean, we own it now but before we met, I bought it, fixed up the house and fencing, and the barn. I put my life savings, my 401K and my inheritance into the farm. Things were great for a while. We adopted a young girl who we both knew. She worked at my farm and my husband kept an eye out for her when he moved in across town. She comes from a terrible home situation and she's the sweetest girl, well, young adult now. But.

She stopped when she felt the pre-tear sting in the back of her eyes. *No. Not now.* She shifted then. Yes, in her chair, but also into adrenaline and deep pain. "My husband has a daughter from his first marriage. Grace. She's terrible to our daughter, Hope. Thankfully, she moved back to California but the damage she's done was awful. Anyway, since she left, Eli threw himself into his work, his research, and he wrote a book. He's not around much and I ....

She stopped. Hearing her own words, she realized she wasn't very convincing. *Maybe this was a mistake.*

"Go on. You're doing fine, Rebecca."

She let out an audible sigh. "Well, I mean. I don't know what's happening. I had concerns recently. He got an office downtown but whenever I've swung by he isn't there. He comes home early sometimes then goes out but I don't know where. Says he's going back to the office or over to the rental we own. His house, before we married. Anyway, the reason I'm here is. She opened the photo app on her phone then, to remind herself she wasn't fabricating anything. She saw what she saw.

"So I found some paperwork behind my shoe rack in our closet. It's important paperwork. I don't know why it'd be behind my shoe rack. It's our marriage certificate, the titles to our vehicles, one of many folders that belonged to a man who was Eli's mentor and the great-grandfather of the girl we adopted. He passed last year and all of this stuff. This paperwork. It. It was all in our safe. It just makes me very uncomfortable. And when I looked in the safe," she stammered. Tears clouded her eyes now as she looked back down at the enormous desk. "When I looked in the safe, almost everything that had been in there was gone."

"Okay. You're fine. This is good info. It seems to me that maybe you feel like maybe this is out of character for your husband?"

Rebecca nodded, not wanting to even face what this could mean for her, for the farm. For Hope.

"Well, I can tell you this. If you retain MacLean, MacLean, and Howard, we will do everything we can to secure what's yours, Mrs. Cranston."

49

"How was the date?" Eli asked in a nonchalant, almost un-interested way. Teresa was in jeans, a t-shirt and flip-flops, more relaxed than usual. She picked at the piping on the edge of the blue chair, contemplating much that Eli wasn't privy to. She looked up and answered, "It was fun." She shrugged like a kid who has to choose between homework and taking out the trash. Eli waited an uncomfortable minute. His phone buzzed. He ignored it. Teresa looked past him out the window. "Can I ask you how you met your wife?"

Eli wasn't expecting such a direct and personal question. He responded with, "Can I ask why you want to know?" Teresa immediately looked away, feeling she'd misstepped. She straight-ened in her chair, nervous. Eli was seeing the Teresa from the pandemic years. *What happened?*

Eli softened his shoulders and gaze and flipped a page in his appointment book that he used as a prop, a distraction. "I met my wife at the farmer's market when I moved to Bar Har-bor." No response from Teresa. He added, "She didn't like me at first."

Teresa's eyes flashed a quick second at Eli's face. She crossed her legs and looked again. "Really?"

Eli nodded. "Yup. She had these concoctions I had never seen. Granted, I had lived in Los Angeles my whole life before moving here. It couldn't be more different, which is what I wanted. However, it took some getting used to. Have you heard of Fire Cider?"

Teresa giggled. "No. What is that?"

Eli smiled, "Let's just say it is in fact good for you but it's basically all the hot, spicy things you have in your spice rack plus garlic, honey, and apple cider vinegar. Oh and it sits for weeks before you drink it. " He stuck his tongue out for effect.

That did it. Teresa exhaled, laughed, shifted herself in the chair again and uncrossed herself. "That doesn't sound great. So how did you get her to like you?"

Eli quickly answered, "Not by trying Fire Cider! No, ma'am. It was a year and a half before I was able to stomach the thought. It's actually not so bad."

He took a deep breath, Teresa following. "So, date was not so good?"

Teresa smirked. "No, it was good. Really good."

Eli waved his hand like a magician, "And?"

"And, I just think it'll go the way all my relationships do. Start out fun and then before you know it, I'll be paying for dinner, groceries, the rent, his issues." She shook her head at the very thought of being stuck in a sickening cycle of trying to help someone who will punish her for it.

Challenging her thinking, he asked, "Well let's start with last month's list of worries: Is he allergic to your cats? Is he employed? And does he do any drugs?"

Teresa snorted at her own list of fears. When she heard them out loud she understood her thinking wasn't very solid. No, in fact, it was tainted by so much of her past.

"Ryan is not allergic, has a job, and no idea about the drugs."

Eli nodded emphatically. "Okay, well two outta three isn't too terrible. So now we work on the part about you creating a future you actually want. Next session, we will start FLP again. What do you say?"

Teresa's eyebrows indicated her approval. "Okay. It really did help before. My life is so different now."

"You have to trust yourself more. That's the key. Trust that you won't allow yourself to walk through doors that are not for you."

Eli's phone buzzed. Rebecca. *She knows I'm working.*

"So tell me about the date. I mean, not all the sordid details, please." Eli put his hand up like a cop stopping traffic. Teresa laughed now, the part of her that was just reawakening. The part that wanted to enjoy life again.

"Well, he picked me up, brought me flowers. It was nice. We went to McKay's." She stopped.

"And. And I was able to eat clam chowder. Almost the whole bowl and only had to sip water to get it down twice."

Eli nodded, knowing that anyone else who might hear such a drab sentence would laugh at the simplicity. How blasé. For Teresa, however, it was Everest. And to Eli it was proof he was helping her heal.

50

Standing in the center of the arena, Hope loosely held the lunge line as Pirate trotted around her, stretching his legs, head low, blowing air, warming up. Piper sat on the director's chair at the opening between the arena and barn, replying to clients' texts and answering questions from the group about the class the night before.

"Hey Hope, do you remember the little boy who was here yesterday? My 2:00 pm session?"

Hope looked over her shoulder at Piper. "Yea, he was so cute. What about him?"

Piper said, "His mom says he won't stop talking about you. Haha, he has a crush on you."

Hope laughed, "He's not my type," she surprised herself by saying it out loud.

"Well, do you have a type?" Piper stared at the side of Hope's head and waited.

Slowly Hope walked in front of the line so that Pirate turned in toward her. She looked back at Piper, "I like boys who don't talk much. Why do they talk so much and why do they talk about such dumb things?"

Piper hadn't expected such a response from Hope. She'd been at the farm for about three weeks and was just starting to relax. John could make her laugh but Piper kept their relationship more business oriented until now. She leaned back in the chair and let out a genuine laugh that made her look like she was howling at the moon.

"I guess I don't have an answer to that but I think a lot of women wonder the same things."

Hope pulled her stirrups down on each side of her saddle, tightened the girth a notch and gathered her reins, ready to hop on. Pirate's head shot up as he turned his body away from her. She looked in the direction his ears were pointing to see a man leading Oliver into the barn from the pasture. "Don't be scared. It's just Ollie." She circled him back to where they started and mounted up. Pirate called loudly; she could feel the vibration against her calves as his barrel expanded with breath. She scratched the Morgan's withers and told him to get over himself. He walked forward and after a few strides, lowered his head.

"Hope, come over here for a minute. I want you to meet someone." Piper waved her over and Hope could see the man who was now standing with her.

"Hope, this is Slade. He's one of my clients and Oliver's clear favorite."

Hope furrowed her brow and played with the visor of Hope's helmet. *Slade? Slade. Slade.*

"Hi. This is Pirate."

Slade reached up and shook Hope's hand. "Nice to meet ya. I saw your horse the day after he arrived. He's really beautiful even though Oliver seems to have beef with him."

Hope covered her mouth and giggled. She hadn't heard anyone use that word since middle school. "Thanks. He's the best boy. I mean I love Ollie, too. He's definitely alpha. Pirate is more like a pissy mare."

"Oh my God, young lady, who *are* you?" Piper swatted her boot with a crop.

"Well, it's true!" Hope was happy to be with people who spoke the language of the horse world. It was her world. She didn't know much about anything outside of it.

"Well, I have to get back to Oliver. Nice meeting ya, Hun."

Hope squeezed her legs against Pirate's sides to move him back on the rail. She twisted her torso back toward Slade and Piper and placed her hand on Pirate's rump.

"Nice to meet you, too. And—it's Hope." Slade straightened his back and said, "Yes, ma'am. Hope."

51

Missy Barlow sat on the edge of the bed in her estranged husband's apartment, fed, clean, hungover. She lit a cigarette and pulled on a t-shirt from Stan's laundry basket while Stan's CPAP machine muted any of the noise she might make. *Never bothered to do a damn thing about that snoring when I had to try to sleep all those years.*

She walked in the dark to the kitchen, stubbing her toe and stifling a yelp. The refrigerator wasn't well stocked but it was more than she ever had at any one time since she had left the cabin they lived in on Mt. Desert Isle.

Day drinkin's a bitch especially when ya can't sleep. Must be gettin' old. She took a beer and made herself a ham and cheese sandwich. She sat in the dark living room and looked at her phone. Nothing. Relieved to have tracked down Stan and grateful he let her in the door, she didn't yet know her next move. For now she would ride out whatever attitude and anger he threw at her for disappearing seven years ago. She knew how to handle him. *Plus,* she thought, *he is set up pretty good. Government housing, his military pension, social security, and the money he got from the builder he sold the land to. If only he had had his shit together when I needed him to.*

She opened Instagram to see if Hope had posted anything about the new place. *Kid thinks she's got it made in the shade. She hasn't blocked me. That's good. No new posts. Must be busy making everyone feel bad for her.*

Missy silently admonished herself for thinking that way.

She loved her daughter but she hadn't expected to find an adult when she came back home to ask for help. *I don't know what I expected.*

She wiped crumbs off Stan's t-shirt and walked back to the kitchen, this time using the light of her phone to avoid smashing her toes again. She scanned the kitchen. *Ha, ah ya kiddin' me?* She walked to the small round table by the sliding glass door and picked up the brown wallet, curved and cracked, sitting next to Stan's keys. It had been years since she'd seen Stan's wallet sitting out in the open. Soon after she moved in with him, he realized his mistake in trusting her with anything important. She flipped it open. *A credit card? Shit.* A few twenties and his license. She looked in the billfold and pulled out a small picture. Her bottom lip lost all control and bobbed up and down like when you hook a fish. She ran her finger over the tattered picture. Hope was just three and Missy, barely twenty. *God we were just kids.*

She tucked the picture away and closed the wallet. "Not tryin' ta get kicked outta here," she muttered.

She stepped out onto the tiny deck on the other side of the slider and dialed Hope. She quickly hung up. It was 3:30 am and no one in the world would pick up for Missy Barlow. She knew this. *Shit, the bridges I've burned.*

52

Rebecca pulled into the driveway at Full Circle Farm and sat in the truck for a moment remembering the first time she had laid eyes on the house. The realtor had been sweet about it, almost trying to talk her out of it. "Well, I mean there are a lotta farms that go the way of progress around he-ah. Guessing a contractor would be the best buyer here. Ya know, there is a gentleman's farm coming up this spring, a small barn and a few acres ready to go. Probably will be on the market in a month."

Rebecca asked if she could see the inside before the realtor said anything more. She'd been determined to make it work from the moment she saw it on the real estate app while sitting in Route 3 traffic, knowing she was done with her corporate sentence and the dumpster fire relationship she had just doused.

She sat in the truck, admiring all the work she'd done even before Eli showed up. The satisfaction of not only painting all twelve rooms but hiring Clem for repairs and getting to know him, Annie, and other locals. It had been a whole new life and it was the beginning of a healing journey she had no idea would lead her to marrying a man the likes of Eli and adopting the most perfect child. She covered her face with newly manicured hands and let herself cry. The wisdom deep in her bones knew she would be just fine but that part of her that was still a girl who'd had her heart broken too many times needed to be heard. So many hours, so many years, so much work. "And it's not even my body that's tired!" She screamed into the palms of her hands that smelled of almond oil. "Why? Why is my life like this? Where is my break?"

The rap on her window startled her but she kept her hands over her tear-soaked face. She waited.

"Rebecca, open the door. What's wrong? Rebecca, open the door!" It was Jack. She wiped her face with her sleeve and rolled her window halfway. "It's okay, Jack. I'm fine."

"Are you sure? Eli has been worried. He asked if I knew where you've been." Rebecca recoiled. *What?* "It's fine, Jack. I just called him. He knows where I was. I just spoke to him. Just visiting friends in Boston."

Jack looked at her with eyes that clearly knew she was lying. He had known her a decade or more. He had grown up working in the farm store and had watched her business grow from a single hardworking employee to seven employees and a booming cafe and ice cream window in addition to the farm store. He knew to leave this alone, instinctively. He said, "Oh, okay. I must have misunderstood. So anyway, the electrician installed the broaster but I think there's gonna be a learnin' curve to it so we can tackle that this week if you want. I'm just gonna process those chickens that I pulled from the ice. Okay?" Rebecca smiled at the person she realized was more dedicated to her than anyone in her life had ever been. "Jack, end of the week, we need to talk. I've been thinking I need to make you manager here. Let's talk about it, okay? Obviously, a raise and benefits. It's long overdue. I have some things that need my attention and I trust you with everything in that place."

Jack's eyes conveyed his surprise and also the fact that he wanted to understand what on earth was going on.

53

"Hey Slade, can I ask you a question?" Hope had her gloves in her mouth as she tightened Pirate's girth and realized she sounded like she was underwater. She opened her mouth and let the gloves fall to the aisle below.

Slade shook his head, bent to pick up the gloves, and asked, "Were you born in a barn or somethin'?" Hope shook her head. "That would have been cool, but no. I'm just wondering about the group that Piper has here on Thursday nights. I mean, not my business and I don't ask, but one of the women told me I should go one of the nights."

Slade shook his head and looked over his shoulder to be sure no one else was in earshot. "I don't know for sure. I think it's like, I don't know, like Hogwart's or something." Hope put her gloves on and smiled. "Hogwarts!" Slade laughed, "Like I said, I don't know but the ladies who show up are always excited and talking about cards and messages and I don't know, maybe it's like a seance or somethin'. You should go."

Hope's mouth dropped open. "What? It's like a *seance* and I should go!?"

Slade shrugged, "You asked! Why don't you ask Piper?"

Hope shook her head. "Nah, it's her thing and if she wanted me to know about it, she'd tell me. Plus, Thursdays the house is empty. John goes out with his buddies so that's when I bake."

"Bake?" Slade laughed at the meaning that popped into his head and thought she wouldn't understand. "I don't mean ..."

Hope stopped him in his tracks. "I don't smoke. I bake sour-dough and banana bread for the week." She led Pirate past Slade and out the door into the July sunlight. She mounted up with just one bounce on her left foot. Slade wondered what it would have been like to have learned to ride before his injury and then realized it was only his injury that would have gotten him to even go near a horse.

"You heading out to the trails?" Slade asked her and picked up a bottle of fly spray.

"Yea, I need to get Pirate out of the ring or he will get bored and cranky."

"Standby," he said as he grabbed a rag from Hope's brush caddy and soaked it with repellent. He gently wiped it over the horse's ears, neck, and flanks. "Be careful out there. Knuckle-heads on dirt bikes don't always know the rules." Hope wasn't sure how to react. Did he think she'd never ridden trails alone? For hours and hours since she was twelve years old, she certainly had. She turned Pirate out toward the pasture. "K. Thanks." She circled Pirate back at the bottom of the hill. "Really think I should go to that group?"

Slade shrugged, "I mean, I haven't seen any banana bread and you've been here a month, so— doesn't matter to me."

Hope rolled her eyes. "Walnuts or raisins?"

Slade smiled. "Both, please."

54

John settled into the chair at his desk and checked his microphone, ear buds, and recording equipment. He was particularly interested in this morning's session. He had discovered over the years that past life regression isn't what each client needs. It's the work he learned from his father that gave him the foundation for his life's work. As with any generation, he built on what he was taught. He honed his own gifts and added his own ingredients.

He flipped through the intake form and crossed some information out and made notes on some items he wanted clarification for. Glancing at his clock, he decided he had time for one more cup of coffee.

In the kitchen, Hope was pulling on her boots. "Morning, Hope!" She looked up at him, almost falling against the wall, one boot was always a bit tighter than the other. "Morning. You're up early."

John laughed, "I don't know who gives me a harder time—you or Piper. You just love to make fun of me for sleeping normal hours. It's you horse people getting up before the sun that are not normal."

Hope giggled. "Hey, at least we go to bed at a normal hour. You're like a vampire." John tilted his head, "Touchè."

Hope took an apple from the counter and went out through the mudroom off to the barn smiling. She hadn't expected to feel so comfortable here even though she missed home. Rebecca mostly, but Eli and Peppercorn, too. The image of Ink's and Smudge's faces brought tears to her eyes and she pushed it all away. She knew they were fine. She knew she was also fine except for the phone notification from her mother at 3:30 am. It grated on her heart like a block of romano, which she was thoroughly allergic to.

John took his coffee back into his office and stood at the open windows. The fox kits he'd seen in early spring were back. They had shed their fuzzy gray coats and no longer had bright blue baby eyes. Still small, they were now a beautiful copper, their eyes a stunning amber. No vixen in sight, he watched them pound and pound on the ground under the arborvitae that lined the front of their property. To his surprise, one of them snapped up a field mouse and pranced away, head held high, its siblings in hot pursuit. Soon they would retreat to the woods where somewhere they had a den. For now, they were learning to hunt. He knew their mother was likely watching, not too far away.

The knock at the door set him into motion. He swung the front door open, "Good morning, Sir. Come on in."

Slade stepped in. "No need for Sir. I'm just a grunt." When he shook John's hand, he was not aware that John could feel his fear, his hesitation.

He led Slade the ten steps to his office and closed the door behind him. "Good to see you. You're more than welcome to take a seat in a chair or get comfortable on the couch. Most people prefer the couch for the actual session once we get rolling. Up to you."

Slade froze for a moment, not sure if he was going to regret this. His psychiatrist had given him the go ahead and had an extensive consult with John. When his doctor asked if he trusted John with his trauma, Slade's response was, "My life has only gotten better since I turned down Farm Road."

John outlined the process he used with all his clients who came for hypnotherapy. "You're in control the entire time. You won't be asleep; that's a common misconception. You'll be very relaxed but aware and you can stop at any time you feel uncomfortable.

Slade nodded. "Let's rock 'n roll. The longer I wait, the less chance I'm gonna go through with it but I want to. I think it will help me. God knows the horses have changed me in a way I can't explain." Slade had indicated early on that it was the time period he returned from Afghanistan that he wanted to start with.

John paid homage to Piper's work and the dedication she had to helping people heal with the help of the horses. He wasn't sure how much Slade knew about Piper's journey and he didn't ask. For the time that Slade was in his office, it was all about Slade and his needs.

"Okay, so this is usually when people lie on the couch and get comfortable. You can put the headphones on so there won't be any distracting sounds, just my voice as I guide you."

Slade listened as John instructed him to breathe deep into his abdomen and let all the tension in his muscles wash away in the river of gold light that gently flowed through him.

John gently guided him through a meditation to help his mind relax and to lower his resistance. "Now that you've reached the bottom of the staircase, I wonder what it is you see there. Who is waiting for you on this perfectly beautiful day?" Immediately Slade said, "Moose and Ashley and my girl, Kristi." John was impressed with his quick response. He watched as Slade yawned and swallowed, indicating that his nervous system was relaxed.

"I wonder if you can recall the details of that day. Whatever comes to mind, just relax and tell me: sights, sounds, smells, all of it."

Slade took a deep breath and said, "I hadn't seen Moose since I was medevaced. Wasn't sure how he'd react to seeing me in swim trunks and a prosthetic leg but he was cool. He's about ten years older than me and he saved my life. He was on his third tour and it was my first and only. I always kinda felt I ruined something for him that I don't know about. So Moose and Ashley are waiting for us at their house right along the river. Me and Kristi drove up in our swim suits and we just had my rucksack stuffed with what we needed for the week. Not much, just a couple a pairs of shorts and t-shirts and beer money. Ashley was Moose's dream girl. He talked about her all the time in the sandbox. I mean all the guys talked about their girls back home but Moose had a plan. I looked up to him for that. I didn't have a plan. Kristi was cute but she wasn't my dream girl. She was fun and we had the best week up there with them. Moose's grandfather left him the house and they were in the middle of renovations when we were there. It was definitely a family heirloom. Moose was into it. He wanted the big family and deserved it, too."

John waited, then asked, "What did you do that day besides canoe? What was it like to be there?"

Slade picked up where he had left off, "We fished and cooked on the grill that night, talked about the war and where it was all going. It was a mess. I could tell Ashley was upset that Moose kept talkin' like he was goin' back. He wasn't but everyone knew he wanted to. It's hard to explain but he never really was home when he was home. His mind was with his unit back there and with the ghosts of the guys who would never come home. Not me. My leg was back there, probably choking a camel herder who cooked it over a fire in the desert. I was done when I got home. Me and Kristi slept on the sleeping porch and listened to the river, buzzed, and not a care in the world. It was a good week."

John said, "Sounds like a perfect week. Let's move to the last day you were there. What happened that day?"

Slade started tapping his foot on the couch. John said, "Big breath in, good. Let it go and tell me."

"Well, we took a spin around town after breakfast. Kristi said she wanted us to move up there. She got pissed when I said I had a job at home. Anyway, Moose and Ashley made us promise to come back the same week every summer so we could be sure to stay in each other's lives. She said they would probably have a baby by then so we might not be drinking as much. Ha! Moose said if they had a baby he'd be drinkin' plenty. And then we got in my truck and drove home. I've seen Moose since then but me and Kristi, we never had another week on the Kennebec together."

John looked at his watch. He didn't want to end there but felt it was probably a good spot to wrap it up. "Okay, I wonder if you can see the staircase again, the one you walked down earlier and just put one foot on the first step."

He guided Slade up the staircase and back to the office. Slade opened his eyes and yawned, sitting up, a little self-conscious. "How'd I do, doc?"

John smiled, "You knocked it out of the park. You did great. So I'm going to go over the recording and I can email it to you if you want to listen to it before our next session. How do you feel?"

Slade stood, adjusting to being on his feet and shrugged. "Good, I guess. I don't know how I'm supposed to feel but I think there's probably more to talk about."

John nodded, "There always is. Let's see what next week brings."

55

Hope turned out the banana breads onto a cooling rack and inhaled the sweet aroma of what, to her, was a direct portal to Full Circle Farm. Closing her eyes, she imagined being in the farm kitchen, hearing Jack place orders with vendors, smelling the brownie batter and hearing small children beg their mother to buy a carrot to feed the donkey. Rebecca had packed some essentials for Hope to take from the farm kitchen, though Hope had protested. Two loaf pans, a baking sheet, a cake pan, and a beloved bean pot. "It's not like you're leaving forever. You're just borrowing them," she had said and tapped Hope on the nose, the way Hope tapped the barn cats, minus the "boop."

The screeching of a blue jay outside brought her back to Piper and John's kitchen at All in Time Farm. She reached into a drawer and found the plastic wrap was empty. She checked the other two drawers and found in the back of the bottom one, a single cocktail napkin, one that Piper kept for posterity, that read Black Whores Farm. With wide eyes, she placed it back in the far reaches of the drawer and closed it. In the pantry she found what she was looking for and wrapped the bread containing nuts and raisins and left the one with nuts only on the rack. Piper hated raisins.

She grabbed a sticky note from the drawer, reminiscing about the sticky notes she had left on Eli's door, begging to take care of his ponies. Reflecting on a time long ago with the perspective of early adulthood, aided by copious hours of therapy, she realized just how perilous her childhood had been. On the note she simply wrote a capital letter S and headed out to the barn to leave it in Slade's tack locker. Curious if the women from the group would arrive before she got back into the house, she took her time. The hydrangea she had uprooted from home was well acclimated, yet wouldn't likely produce blooms this year. *Why did I take it with me? Am I really going back to Full Circle Farm or will I stay here? Do they want me to stay?* She recognized the hallmarks of anxiety and knew that Eli would guide her to take a slow, deep breath, so she did. The inside of a barn was always the balm her soul needed. Cool, serene, gentle, and timeless, mixed with the scent of pine shavings and alfalfa, it was instant calm for her troubled heart.

She looked in on Pirate, chewing his hay like it was his job. The deep nicker vibrated in her chest. He stepped to the bars on his door, his muzzle and whiskers determined to attract a scratch or better yet, a treat. Hope kissed the velvety nose and promised him some leftover raisins in the morning. Inside the tack room, she placed the still warm bread in Slade's locker. Inside she saw a piece of paper with a phone number on it. (207.) *Hmm. Maine.*

She closed the door when she heard voices. The chime of the alarm sounded and up above she could hear Piper walk to the door of the office Hope had never seen. She stood with her eyes closed for a moment, feeling she shouldn't be in the barn but chastised herself. *Why do I never feel I belong anywhere?*

Camille, the young woman who had first invited Hope to join them some evening, stopped in the aisle as Hope stepped out of the tack room. "Hi Hope! You're coming to class!?" Anne and Jamie waved her over. "So exciting! C'mon!"

Hope shook her head. "Oh. No, I was just finishing up some ...," she stalled. Piper stepped off the bottom step and into the aisle. Jamie said, "Hope's joining us? How fun!" She walked past Piper and started up the stairs, followed by Anne. Claire waited, sensing tension. Piper looked at Hope and raised her brows. "Would you like to join us tonight? You're more than welcome, Hope."

Claire, normally reserved, walked across the aisle, took

Hope by the hand and trotted her up the stairs to the office.

Piper took the lone chair from the closet and set it in the spot the members cleared for her. Hope sat on the edge of the chair, tapping her hand on her knees, looking for signs of anything that would suggest a seance. Anne handed Hope a slip of paper, a pen and explained how to write an intention. Piper sat back and admired the love the group had for a total stranger. The scent of burnt raisins, mostly forgotten but instantly recognizable washed over the spot behind her nose. *Why?* She misted her palo santo spray around her desk and chair as the group drew some cards from the table. Hope looked at Piper and quickly looked away. Piper smiled. "If you want to, take a card. No pressure." Hope shook her head and smiled.

Piper closed her eyes and felt for the direction the group needed. She swayed slightly to the music she had chosen, titled "Spring Reverie."

She waited until everyone had written in their journal and softly said, "Okay, so I'm being guided to have us use a different deck tonight." She reached into her desk drawer and pulled out the first deck she had ever used. It was from a friend who had watched her struggle when her life began to crumble after Paul's death, and everything she believed to be true proved to be the opposite.

She shuffled the deck and handed it to Anne who sat to her right. "Everyone take a card but don't look at it yet. Jamie said, "Oh! I love when we do this." Hope looked at her in disbelief. *Do what?*

Hope took the deck from Claire and slid a card from the middle before passing it along. She put the card face down on the table in front of her and waited. When the deck reached its starting location, Piper said, "Okay, pass your card to the person directly across from you. That's the message you are delivering tonight." Anne stood and reached across the table to Hope and smiled at her. Hope reached down for the card on the table and handed it to Anne. Once everyone was seated again and the chattering stopped, Piper instructed them to look at the card that was given to them and journal about it while the music played. Anne looked at her card and whispered, "Oh my gosh." She looked at Hope and smiled. Hope was stunned to see the woman's eyes glinting in the dimly lit room. Hope watched as the women began to write. She didn't have a journal and was nervous to turn her card over. Her breath quickened. She reached for the hair tie on her wrist and snapped it. Piper handed her a small journal with the words "She's a Wildflower" on it.

Hope opened the journal and wrote the date, the time, and her name. She felt like she was back in high school. She turned the card quickly, the way one might tear off a sticky bandage. It read, simply, "Mother."

Hope began to write, not expecting much but much was there and she wrote until she heard someone whisper, "Wow. She's getting a lot."

When it was her turn to share, Hope simply said, "My card was Mother and I just wrote that I need to call her back. She called me the other day and I have been busy."

Claire said, "Cool. See how it pertains to what you need in the moment?"

Hope nodded but thought, *My mother is the last thing I need. My mother always needs something from me.*

After their meditation, during which Hope was able to sit comfortably further back in her chair and relax, the group was buzzing with energy and hoping there was another activity left as they wrote what they experienced during the guided meditation that brought them to a cozy beach house in which they would meet someone who had a message for them or someone in the group.

Piper looked around and was happy to see Hope had color in her cheeks and was enjoying the evening, the women sending almost visible comfort to her, intuitively, instinctively, maternally.

"So, let's just go around the circle and share anything that came up for you. Anne, let's start with you."

Hope listened as the women talked about colors and places, names of people, and dreams they'd shared. One woman cried about a great aunt who gave her a chore to do this week: to visit her sister she no longer speaks with. The group spoke in hushed voices, words of support and empathy, "It's okay. I know it's hard. Forgiveness is so freeing. It's about you, not her."

Hope thought, *That is not at all what I experienced.*

Piper looked at Hope and smiled, "Do you want to share anything? You don't have to."

Hope took a breath and looked around at all the faces of the women who she felt were genuinely eager to hear what she had to say. They giggled at the comical expression on her face. She let out a loud sigh and giggled. She shook her head and said, "I don't think it will make any sense."

Claire said, "If there's one thing we have learned here, it's to say everything. It might make sense to someone else."

Hope looked at Piper and said, "I just heard a man say, 'You've learned your lesson of patience. Now, you need to learn to put it all together: Patience, action, and healing. They are not separate.'" Hope stopped and looked at the words in the journal. She had underlined the next few sentences. Without looking up, she said, "The farm was just the beginning, Paris was a piece of the puzzle but the rest is right here under your roof. I was happy to be a part of it all but you still have work to do." The silence more than uncomfortable, Hope wished she was back in the house washing pans and spatulas.

Piper asked, her signature poker face on point, "Anything else?"

Hope read the last line from her journal, "Paul wants you to know Philip has come back to you but not as a little boy."

56

"I'm not sure, Dr. Cranston. I feel like I'm turning a corner but I'm not sure where I'm going." Lois smoothed her hair and rubbed her nose. The late afternoon sun was in her eyes. The sneeze surprised her. Eli stood and closed the blinds enough to shield her from the bright western sun as it set.

Lois said, "Thank you for seeing me later than usual. My schedule has gotten better but it's not the same hours. I took your suggestion to shake things up a little bit."

Eli nodded. "That's good. Change is challenging but it pushes us in new directions we have never considered. How are things at home?"

Lois shook her head. "I am not there much so I can't really say." Her mouth opened wide and her laugh was comical, like a cartoon character's perfect "Haha"!

She clasped her hand over her mouth then. "Oh my gosh. I'm sorry. I don't know where that came from." Her cheeks colored and Eli recognized the nervous system trying to adjust itself. "Laughter is good! So is a yawn or a sigh. All three are good signs."

Lois smiled then. "I am really trying to let my son figure things out on his own. Now when he texts me questions I feel he should know answers to, I just don't answer."

Eli asked, "And what happens?" Lois became animated, her arms shot up in the air, again cartoonishly. "He texts back to say never mind, he figured it out!"

Eli nodded. "How 'bout that."

Eli's phone buzzed on his desk which made him glance at the clock. *Oh geez, over time.*

After wrapping up the session and collecting the co-pay, he wished Lois a good week. She was still chatting as he saw her to the door. "Watch your step."

He turned back to his desk and saw it was Becca who'd texted. He used his phone to deposit the check Lois wrote him into his bank account and when he heard the door open, he assumed it was Lois with one more thing to tell him.

Instead it was Rebecca.

"Becca!"

She looked frightened and disheveled.

Eli went to her, concerned. "Becca, sit down. What's wrong? You look like you've seen a ghost."

Becca sat stiffly in the chair Lois had just vacated.

"Is it her?"

Eli's head bobbed like the little bobble head toys Gracie used to have on her dashboard.

"Is what, is what who?"

They both found that funny but the noise Rebecca made was not akin to laughter.

Eli touched her hand, "Becca, *what is* going on? Did something happen in Boston? I thought you were staying another night?"

Rebecca could not have guessed she would ever feel this way again. Leaving the man she narrowly escaped marrying so long ago and then uncovering the secret about Grace being in prison, when Rebecca thought Eli was writing to his ex-wife for years. It was shocking because she had felt certain she knew what was happening. But as it turned out, she was way off the mark. Right now, she felt like a scared little girl. She couldn't imagine that she was that far off the mark this time. This man she entrusted with her life, her future. *A good man, no less. It's not as hard when you realize a person is a jerk, but he's not. Not to other people, anyway.* All of this was racing through her head and it reminded her of the time when she was certain Eli was still in love with Antigone, sending her dozens of cards and letters that were sent back and stored in his desk drawer. She couldn't have been more wrong then and that thought was throat punching her now. "Could I be wrong this time, too?" Her eyes scanned the painting of the sailboat that hung on the wall of the office. It had been in Otto's study. She recognized the significance of the boat in rough waters. The sun poking through the storm clouds, promising to come back and settle the seas was what she wanted right now. Sun, warmth, and laughter. There hadn't been much of that lately.

"Becca, I'm really getting worried here. Has something happened I don't know about? What's going on?"

Rebecca Treadway Cranston concentrated on keeping her eyelids from splashing the tears that teetered and threatened, balancing on the rim of her blue eyes.

"Eli, where is the deed to my farm?"

57

Missy left the apartment early, before Stan awoke. The weeks had gone by quickly and to her surprise, Stan was happy to have her there. He fed her, bought her a new pair of sandals, kept her in cigarettes and brought her to his AA meetings. Missy had always done what she needed to do to get what she wanted and if AA meetings three times a week would keep a roof over her head, she would attend. She waited patiently for him to ask about Hope but as the days passed, she realized that he wasn't likely to.

The sun was warm but tolerable this early, which allowed her to take the longer route toward the old house.

She walked along the street she thought she had recalled perfectly in her mind for so many years. The blue house on the corner was no longer blue but it also was no longer a Colonial. She shrugged and turned in a circle. Maybe she was remembering the other end of the street. The sun warmed her face as she strolled; she could see her younger self two decades earlier, skipping along the water's edge, thinking how life was finally beginning for her. Away from the watchful eyes of her grandparents and far from her joyless, uber accomplished parents in New York City, she was free. She watched her sixteen-year-old self walk into the deep blue water, peeling off her t-shirt and denim shorts to reveal a pink bikini. *I was so freakin' young.*

Missy continued walking, wondering what it would have been like if they'd stayed here, in Bath. She knew they couldn't have. Even then at sixteen, she could understand that what

Stan had been through in that house, it would never make for a happy home. As long as she had Stan, she didn't really care where they went. Or so her teenage self had believed.

As she approached the old house, the one they stayed in until three nights before Hope was born, she stopped. *Why am I doin' this? I don't wanna see who lives there now.* She turned back and headed south down Front Street. She looked back to the water and saw young Missy slowly sink beneath the water, nose pinched. She surfaced, leaned back into the gentle blue and watched her pregnant belly rise to the surface, buoying her there along the craggy shore of the Kennebec.

58

Slade could feel his muscles letting go as he let the couch fully support him; he had come to enjoy listening to John's voice and trusting the process now. John's voice was comforting, a rarity in the harsh world where Slade lived. "I want you to take me to the next time you see Moose. What is happening on this day? Take your time and be there in that moment. Sights, sounds, smells. When you're ready."

Slade took a deep breath and his tapping foot slowly came to rest. He said, "I'm nervous to go to the door. I know Moose needs me in the way I needed him back in Afghanistan. But ... but I had only lost my leg. Moose. God, Moose lost his wife and his baby. I just don't know how I'm going to be able to sit with him or what I'll say."

John asked, "How long ago did he lose them?" Slade answered quickly, "Four months ago. I had just had another surgery so I couldn't get to the services. Then I had to have another surgery because of an infection so it took me some time to get up there, but I did. I think that counts. I hope so." John reassured Slade, "Of course it counts. You did what you could do when you could do it. I'm sure Moose understood. What happens when you get to the door?"

"Moose comes out on the porch and hugs me. He's lost weight and looks awful. He's crying and saying he doesn't wanna live. He can't live without Ashley. How can he live without her? What good is he without her? I try to console him but he's a wreck." John moved him along. "So tell me what's happening now. I wonder what you say to Moose."

"I told him we are going to the bar we go to when I visit. We have a beer and he starts to seem more like the sergeant I trusted with my life. He talked about moving, not wanting to stay in the house with all the memories. The bartender brings another round and tells us it's from the guy at the end of the bar sending his condolences. We toast to Ashley and the baby who was going to be named for Ashley's father." John pushed him along. "Okay, is there anything else that happens on this night? Anything significant that was said or ...."

Slade interrupted him, "Hell yeah. We meet some girls at the pool hall later. They are there when we walk in. We're drunk and the girls are young. I mean, Moose has twelve years on me so they were a lot younger than him but still really young to be in a pool hall at midnight."

John pushed him to explain what happened next.

"Well, we invited them back to Moose's house and they came with us. I knew it wasn't right and I passed out on the couch anyway." One of the girls left as soon as the sun came up but the one that stayed was in bed with Moose. So I took myself out to find a Bloody Mary and something greasy to kill my hangover."

John was relieved to hear this and wasn't surprised to see Slade's foot tapping again. He pushed him forward once more. "So now let's go to the end of the weekend when you're ready to leave Moose's house and come back to Massachusetts. Take me through that time."

Slade hesitated, then said, "I told Moose I would always be here for him, no matter what. Told him to be careful 'cuz that girl isn't nineteen like she told him. I swear she looked like a kid. Moose laughed at me and told me to bug off, he knows what he's doing. So I got on the road and headed home."

John said, "Okay. Did you and Moose make any plans to see each other again?"

Slade wiped his face. "Yea, sure. Every summer, that's what we promised and even if Ashley was dead and Kristi broke up with me, we were brothers and we made a promise. But after that, things went sideways like a truck on black ice. Cluster fuck."

59

The certificate of training hours completed in Therapeutic Horseback Riding awarded to Hope Cranston as a preliminary instructor was pinned to the cork board in the tack room. Hope wasn't sure what made her happier: to see her accomplishment or to know Piper had immediately displayed it for everyone to see. It was only last night that John's printer slowly spit out the special paper he bought for the occasion. Hope took her saddle and bridle from her locker as she listened to Becca fill her in on what was happening at Full Circle Farm: the broasted chicken and potatoes debut, celebrating Jack as general manager, and adding three new ice cream flavors. Hope was suddenly home-sick all over again. "Oh, I miss being there, Becca. It's been great here but I can't wait to come home." She could hear Piper's first clients of the day through the window of the tack room as they arrived. Becca said, "We miss you, too, Hope. It's not the same here without you." Hope sensed Becca wasn't telling her every-thing. No mention of Eli or the ponies. She bent down to tighten her field boot laces and when she did, she saw a receipt that had been swept into a pile of dust and hay but not thrown away. *Lazy kids,* she thought. Dunkin' Donuts on one side and an address on the other. Atlantic Townhouse Apartments, *127 Draydon Road, Bath. Hmm.*

Hope shivered, unconscious of the oddity in the heat of the day. She asked Becca to give Eli and the ponies a hug as she swept it all into the dustpan. "Love you, Becca." As she emptied the pile into the trash can and grabbed her gloves from her locker, Becca told her, "Hey listen, when you have some time this week, I want us to talk about a couple of things, okay?" Hope noticed the goosebumps on her arms. "Okay. Is everything all right? Like, should I be worried?" Rebecca reassured her that it could wait until later in the week. "Go ride and say hi to Pirate for me. Love you."

Hope tucked her phone away and as she closed her locker, a slip of paper floated out. A little messenger fluttering to the ground. She scooped it up and saw that the date was a week ago.

Hey Hope - thank you for the banana bread. It was delicious. You are a good cook! You must make your old man proud. - Dennis

Hope stared at the paper in her hand. She turned it over and back again as if more information might appear. *Dennis? Old man? What?* She fished the receipt out of the trash and compared the handwriting. She tucked them both into her breeches pocket and went to tack up before the kids descended on the farm.

Piper was in the aisle, setting up equipment and grooming Domino, her truest, most even-keeled pony for her first client. "Morning, Hope."

"Morning! I will get out of the way as fast as I can. I was just admiring my certificate. Can't believe I finished all my hours."

Piper looked at her with a beaming genuine smile, "Congratulations. Job well done."

Hope had been wanting for a week now to ask if she'd upset Piper about what she had written in her journal and read aloud at the end of the class. Every time she thought she could get the question out, there was an interruption and here she was a week later, wondering. Instead, she asked, "Is Slade's name really Dennis?" Piper laughed, "Yes, Dennis is his first name, but he only uses his last name, I guess."

Hope wondered why but didn't ask. Piper said, "Have you done any sessions with him yet? I think it would be good for you to get some practice with adults, too." Hope shook her head. "I could, if you think it's a good idea. I mean, I like the kids but if you think it'll help?" Piper nodded, "Yup. I think it will. John mentioned it, too. He's been working with Slade. Not sure if you knew that. It's sort of a team effort."

Hope slid the bit into Pirate's mouth and pushed the headstall over his ears. "Sure. When is he coming next? I'll put him on my calendar."

Piper greeted her clients. "Hope, let me text you later. Oh, and class is tonight if you're still interested."

Hope led Pirate out to the sand arena to warm up. The creaking of the leather as she mounted up would always relax her instantly. *So Slade's name is Dennis, Piper isn't mad at me, and Becca has something she needs to tell me but not yet.* As she walked on a loose rein, she looked at her phone. Another call from Mom. *Perfect.*

60

Not sure why she felt the need to but doing it anyway, Rebecca took photos of the items still in the safe and the items that were still sitting behind her shoe rack. She scooped them up and returned them to the safe. *If Eli is going to play dumb, then I will just have to piece together what I can on my own.* She couldn't shake the look on his face when she had accused him. *Just like the time I accused him of sending his ex-wife birthday and Christmas cards every year when it was really his daughter.* She shook her head in disgust. *No. Don't let him off the hook. He had no explanation to offer. None! Ed MacLean said he's seen this scenario time and time again.*

She backed out of the closet and took one last picture, again, not sure why. Her phone was on the nightstand, where it sat, buzzing. *Not answering, Eli.* She stood at the bedroom window and watched Cayenne rolling in the pasture, Ink and Smudge grazing near the pond. This was her dream home and she was not prepared to leave it. Or split it.

Her phone buzzed again. Annoyed, she picked it up, ready to scream at Eli about how unfair this is and why would he do this to her? Instead, it was the Law office of MacLean, MacLean and Howard.

"Yes?" Her voice was timid, uncertain. "Yes, this is Rebecca. Uh, huh. I'm not really sure. Yes, I can get a list together. Okay. A retainer? How much would that be? I will let you know. I have some things to figure out here." She was impatient now, pacing, hand on her forehead. "Okay. I understand. Yes, I will."

Standing in the late afternoon sun of the bedroom that she imagined one day in the far future, she would die in; suddenly she sensed she wasn't alone. Startled, she turned to see the man she had trusted and loved for over a decade. *How can everything change overnight? Was it overnight or have I just had blinders on the whole time?*

"Eli. What are you doing?" Her voice betrayed her. She didn't mean to sound accusatory for the sheer fact that she wanted this conversation to go as smoothly as possible.

"I'm worried about you, Becca. I don't know what you think is going on, but until you figure it out, I'm just here, concerned."

She quickly looked away from his pained expression. *Not getting sucked in!*

"I am not yours to worry about, Eli. I was fine before we met and I will be fine when this is finished. I just can't believe this is happening." Still looking at the floorboards they had stripped and refinished by hand over many days the first spring Eli spent at the farm, she heard him walk further into the room and stop. "Becca, I don't know who was in the safe or what happened to everything in there but I'm as concerned about it as you. You might not believe that, but it's true."

Becca wiped at the tears she didn't want to shed in front of Eli. "I can't talk about this right now. I am in shock and honestly, I don't know what to think. If it wasn't you, who would it be?"

Eli put his hands in his trouser pockets and shifted his weight. "Well, there are only two people I know of with the combination: Me and you."

She looked at him then. "Yes. Me and you and I didn't open it! I didn't take those things. Why would I want Otto's things? Those are precious things that were left to Hope! The deed to my farm? Really? I didn't move those things!"

Her voice rose alongside the anger that animated her arms and seemingly her hair, too. For a moment, Eli saw Antigone in a way that he never rally saw her when they were married, shortly after law school. *Perspective offers so many clues,* he thought.

The flash of anger, the wild mane waving as she whipped around to face him, the betrayed look on Antigone's face when Eli couldn't keep Gracie out of prison. There was no calming her down and there was nothing Eli could have done to make it right. *Do something, Eli! For Christ's sake, fix it! I don't care what you need to do—just fix it!* Eli took a deep breath, knowing he couldn't fix what was broken so long ago, nor could he have avoided the consequences that followed. For him, for Antigone. For Grace.

"Rebecca!" he stopped and cleared his throat. He rarely used her full name. "Becca. Let's think about this, okay? A lot has happened in the last few months and ..." Rebecca cut him off then, angry, spiteful, in a rage, she screamed, "A lot has happened? Tell me, Eli! What has happened?! I want to know! I want to know who Darcy is! I want to know where the hell you are when you leave the front door because you sure as hell aren't in the office all the time! I've come by there to surprise you half a dozen times and you aren't there! Melissa Barlow blows into town and suddenly, our lives fall apart? Hope, for God's sake. She didn't deserve to deal with any of that and we sent her away? What kind of parents are we? She probably doesn't even want to come home! I wouldn't!"

Eli's eyes widened. *What is she talking about?*

"Becca, please. I think there is going to be an explanation, but we won't get to the bottom of anything if we can't talk rationally."

"Well, Eli. Tell me. Rationally. Who opened the goddam safe?"

61

"Yea, we can hit the trail. It's early enough to miss the deer flies. Well, maybe not miss them completely, but it's better than the afternoon." Hope handed Oliver's lead to Slade and she held onto Pirate.

They tacked up in silence, doused the horses in fly spray, and walked them out toward the pasture.

Hope asked, "Is this your first trail ride?" Slade nodded as he buckled his helmet. "Sure is. I'm psyched."

"Let's see if Ollie will follow. I don't think he'll want Pirate on his tail." She moved Pirate past the pasture gate along the well-trodden path toward the woods that surrounded the farm. Hope turned herself sideways so she could talk to Slade about the importance of relaxing on the trail but keeping good contact with his horse's mouth. "It's a way to communicate and on the trail, I mean it depends on the horse, but they sometimes spook at things they see." Slade sat up straight and gathered Oliver's reins, suddenly nervous. "Give me an example of things they might spook at, " he asked but wasn't certain he wanted an answer.

Hope, straight-faced, said, "Rocks, trees, rabbits. The wind." She giggled and added, "I mean, they *are* prey animals but they do a lot better with a buddy, so they'll be fine."

Remembering the things Piper told her to work on, she asked, "Do you have any anxious feelings or thoughts right now?

Slade answered, "Uh, well I'm wondering which tree is gonna do us in. Otherwise, not really."

Deciding they could take the longer loop, Hope, tried again. "Do you have any riding goals, now that you obviously know the basics?" She looked back at Slade again. He nodded and said, "Actually, yeah. I was thinking of asking Piper to sell Oliver to me."

"Really?! That's exciting!" Hope flashed a toothy grin, a clear approval. "What did you do in your spare time before you started at the farm?"

Slade looked around, quasi-relaxed. "Just work mostly. Go home, walked my dog when he was alive. Thought about getting another one. That's it. Watch TV, sometimes shoot pool with the guys. What about you? You ride your whole life, I bet."

Hope turned Pirate toward the brook that would allow them to avoid the bridge ahead, unsure how Oliver would react. "Yea, pretty much." The thought that Slade would ask her questions hadn't occurred to her. "Okay, so just lean forward and grab a handful of mane as we go down the bank here. I don't think he'll jump over the brook , but just in case." Slade immediately pulled back on his reins. Oliver answered with a little jig that of course made Slade pull harder. Hope said, calmly, "Loose rein. It's okay. Eyes up, that's where you're going. Remember that. He isn't sure why you're pulling him up and he wants to go. You just tell him what you want. He trusts you. He will always react to your energy. Settle and he will settle." Slade said, "I don't want to jump the brook, I can tell ya that!" Hope giggled, "Well, we can hop off if you want but I think it's fine. Watch how Pirate goes and you can decide." She put her leg on Pirate who lowered his head, walked into the brook, stopped and drank from the moving water. "Well, shoot. I didn't know that was an option," Slade said. He looked up, over the brook and moved Oliver closer and found that the tried-and-true Iberian had no interest in drinking or jumping. He stood in the brook and looked around, then lowered his head and hopped up the other side, Holy shit!!" Slade shouted.

Hope said, "Nice job! Maybe you need to start some cross rails soon. You know, actual jumping." Slade shook his head, "Nah, I like the trails. This is more my speed."

They walked in silence for a bit, listening to the rhythmic hoofbeats as they made their way through the well-worn path around trees, over rocks, through brush. Slade thought about a trip he was going to take at the end of the month while Hope looked at the messages on her phone.

Slade continued with, "So tell me about your folks."

Hope didn't turn back toward him this time. She just asked, "Which ones?"

Slade laughed, "Uh. I dunno. How many you got?" Hope laughed to herself. "My adoptive parents have a farm in Bar Harbor. I'll be going back soon. Not sure when. I just finished my hours for my certificate, which is why I came down here in the first place."

Slade waited for more and when it didn't come, he pushed, "So what about your birth parents? Are they alive?"

Hope looked over her shoulder and said, "I guess so."

Meandering around the stand of giant oaks and back toward the farm, Hope warned, "They are going to want to go faster toward home. They always do. It's good practice to make them walk."

Slade said, "Good to know. I'm thinking I'll learn more out here than in the arena."

Hope thought how interesting it was to watch an adult learn to ride compared to her experience starting as soon as she was able to find someone to let her up in a saddle.

Pulling Pirate in a tight circle to remind him she was the one setting the pace, Hope giggled. "See? They will get away with murder if you let them."

She looked back to Slade and asked, "Do you have kids?"

Slade shook his head. "Nope. No kids." Hope waited to see if there was an explanation or reason. Slade added, "I got two nephews and a niece. They're pretty cool. I help them with their cars, used to take them fishing when they were younger."

Hope led them into the arena to finish their ride. "Let's make them work a little. We don't want them to always see the barn as the end to work. They should always be willing to work. They get stubborn, sometimes."

Hope showed Slade how to ride a serpentine and promised to set up a trail course before she left at the end of the summer.

Slade guided Oliver to the mounting block to dismount, which Hope found strange. She watched as she ran her stirrup irons up and loosening her girth.

"You don't have to dismount on the block," she said, as a matter of fact.

Slade stepped down from the block and pulled his pant leg up, revealing the titanium prosthetic. He bent down and tapped it with his hand. "Makes it a little easier with this thing."

Hope gasped. "Oh! I'm so sorry. I didn't know." Her heart, like a homebound pony, plunged ahead. "I'm such a jerk."

62

Claire and Jamie exchanged glances as they each pulled a card for Hope after asking if she would like them to. Hope opened her journal and wrote the date and Class #5 at the top. She turned the first card over. On the card was a picture of a young woman walking toward a beautiful lake, a deer watching from the side of a steep hill. There was only one word on the card: *Perception*. She wrote in her journal and then turned the second card over: this one showed a woman standing at a gate on a hilltop overlooking a village full of people inviting her to visit. When she saw the words "Find Your High Places," she understood immediately how the two cards related to each other and herself. Jamie said, "Look at you, Girl. You're going to be mayor of that village." A collective laugh made Hope feel that this was the village that was helping her find her place, her way. Anne said, "Yeah, you can't go back to Maine!" Hope's cheeks flushed, not sure what to say.

Piper looked at the clock and moved them forward. Again, she heard "compass" and this time asked the group if it meant anything to anyone. She saw only quizzical expressions but felt someone wasn't ready to claim the message yet. "Okay. So if everyone would like to chime in with any message, feeling, name, or anything at all, we can wrap up with that."

Deep breaths, eyes closed, pens scribbling, Piper looked at her phone. A text from Slade: **I think I scared Hope. She didn't know about my leg. I don't want her to feel bad.**

She replied: **She's tougher than you think but I'll let her know you texted.**

The group took turns with the messages they got in their brief moments of connection. Anne said, "Jamie, I'm not sure why, but I feel like your career is going to change, but not. I know that's weird, isn't it? I see an old stone building, like a mill, but maybe it had a different use at some point? I don't know but I see a store or shop or something. Does that make any sense?" Jamie looked at Anne and said, "You have no idea. Oh my goodness. I'll share next class but, yea, career change and shop ... you can't make this stuff up."

Jamie turned to Claire and said, "Have you met someone new? I know, super personal but I feel like if you haven't, you will soon and I get the name Gary." Claire rolled her eyes. "That's my ex!" More laughter and this time Jamie said, "Oh no! Maybe it's a new Gary."

Hope was fidgeting, uncertain if she had anything worth sharing but remembered the sentiment, *Say everything.* Piper raised her brows and asked, "Anything?"

Hope said, "I just got, 'Not everything is cut and dried? You have to be open to seeing how the pieces fit together.'" She shrugged her shoulders.

Claire looked at her, "Funny you say that. The reason I wanted to pull a card for you is that I was feeling like someone wanted to show you that things from your past aren't exactly as you remember. I saw a man yelling at a woman but he was just trying to keep her safe because she always put herself in harm's way. And then I saw him hiding money from her, saving it for something for his daughter but the woman took the money and used it on something, not sure what. He seems like a good guy who had bad things happen and no one could understand why he was the way he was. He needed healing but he didn't know where to turn." The room was silent. Claire asked, "Does any of that make sense?"

Hope looked out the window behind Piper and said, "No."

63

The parking lot was buzzing with vehicles. Massachusetts, New Hampshire, Maine plates mostly on any given day, but on Labor Day Weekend you could count at least fifteen different license plates at the State Line Liquor Store in Portsmouth. Hope sipped on her iced coffee and watched for the Full Circle Farm truck. Rebecca promised to bring Peppercorn so she could see the old dog she missed terribly. Wearing her All in Time Farm ball cap, denim shorts, and a Bar Harbor tank top, she felt too hot already. She glanced at her phone. A text from Slade: **Hey - Piper wants to know if you want Pirate's fly mask on or off?** She closed her eyes and inhaled deeply. *She knows the answer is yes. Why doesn't she text me herself? I know what this is about. She doesn't want me to go to the group anymore. I don't want to go anyway. I want to go home.*

Before she could text back, another text from **Slade: BTW thank you for the banana bread. I'd give it a 10/10 again."**

She smiled, then. *Why couldn't my father have been like him?*

She replied with: **Yes and you're welcome.**

"Hope!" The voice she would know anywhere called from across the lot. Hope looked up to see Rebecca carrying Peppercorn and waving to her.

"Becca! Hi Pep, Buddy!" She scooped up the barely there, old dog and hugged him as his tail went into overdrive. Rebecca wrapped her arms around them both. "Hi, Honey. I've missed you so much."

Hope held back tears. Not realizing how much she had missed Becca until she was there with her, she clung a moment longer. "Is Eli here?" Hope asked. Surprise lit up Becca's face for a microsecond but Hope felt it with her entire being. Her eyes scanned Becca's, looking for the clue that would match the feeling of anxiety she was fighting.

"No, he has some clients today. He's so busy but he sends his love. He said he called you the other day?" Hope nodded. "Yea, for a few minutes."

Becca looked at her phone and squinted at the sun. "Let's get lunch somewhere cool."

The drive to Bennett's was full of small talk, mostly about Ink, Smudge and Cayenne, Jack, and the store. Hope wanted to ask more about Eli but got the feeling Becca was avoiding. "Dogs Allowed," Becca read the sign and kissed Peppercorn on the top of his head.

They breathed in relief for the cool interior. Pep was served some water and then the waitress left Becca and Hope, seated across the table from one another, to themselves.

Becca cleared her throat and diverted her eyes to the specials posted on the table. "So tell me. How has it been at Piper and John's? Has it been worth your time and effort?"

Hope's slight recoil was not intentional but certainly not invisible. *If you didn't think it would be worth my time, why would you send me there? Why am I so confused?*

She gave Becca a forced smile. "Yea. It's been good. I got all my hours so now ..." She wasn't sure what to say but was wondering why they hadn't set a date for her to return home. All at once, the thought that perhaps she wasn't going to be going home crept into her thoughts, knit her brow and stabbed her eyes. *No, I'm not crying!*

"So now what? I mean. Is that why we're meeting for lunch? Am I not coming home?"

Her lip danced furiously. Embarrassed, she sipped her ice water, then scooped up Pep and let his fur hide her face.

"What? Of course you're coming home. Hope! That's what I wanted to talk about. Oh my gosh."

Hope focused on the dog. *I don't believe you. Something's wrong.*

The waitress cut through the tension, took their order, and left a biscuit for Peppercorn.

"I just feel like something's off, Becca. You'd tell me if something's wrong, wouldn't you?"

Becca reached across the table and took Hope's hand. Two farm girls, tanned skin, broken nails, and intuition in spades, sized each other up, the months apart revealing much.

"Hope. You're right. There is something, but I'm sure it will be fine. I just need to figure out a few things and ..." she stopped when Hope withdrew her hand like a dog snatching a chicken leg off a picnic plate.

Agitated, Hope squinted her eyes as if Becca's gaze would burn like Missy's did. Like Stan's did. Like Piper's did when Hope delivered her first message to the group. But, as she forced herself to stay locked onto Becca's kind face, the tide of a time forgotten washed through her and she was twelve again, then ten, seven, six.

Becca was, when first they met, and every day hence, sweet salvation. Lost, unable to find her mother, six-year-old Hope stood under the market umbrellas at the Eden Farmer's Market, wailing the song of those who knew they were, in many ways, abandoned. Salted rivers cut through the unclean canvas of the frightened girl's face, unspoken weariness and dread, a neon sign only the empathetic can see. Rebecca had knelt in front of her, soothing her, promising to help. Finally, as the hitching sobs gave way to a deep yawn, Hope sat on the ground and surrendered the strangled 10s and 20s she'd stolen from Rebecca's table.

Her job as the daughter of Missy Barlow, was to steal, swipe, and swindle. Her reward, a candy apple, a piece of taffy, or if she did really well, a genuine smile, the kind Hope could feel in her chest. It wasn't the first, nor the last time Rebecca waited with her until the green Corolla came screeching back, Stan Barlow making excuses as he ushered the sleepy child off to the cabin tucked off Ogden Point Road.

Childhood in the flash of an eye, fading. *A lifetime ago.*

"Hope. I need you to tell me something." Becca's sobering voice reeling her back to the current moment.

Anything. I'll tell you anything as long as you still love me. Please.

Hope slowly allowed her eyes to close and open in the present, her lunch on the table, Peppercorn at her feet.

Becca leaned forward, revealing the smile from which Hope could always find comfort.

"I need you to tell me what happened to everything in the safe."

64

"Moose didn't know. Christ's sake, I knew the *minute* she called me, she hadn't told him. She was scared out of her mind." Slade lay completely still on the couch. "I picked her up at the train station and thought, *Man, she is trouble.* Told me Moose threw her out but didn't tell me why. Shit, I don't think I would have let her in my car if I'd known. I woulda brought her to the police station and let them sort her out. She was a kid! Moose insisted she wasn't underage but I knew better. She didn't even have a driver's license.

She said she needed a place to stay until she could figure out how to find the money for an abortion." His voice trailed off, his foot taking up the energy, enough to urge John to remind him to breathe. "Deep breath. You're doing great."

Slade continued, "So I tell her she can stay at my apartment but that she has to stay inside, no going out, no messing around. I mean it's a small town and I don't need people seeing a pregnant chick coming and going from my place." John recognized the rule follower, the integrity that was woven through Slade, despite the tragedies he had survived. "So now what happens? Take me through the time she is there with you."

"What happens?" Slade quipped. "What happens is she is just as wild as I knew she was. Smoking, asking me to buy her beer which I didn't. She was like a cat, just wild, looking to kick up any kinda drama she could. After a week, she said, 'Hemi, you're gonna marry me.' That's when I knew I needed to get her back to Maine. I mean, a pregnant minor, out of state in my apartment? Nah. Not happening. I took some money outta the bank, and drove her back to the train station. She was going *home*." He took a deep breath, one hand was grasping the edge of the couch. "That's good Slade. So she called you Hemi?"

Slade answered, "Yah, that was my nickname when I was in the service. Hemi. Only Moose still called me that after I was shipped home. I told her never to call me Hemi. So I drive her back to the station and give $300 for whatever she needed to do and told her to have Moose call me when she made it back to Maine. Asked her if she wanted me to call Moose when I got back to my place. She spit at me and took her bags out of my car, slammed the door. Ha! She was a pisser."

John looked out his office window. Late summer was begging fall to come change everything, to color the landscape and cool the uncomfortable days. In the flash of a single moment, John watched as a coyote snapped at one of the almost grown fox kits. John quietly stood, distressed. He watched as the larger canine flung the stunning red fox to the ground, another coyote lying in wait for his turn. The cry from the fox was pain and pure terror. John turned the meditation music up for himself, Slade unable to hear anything but John's voice. "So Moose's girlfriend went back to Maine? Did you ever hear from her again?"

Slade was silent. His body was still, relaxed. John waited as he watched out the window as the other fox kits hopped and circled as they followed the scent of their brother. John understood that loyalty can lead to downfall. *A cruel truth.*

Slade cleared his throat. "Yea, I saw her a few hours later. She knocked on my door."

John, surprised, asked, "What then?"

Slade hesitated, lifted his hand and wiped at his mouth and the hint of a beard.

"She lifted her friggin'shirt, no bra on. Got a goddam tattoo with the money I gave her. If she's still alive, there's a woman out there with SLADE inked on her breast with a husband, *the man who saved my life,* who thinks I'm the father of the kid he raised."

65

The vet gently put his stethoscope on Smudge's belly. "I'm not hearing much sound in there. How long's he been down?" Eli pushed his fingers through his hair and looked around at the barn clock. "Uh, not sure. I came out to feed and saw him down already."

The vet was busy getting Banamine ready. "Okay, this will help with the pain. Poor baby." She stroked Smudge's neck. She started to pass the tube down his nostril. Ink was in the adjacent stall circling, pawing at the boards dividing him from his shadow, his brother. Eli scratched Ink's forehead to calm him. He tried Becca again but got her voicemail. "Becca, call me as soon as you can. Tell Hope I miss her." He knew she was upset with him but felt she ought to be answering his calls and this was urgent.

The vet slowly pumped the mineral oil down the tube into Smudge's stomach. He groaned, his eyes watching Eli, now crouched on the shavings next to his first friend in Bar Harbor. "It's okay, Buddy. I'm here. You'll be okay." Another groan. Eli watched his long eyelashes as they danced up and down as his eyes focused on Eli, then the vet, then the sound of Ink shrieking. The vet tapped Eli's shoulder. "We have to get him up, walk him." Eli knew this. He'd watched Hope and Rebecca walk Cayenne when he colicked many years before. He couldn't bear the thought of forcing his little pony to stand when he was in so much pain but knew that if he didn't, he would die. He stood and clapped his hands, moving toward his tail. The vet pulled on his halter and directed Eli to grab his haunches and lift. Smudge groaned as he heaved himself up. "Hooray! Good job, Smudge. You can do this. I got you, Buddy."

The vet instructed him to walk him down the aisle, the driveway, around the barn, wherever, just keep him walking. "How long? I have clients. I mean ..." Eli's voice trailed off, realizing then that Hope and Rebecca did the farm work. All of it really and they weren't there. The vet answered, "Depends. Could be a few hours, up to twenty-four."

Eli's eyes bulged, "Twenty-four?" The young vet looked at him, all business. "Yes. That's if it works. Doesn't always. I have another client cross town with a laboring mare. Call me if he gets worse." Eli was speechless as he watched the woman climb into her truck and drive away. He dialed Rebecca again but hung up after the second ring. She wasn't going to help him. He then called Lois and left her a voicemail that he needed to reschedule her session due to a family emergency. He walked and walked and decided that if Smudge was walking, Ink could keep him company. Together, the three of them walked, slowly around the barn. The afternoon sun in late summer was beyond beautiful, something Eli never tired of. He wished he had on better footwear but he had thought he was just going to toss some hay and grain at the horses and leave for his afternoon appointments.

"Eli!"

Eli turned back toward the farm store. It was Jack, wiping his hands on his apron. "Everything okay?" He shouted up the hill. Eli stopped his caravan for a moment. "No. Little guy is sick. Vet said I need to walk him till he can pass what's impacted in there."

Jack looked back at the store for a moment, then jogged up the hill. He petted both ponies and said, "I can help when I close the store if you need me to."

Eli sighed deeply. "Man, you are the best. Thank you. I could use the help."

Just as the sun was preparing to set, Jack reappeared, apronless, and grabbed Smudge's lead from Eli; Ink had long ago been put back and was happily eating. Eli took off his work shoes that had effectively chewed his feet raw. In his haste, he stumbled backward on the gravel path at the backside of the enormous barn. A brave yet unsuccessful attempt at steadying himself, reaching for a pine tree behind him, ended with him crashing onto what looked like old hay and brush and whacking his head on the trunk of the pine. "Jesus! What the hell is that?" He landed with a thud, on what, he couldn't imagine. The thorny brambles kept him from clearing the brush off his arms and face. He felt trapped, his useless, raw feet now stuck all over with pine needles and sporting a crown of thorns so to speak. Jack's laughter as he rounded the barn quickly turned to concern. "What happened? You okay?"

Eli sat still, wondering the same. "Yah, I just need a hand getting on my feet. Can you pull the branches back?"

Eil pushed his weight to one side and realized that whatever he landed on, sounded hollow. Jack reached forward, hand extended, and pulled Eli to his feet. "Want me to run down to the house and get you some boots or something?" Eli could see why Rebecca made Jack manager of the farm store. His dedication was second to none. "Jack, if you do that for me, I will be forever in your debt."

Jack laughed, "It's not a big deal. Here, hold Smudge."

He ran through the barn, down the aisle past the horses and into the setting sunlight, his silhouette against the gold swath of sky. Eli scratched Smudge's forehead. He could see his sides heaving a bit, tired from walking several hours, still not feeling great. He called the vet to ask if she could give him another dose of Banamine. She agreed to stop on her way home.

Jack reappeared with socks and Eli's slides. "I figured these would be more comfortable." He reached into his pocket and drew out a handful of bandages.

Eli laughed. "Jack. Thank you. If you can walk him one more time around the barn, I'd appreciate it, then please go home. The vet is coming back and I'll be fine."

Jack took the pony and gently prodded him to keep up with his stride. Eli used the flashlight on his phone to look at the brush pile. He could see there was a board or something underneath. *What was it doing under the tree?* Gingerly he made his way down the barn aisle and found a rake leaned against the hose keeper.

He removed all the brush that was covering the piece of plywood. *But why did it sound hollow?* He carefully picked up one corner of the plywood to see that underneath were two deep metal trays from the farm store, the sort they used to bake large sheets of cornbread. *What the hell?* He pocketed his phone and using both hands, heaved the vine and insect covered plywood up and off the trays.

"Holy shit," he whispered as he dialed Becca. Again.

66

She ran her fingers over the nameplate on the back of the saddle, barely feeling the small brass nails that held it in place. For some time, she had quietly envied the girls who proudly displayed their full gentrified names on the cantle of their saddles. She would read them as she circled in equitation classes at horse shows: Anastacia LaFrenniere, Olympia Athanasiou, Tiffany Romanello. For all the money they had, they rarely placed higher than Pirate and her. For a moment she tried to envision adding a surname to the plate, wondering if it would make her feel whole somehow. She thought that it might be impossible to choose without an overwhelming cloak of guilt enveloping her entirely. Barlow or Cranston. Neither seemed to be who she was anyway so she just focused on how grateful she was just to have the Caprilli jumping saddle and matching bridle. Through tears now, she watched as the letters blurred and focused and blurred again.

HOPE

The gift tag read: Happy Birthday and Congratulations! (Come to the arena).

"Surprise! Happy Birthday!" Hope stopped at the entrance to the arena, stunned to see so many people at once. The boarders, the kids who took lessons, Piper's clients, clients Hope had worked with, the women from the development group, Piper, John, and Slade. She stopped in utter overwhelm. Quickly scanning the group, she recognized each person but had a difficult time grasping that they were all there just for her.

Piper and John presented her with a bouquet of pink roses. She hugged them both. "Thank you? I really don't know what to say." The kids came and hugged her, proudly filling her arms up with friendship bracelets, handmade cards, and wrapped gifts. Arms full, she walked to the table and chairs that had been decorated with crepe paper and a watermelon-themed tablecloth. She looked around again as people congratulated her on earning her certificate and wishing her the best year yet.

Slade said, "I hope you like the cake. I baked it myself." Laughter filled the arena as one of the kids loudly and immediately ratted him out. Hope had never felt so self-conscious about her words and actions but she absorbed the love and it helped her relax as John began to cut the cake. Piper yelled, "Wait! The candles!" She fished the small flat boxes out of her jeans pocket and placed them onto the cake. The kids counted out loud to twenty as John lit them.

"Make a wish! Make a wish!" The kids had clearly been to enough birthday parties to know the routine. She stood in front of the horse-themed cake and held her breath, eyes closed. *I wish for everything to go back to the way it was at home. I wish for forgiveness.*

She blew the candles, her ponytail bouncing back and forth, as she tried to get them all. Claire and Jamie leaned forward and helped. She hadn't expected applause. Her cheeks flushed and she smiled at the thought that so many people took time to be here with her.

When the cake had been finished and people had gone about their weekend plans, Hope began to clean up the wrapping paper and boxes, thanking Piper and John again for the saddle and party. "You really went overboard," she said. John shook his head and said, "No such thing, Hope. There is never too much of a good thing when someone deserves it."

Do I deserve it? She wondered.

Back into the barn she walked, a sense of belonging filling her as Slade was grooming Oliver. She held a small piece of cake out for the horse who made quick work of it. He bobbed his head, knowing there must be more.

"Gonna ride in shorts?" Hope asked Slade, knowing he wasn't. She hadn't seen him in anything but jeans. "Nah, I'm just grooming Oliver. I have to be at my niece's going away party in an hour. Off to college." Hope nodded, thinking about her high school friends who would also be heading back soon and wondered if she should think about school, too.

In a moment of bravery or perhaps letting her curiosity get the best of her, Hope asked, "Did you lose your leg in the war?"

Though it was just a second, there was enough of a glitch in Slade's movement that made Hope immediately regret asking.

"Yep. I did. I was around your age actually. Twenty years, one week and a day." Hope picked up a soft brush and gently ran it over Oliver's face.

"Oh. I can't imagine ..." She didn't know how to finish the sentence or the thought.

"Yea, more than half my life without it. Still feels like it's there sometimes. It's weird."

Hope nodded, listening intently. Oliver's eyes closed, enjoying the extra attention.

"Were you shot?" She looked out to the pasture as she asked, not sure if she should even be probing.

"Nope. IED. We were on a mission outside Mosul. Nighttime. A kid jumped out of this shitty little car we had passed a few clicks south and ran at us. Right at us, like a running back. Shit, I knew then our mission wasn't going to plan. Then, boom! The kid blew into a million pieces and my leg went with 'im."

Hope recoiled at the thought of a child dying that way. Her civics teacher in school had been in the war and shared some stories of the Taliban and their tactics but they just seemed like stories to her at the time.

"My God. That's horrible," she said. "How awful."

Slade had told the story so many times to so many people that he knew the responses before people could say them.

"Yea, it was scary. I don't remember all of it but I remember my unit leader, Moose, telling me I was going home, that I would be okay."

"Moose?" Hope looked at him as he brushed Oliver's tail, untangling the knot that the mud-loving horse made sure he fashioned each day in the paddock.

"Yea, Moose. He saved my life, put a tourniquet on and still managed to pull another guy out of the hell that was showering down all around us."

Hope picked up a hoof pick and stood at Oliver's shoulder. "Sounds like a good friend."

Slade replied, "Yea, the best. I mean we had a job to do and he was a good Marine. We trusted him and we respected him. He was definitely someone I looked up to."

Hope looked at the point below Slade's knee where the prosthetic started. "He sounds like a real hero. Is he still alive?"

Slade picked up the fly spray bottle and waited for Hope to finish Oliver's feet.

"Yea. He is. I just looked him up a couple weeks ago because I was wondering the same thing."

Hope stood back as Slade applied the bug spray and thought that in another month the bugs would be all gone and how she wished she knew someone as brave and caring as Moose.

"Was Moose a nickname?"

Slade smiled, remembering the first time he heard someone call the sergeant by that handle.

"We all had names. Sometimes you lucked out and got a good one and sometimes not."

"Did you have one?" Hope was intrigued.

"Sure did. As a mechanic who loved my Dodge truck, they called me Hemi, like the engine." Hope giggled.

Slade said, "There was a guy we called Bull 'cuz he was a farmer from Texas and a guy we called Skinny, 'cuz he wasn't."

Hope imagined that sort of camaraderie was not meant for her this lifetime.

She watched as Slade took Oliver off the cross ties and asked, "Why did you call that guy, Moose?"

Slade began walking Oliver out toward the pasture. He stopped for a moment, his gaze distant. He said with a quick glance back at Hope, "He was big, you didn't mess with him, and he was from Maine."

67

Rebecca pulled into the parking lot of the Karma Connection and felt uneasy, but it was a feeling she had developed a tolerance for over the last few months.

Eli explained to her everything she demanded, through tears and screams and thinly veiled threats.

"Darcy is a young woman at the book shop in Brunswick, where I did my first book signing. I told you all about her and the guy who wanted to be called Sir. Do you remember? He was the one who announced my award? At the conference?" Eli was shaking his head, incredulous that Becca wasn't grasping any of what he was telling her.

Rebecca was in no shape that afternoon to recall much. She was in survival mode, dependent on adrenaline and cortisol to see her through this mess.

"And here we are," she said to herself in her truck just an hour after dropping Hope off back at the Stateline Liquor Store.

"Let's go meet Darcy." She scooped Peppercorn up into her arms and promised him they would be heading home soon.

She swung the door open, heart racing. *Is she even working today? What will I say?*

The young man at the register looked up and visibly brightened to see the little dog. "Oh, hi there, Buddy."

Rebecca looked around at the customers enjoying iced drinks and books on this scorching day.

"What can I get for you?" Rebecca looked at the young man and wanted to scream but asked for a small iced coffee instead.

Peering around the shop, her eyes were drawn to Eli's book almost immediately. A signed copy sat on the ledge among a dozen other books whose authors had been to the cafe for events. She thought about how impressed with Eli she would be if she had come to an event. She shook her head and pushed the thought away.

A woman's voice behind her said, "Iced coffee's ready, ma'am." Rebecca steeled herself before turning. She snuggled the top of Peppercorn's head and walked to the counter. She approached the young woman, hair pink and blue, lip pierced and a name tag that read "Darcy." Rebecca sighed. Eli didn't have the hair color exactly right but the rest of the description fit. *Oh my God, I have to get a hold of myself. Darcy really is the coffee shop girl. I'm such a maniac. What is wrong with me?*

She situated Pep in his orthopedic dog bed in the passenger seat and turned the engine over. "Okay, Pep. That clears that up. Darcy is not a girlfriend. Now let's go home and see if Hope's story lines up."

Rebecca looked at her crow's feet in the rearview mirror and rather than wondering what to do about them, she wondered what else in the world she wanted more: the thought of being free from all her responsibilities or having people in her life who gave her deep wrinkles and worry lines. People she couldn't live without.

68

"Not feelin' it today. You go. I'm gonna go apply for a job down at the pub, where we first met." Missy watched Stan watching her. She was aware that he knew she was lying. *What does it matter? He could never do anything about it then and certainly couldn't do anything about it now.*

Stan's smirk spoke volumes but he kissed her cheek anyway. "K. Good luck."

"Have a good meetin'," she said as she walked out of the small apartment into the late August sun. Bag on her shoulder, cigarette in hand, she walked down Draydon the way she walked down any street: like she owned it but at the same time, like someone was coming to find her. She fished her phone out of her denim skirt pocket and comically shoved it back when she saw the caller ID: Cranston Bitch. "Weird timin'," she said to the morning breeze. "Weird timin'."

She stopped for coffee and half listened to the voicemail from Rebecca. "God, just get to the point!" Hanging up midway through, impatient and on edge, Melissa walked into the Coastal Trading Post.

She was greeted by the clerk. "Hiya, Missy. You're back."

Melissa tucked her sunglasses into her bag and replied, "Told ya I would be. Cleaning out my grandparents place a little at a time. They had a ton of stuff."

She reached into her bag and gently placed the felt-wrapped items onto the glass countertop of the pawn shop. "These are from Germany. My grandfather grew up there." She fidgeted even if she was speaking the truth.

The clerk gently peeled the cloth from the first item as one would a head of cabbage. His brows raised, barely. Missy was nothing if she wasn't observant. She watched his brows, his pupils, and even the tiny muscle movements of his lips. *He's into it*, she thought.

Brow furrowed, he reached for the glasses which sat atop his mostly bald head. Using his phone to take a picture of the compass before he gently turned it over to view the back, he mumbled and sent the picture to his partner. *Now his brows are poppin'*, she thought. He tilted his head and said, "This is remarkable. I'm not an antique dealer as ya know but you got somethin' here for sure."

Missy turned when the alarm sounded as it had when she had walked through the door. She could feel her heart thumping but didn't think the woman posed a threat. Missy turned back to the clerk, impatiently, "Well, what can ya give me for it?"

Squinting at his computer screen and talking with someone on the phone proved to be too much for Missy. *I'm not lettin' ya screw me like ya did on the other shit I brought in.* She wrapped the intricate treasure she knew was worth at least enough cash to get herself a used car and stuffed it and the other, still wrapped, item into her bag. The clerk, still on his phone, said, "I'm telling you, it's authentic. Take a look at those initials. I think it's a Ludvig Muller." By the time he looked up, the rare compass and Melissa were half a block down the road.

69

"Last class." "Look at you. You've grown so much since you arrived." "I'm so proud of you. I feel like we are all your mothers!" "Promise you'll come back to visit."

Hope had not attempted to keep the tears from falling and as such, sat with the tissue box on her lap and put it to good use.

Piper had excused herself to take a phone call and when she stepped back in, she quietly took a seat at her desk and watched as Hope sat confidently and accepted the warm wishes from the women who, from the outside, didn't seem to have anything in common with her. Hope wiped at her eyes over and over and laughed with the women about the synchronicities that had occurred over the months. "I guess you really can't make this stuff up," she said, voice as steady as a leaf caught in a raging river. "Sorry, I don't know why I can't stop crying." She laughed but she knew why. "I'm going to miss you guys. What will I do with my Thursday nights now?"

Claire said, "You can join virtually! Piper, can she?"

The group turned toward Piper, eager to hear if this was an option. Piper shook her head and said, "I'll get a tripod and we can use an ipad. Sure. You're still in, Hope."

As the chatter dissipated and the women wrote out their intentions and placed them into the almost full prayer bowl, Piper pointed at the decks of cards, inviting the group to begin the work of interpreting their messages and those meant for others. As the music played and the talking ceased, Piper closed her eyes and saw a travel arrow teetering, neither here nor there, balancing on the cusp of fate. "Compass." She surprised herself by saying it out loud. She opened her eyes to see the women looking at her, realizing they were as surprised as she seemed to them. Anne said, "You've said that before." Jamie added, "Like a *compass* compass or the idea of finding your direction?" The collective "oohhhh," was comical, drawing giggles. Piper asked the group, "Who has a compass or had one? I'm seeing lettering on the back. Maybe Latin? It's old and I think it's a collector's piece? I know the message is for someone here." She looked around the circle, the only eyes not meeting hers were Hope's.

"Well, let's keep moving. Let's try the treasure box immediately after the meditation, really put you to the test!" She chose the music and told them, "Focus on knowing what's in the box, relax, and just write or draw anything that comes to you when the meditation is over."

She watched as some women closed their eyes, some stared at the box, one looked out the window and let her focus soften, lids half closed.

Piper scribbled on her notepad: **pine needles, fear, disgust, soil, hidden.**

She shook her head, not knowing what she was seeing. Upon closing her eyes, letting the music take her where she needed to go, the familiar scents of lavender and smoke, burnt raisins, and briny air filled her mind, her soul. The taste of water meeting the shore, the feeling of a long-forgotten tide washing all the losses from her memory and sweeping them back for one last glance, a final au revoir. "Maman! Tu l'as accompli! You have done it!" Piper's heart lurched and stammered. *My boy. My little Philip.* "Maman, I told you I would find you again. There is no time. I was always with you."

Piper's face, awash with fresh tears, glowed in the setting sun as it came, slanting through the office window, telling of the coming change in seasons.

Piper watched the memory, frozen in time, of her and Paul in France. The miscarriage, the realization that there was no baby coming. Her eyes moved back and forth beneath her lids as she tried to piece it all together. Images of Slade, Rebecca, Eli, and a man and woman she did not know all sitting together at the edge of the shore, laughing and promising that in the end it would all work out: that God had a plan and they were the ones who wanted to see it through, to allow themselves to be drawn together in the wildest of ways. Piper was searching, searching, for what, she wasn't sure. The fog rolled in and they were gone. *Not yet. I want to see!* For a moment she was ready to let it fade, to open her eyes and rejoin the group but in the briefest of moments, her shoulder blades twitching, she held on. *Show me, tell me!* She stood on the shore alone, cold, her arms wrapped around herself, clutching the sweater Luuk and Philip once shared. She could smell their straw-colored hair and feel their cheeks against hers but she could not see them. She turned in a circle on the sand, looking down at her bare feet covered in soot and splinters. "Maman!" She looked up now, the fog lifting, sun coming down from the heavens. "Maman!" There, in the distance she saw them playing as they came toward her on the beach. Her beloved daughter Peyrinne, her twin boys, Luuk and Philip and Vander, the love she would choose in every lifetime if it were up to her. She wanted to run to them, to be delivered back through the hands of time and stay with them for a moment or an eternity but knew it wasn't possible. For a moment, everything was still, the sound of the waves gone, no cries from the scavenging gulls. Stunned and not wanting them to leave, she held her breath, clutching at the single pearl around her neck. And then, as the sound began to softly return, from behind Vander and their children, came an elderly couple, hand in hand, carefully making their way toward Piper and gently reaching back to a younger couple she hadn't recognized and still didn't. They stopped yards away from her and turned, gently pulling their gift through the sluggish fog.

Piper watched in disbelief as Hope took their hands, wanting them to move forward with her. The man and woman shook their heads "no" and smiled. They gently pushed her forward. Anne's voice came then, "Piper, are you okay?" Then Claire and Jamie, "Where did you go?" a nervous laugh from the group followed.

Blinking and tapping her foot to be sure she was really there in her office, she took a breath and smiled. She straightened in her chair and cleared her throat.

"Okay, well," she stammered, wiping at her eyes. "So tell me, what's in the box?"

Without a moment's hesitation, Hope said, "Echoes."

70

Sitting on the curb waiting for the Antiques Emporium to open, Missy scrolled through Hope's Instagram account and wondered why her kid was so boring. *Not in a bad way, but Jesus, live a little.*

Horses, a new saddle, banana bread, and a box surrounded by crystals and a bunch of dull-looking women in business attire.

The sound of several deadbolts unlocking sent lightning through the backs of her eyes as they focused on the storefront. Despite the abuse Missy had put her body through, she could still spring up from the ground like a kid on too many Red Bulls. She rushed to the door as if the owner might decide on a beach day instead. Pushing the heavy wooden door open, she felt the chill of the temperature-controlled space. The green velvet couch in the center of the room assaulted her senses. *Oma and Opa's house. Nehmen sie auf dem sofa platz. No thanks. No more lectures on how to live a proper Jewish life.*

"Good morning!" The woman behind the counter was as cheerful as Missy was agitated. This was her second visit. The first was wasted time and Uber money. "You the aprraisah?" Missy had no time for pleasantries.

The woman's brows furrowed, lips pursed. "No, I'm not. Can I help you? Do you have an appointment?"

Missy placed one item on the counter before the woman could finish. "Yes. I was told the aprraisah would meet me here at 9:00 am." She looked at the array of clocks behind the counter and pointed. "Looks like it's 9:05."

"He'll be out shortly. Can I take a look?" The woman was reaching for the felt covered item. Missy bit her bottom lip. *Shut up Melissa Gunther Barlow. Shut.Up.*

Nodding and smirking, she stepped away from the counter, wanting a cigarette. She ran her finger over the cedar chest that sat atop a clawfoot dining table. An arctic shiver ran head to toe. She reflexively drew her hand back. The woman watched her as she gently peeled back the cloth. Melissa turned her back then and gazed at the pictures hanging on the wall. Squinting, she examined oil paintings, cuckoo clocks, and other items she imagined once meant something to someone. From behind her, she heard a low murmuring. Whipping her head too fast, darkness enveloped the room. Annoyed, she stood still, waiting for her heart to pump blood up to her brain. Slowly, the staticky dots gave way to a man with a lighted magnifier looking at her grandfather's prized possession. The coppery taste in her mouth and pounding headache reminded her she needed to turn these things into cash as soon as possible and be done with it. *No squabbling!*

Back at the counter, Missy felt the old familiar burning lens of judgement on her as she rifled through her bag, making sure she didn't lose her lighter, phone, and wad of singles she'd been skimming off the top of Stan's grocery money. She lifted her chin and leveled her gaze first at the man, then directly at the woman who was clearly suspicious of Missy.

"What a ya think, huh? My grandparents had a lotta cool things from the old country. Germany. My grandfatha was a well-known psychotherapist. Otto Gunther, ever hear of him?" The man, yet to lay eyes on Missy, shook his head.

"This is an interesting piece. It's a Muller. It's in very good condition. Are you looking to sell or just have it appraised?" *Music to my ears,* she thought.

"Depends. I got another guy wantin' to take a look in an hour. I need a written appraisal."

The man, still studying the inscription on the back, asked, "Do you have paperwork?"

Indignant, Missy replied, "Paperwork? There's no paperwork. This was handed down from my great-grandfather. If you're not going to appraise it, don't waste my time!"

The woman busied herself with a customer who'd come in with two paintings and a Queen Anne's chair.

"Six. I'll give you six for it." The man's mustache flinched on one side only. *Like a dog,* she thought. Missy was not ignorant but she had been without a fix for almost two full days and feeling it. "Listen, I'm not here ta bust ya balls. I just want what's fair."

The man scanned pictures into an app and for the first time, looked at Missy.

"I'll give you a check right now for $6500 or I can give you $5000 in cash."

Missy's head throbbed as she stepped onto the sidewalk, hand inside her bag, securing her healthy handful of cash, lighter, and the half a joint she started at breakfast. She called an Uber to take her to the airport. There had been times of great clarity sprinkled throughout Missy Barlow's life, but even all rolled into one lump sum, they could never counteract the fog in which she made most of her life's choices. She called Stan, knowing he was in a meeting and wouldn't answer. "Hey ah, I'm just callin' to say thanks for everythin'. You and I both know I can't live that sober life shit but ah, I'm glad it's workin' for ya. I gotta be gettin' back to my life now. I know ya never undahstood me. No one has, really, but it's okay. I left the key on the countah. Bye-bye fa now, Stan."

The owner waited for Missy to leave before angrily telling her husband that he should have called the police.

71

Sitting on the familiar leather sofa in the morning sunlight, Slade waited for John. He looked up at the various diplomas and awards and wondered what made a man become a hypnotherapist versus a mechanic. He laughed at himself, realizing he'd never wondered that before. *These sessions have made me wonder about a lot of things.*

He rubbed the side of his knee, more out of habit than anything else. His phone reminded him he hadn't turned off notifications. **Hey Hemi - Doing good. Hope you are too. Weird you texted. Was thinking about you last week Brotha. Call me some time.**

John came in with his coffee mug. "Hello Slade! Are we ready to go?" Slade nodded. "I sure am. I'm sleeping better, did I tell you that last week? Feeling good, so every session is doing somethin'. I'm really shocked."

John nodded as he reviewed notes he'd made the night before.

Slade was already lying back on the sofa, stretched out, breathing, centering himself.

John looked at his notes. **Needs to view Moose realistically. From adult perspective. Real Name?**

John's voice was the only thing Slade could hear through the headphones. "Take me to that day. The day you realized Moose was just human and not the sergeant you thought could fix everything."

John was the ultimate professional yet couldn't help but

feel like Slade was a victim of his circumstances, his patriotism, and his own core beliefs. If ever he rooted for a client, it was Slade.

"It's Thanksgiving. I'm alone. Don't feel like being around anyone. My parents stop by and I won't answer the door. I'm looking out the window at them leaving me a bunch of food and," he cleared his throat. "And I see my father reach into his wallet and leave some money. I feel like a sad sack. A loser. Now Moose is calling me."

John noted the inflection in Slade's voice as he mentions Moose.

"I answer and he is telling me the baby was born in August and that he's not sure if it's his kid or mine. He told me to swear on the Bible and then answer him. I'm telling him over and over that I never touched his girlfriend. I remind him that I told him the very night we met her in the pool hall that she would be trouble for him and that he didn't listen to me."

John moved him along. " Okay, I'm sure Moose eventually realized he'd made a decision that might not have been the best for him but he was grieving at that time. People do things they wouldn't normally do when they're grieving."

Slade shook his head. "He said to me, 'Dennis, if this is your kid, you need to come get it. I don't want it if it ain't mine. Mine died with Ash. I don't evah wanna go through that again.' So I tell him I'm not lying, that I'd never lie to him. And then I asked why he was calling me by my first name. I feel like there was somethin' broken that couldn't be fixed."

"Good. Okay, so you see how Moose's pain was a big factor in his decisions? I wonder if you can just see him while he's talking to you on the phone. Picture him in his house, talking to you."

Slade said, "They had just moved north before the baby was born. Couldn't have the baby in the house he and Ashely were planning to raise their baby."

John took notes and asked, "Okay. Where did they go? Where is he now, the day you are talking to him?"

Slade's foot began to tap nervously on the arm of the leather sofa where his feet were. "They went up to Mount Desert Isle. He needed a fresh start up there. Needed to get away from Bath."

A familiar sense behind John's eyes taunted him to pay attention, but the sound of Piper's truck pulling down the gravel drive past the house to the barn tugged his senses back to the room. He put up a fight. He could hear his wife's voice, "Say everything."

He looked back at his notes again and traced the question mark after **Name** over and over again until he wore a window onto the page below.

"John, what is Moose's real name?"

Slade's hand over his short beard sounded like shears on delicate paper.

"Stan. Stanley Barlow."

72

Rebecca pulled up to the barn and threw the transmission into park. Her door was open before she turned off the engine. She ran into the barn. "Eli! Where are you? Where's Smudge? Eli!"

Running back out in front of the barn, she scanned the farm store lot and the driveway at the house. Seeing Eli's truck was a good sign but where was he? The shrill call from Cayenne at the gate turned her around and there she saw Smudge and Eli coming up the hill to the barn. She waited, watching Smudge's gait and behavior until they reached her. She immediately greeted the pony and bent down to put her ear to his belly. "I just got off the phone with the vet. She said he seemed better?" Eli waited, knowing that a worried Rebecca would not hear a word he had to say. When she finally looked into his eyes, what she saw there darkened the doorstep of her heart. *I have so much to explain,* she thought.

Composing herself, she walked around Smudge and hugged her husband. Instant tears betrayed the tough exterior she'd been sporting.

Eli said, "Hi Becca. I'm glad you're home." She stood back and wondered as she searched his face if she'd started something she might not be able to put a stop to, a runaway train of suspicion and accusations.

He continued, "Yea, he's been clearing himself out. Vet said he is out of the woods. Bran mash for a couple of days and he'll be right as rain."

She took the lead rope from him and returned Smudge to the cool safety of his stall.

"Eli, I spent the day with a very upset Hope. We need to talk."

Eli was already tugging her by the hand toward the back of the barn. He said, "Yes, we do. I was trying to call you." He stopped, not wanting to sound accusatory.

Leading her to the tree with the buried treasure, he said, "I am not exactly sure how this got here, but I have an idea. I'm just going to show you what I quite literally tripped over."

Rebecca stepped past him and pulled up the plywood. She said, "Hope told me everything, Eli. It's a lot and I'm still processing it all so please be patient."

Stunned that Rebecca felt she needed to ask for his patience, he sighed and let his shoulders drop. He crossed his arms, unconsciously, and shifted his weight on his throbbing feet. He said, "I'm all ears. Tell me everything because I honestly have no idea what's been happening."

Rebecca looked at the pile of gray Sentry Safe fireproof bags and then back up at Eli. "Hope told me almost everything from the safe is here. She put it out here the night before she left for Piper and John's. Missy forced Hope to get into the safe. Eli, you called it the day Hope told us her mother wanted to come see her. She wanted Otto's belongings, figured they were worth money."

Eli sighed, thinking of Hope and how difficult it must have been for her to be around Missy and how she left for Massachusetts while Rebecca and Eli weren't home. How distressed she must have been. "Well now we know why she left a day early. That poor kid. So what exactly happened?"

Rebecca, half listening, opened bag after bag until she found what she needed to see. She pulled out the deed to the farm, unharmed, as tears flowed unencumbered now, softening the angst and frustration of the previous months.

She turned to Eli when he asked, "What happened?" She took a breath and looked out to see Cayenne patiently waiting at the gate. "You probably won't believe this. Just know all I'm about to say is what Hope told me." Eli recognized her preface. It was the same tone, same words she used anytime she had to tell him some terrible thing that Grace had done.

"Go ahead. I'm listening." He uncrossed his arms then, leaning on the barn for support and rested one sore foot at a time.

"So Grace, at some point, saw that I had the safe combination on my phone. She's heard us talk about Otto's will, our will, other things we put in there. We should have been more careful." She looked at Eli to gauge his reaction. He nodded but she wasn't sure if it was approval or a sign to keep talking. "So anyway, she forced Hope to get the combination from my phone a few nights before she and Grayson left." Eli took a step forward then. "Forced?" Rebecca immediately defended her choice of words. "Yes, forced. I'll tell you more about that later. It's not good." She stared at Eli, not caring if this was upsetting to hear. "She wanted paperwork, court stuff. I don't know why. And something Antigone asked her to find." She looked away when she spoke Eli's first wife's name. Rebecca wouldn't bet her farm on anything but if she had to guess, she'd say Eli would never be completely over Antigone.

"Okay, so that's it? Hope got into the safe then." He wanted to drive home the point that it was not him who moved the deed and the marriage certificate or that Rebecca had been harboring resentment toward him over something he didn't do. But, if anything, Eli had learned and unlearned a lot in his sixty-one years and he needed to practice what he preached: forgiveness and moving forward.

Rebecca moved the plywood to one of the empty stalls inside the barn and wiped her brow, eyes closed. "Twice. She got into the safe again when Missy was here. She pressured her to take Otto's compass and watch and anything worth money. Hope was so scared, she just grabbed it all. Her mother was waiting for her down the road, so she left most of the stuff here under the tree and hurried off because she just wanted to get her mother out of town. But," she stopped and shook her head, wondering where she was when this was all happening. *When I failed her.*

"But she couldn't shake Missy. She gave her the things but Missy wanted cash. She told Hope there must be cash somewhere, that Otto was loaded." Eli's laugh shocked them both. He shook his head and ran his dirty hands over his face, trying to grasp what he was being told. "Then what? Where did Missy end up?"

Rebecca considered stopping there, leaving the details for later but she was already fired up. And, Eli needed to know, once and for all the disgrace his daughter had brought upon *their* daughter's head.

"Missy contacted Grace months before she left here, before Missy blew into town. They hatched a plan together, involving Hope and using her to get into the safe and," she stammered, "and they set up an account with—with pictures of Hope. A subscription site that they were making money from. They blackmailed Hope."

73

The bread was still warm when Hope loosely wrapped it in foil and tucked it under her arm. "Last day," she said to the empty kitchen. The only thing left to pack was the pan the bread came out of. Scooping up her tote bag full of well wishes and slipping into her boots, she pushed her way through the screen door into the subtly warm morning air.

She walked out toward the barn, noticing the early September light hitting one of the flower beds, but not another, reminding her that time moves us all along and there is nothing we can do to stop it. She was going home but not before proper good-byes.

She tucked thank-you cards that she had spent time personalizing for each boarder, student, and client into the "Mailbox" outside the tack room where payments and correspondence were safely exchanged.

She placed the fragrant bread in Slade's locker with a note: The bananas weren't ripe enough so I made you pumpkin bread. Please give some to Ollie, too!

On her way to the pasture to get Pirate ready to load up and head north, she stopped at each horse and pony. Peppermint after peppermint after tearful good-bye, she made her way to Pirate who stood watching the infidelity without much worry. He knew where he stood in the herd.

They walked back to the barn purposefully but not hurried. She was not fleeing Missy or the mess she had escaped months prior. She was going home.

"Hey Hope!" Slade called from the opposite end of the aisle. Surprised she said, "I thought you were working today. I just told Ollie he had the day off!"

As Slade approached, Hope could feel, rather than see, he had something that was about to spill forth. *I am not good at good-byes*, she thought.

"Ha! He does have the day off but I had to come say good-bye and ..." he stopped, holding onto the emotion that had kept him awake the previous two nights. He reached up and peeled the mud-covered velcro closure open and slid Pirate's fly mask off. "And I have to talk to you 'bout something John and I figured out in a session the other day."

Hope was already checking Pirate's hooves, on a mission to be on the road by 9:30 am.

"Oh yea, what did you guys figure out? A price to offer Piper for Oliver?" Hope had learned a lot from Eli and Clem's banter all those years she was growing up listening to them talk politics, farms, and wives. It served her well as she began to navigate the world as an adult but the lack of an answer from Slade concerned her. "No, not that." Slade's voice trailed off but Hope kept her eyes on the shipping boots as she was putting them on Pirate's legs.

"Listen, Hope. Ah, you know my friend Moose I've been tellin' you all about?" Hope visibly relaxed. Still on one knee in the aisle, she stopped a moment before proceeding to the next leg. "Yah. Of course."

Slade took a deep breath, not sure how to proceed but knowing he must. "Well, in my session, John asked me Moose's real name, which, I never use. I mean, to me he's always gonna be Moose."

Hope stood now, uncomfortable only because this didn't seem like something anyone would miss work to tell her.

She looked at him, not certain if what she was feeling was concern or impatience. Slade raised his eyebrows and shifted his weight. "So anyway, John told me that Cranston is your adopted name and so I never put two and two together."

Hope let the cross ties hit the stall doors and immediately

walked past Slade, almost knocking him off balance. The pressure of the tide rising and the destruction that almost always followed was something born inside Hope. It wasn't anything she would ever find words for, no matter how hard she searched or how far she traveled. It was more often than not the first fluttering beneath her skin, the bitter taste that arose on her tongue, the dread that anchored her to the earth, that foretold of news that would once more change her course, her direction.

"Hey, hold on a sec," Slade laughed but quickly intuited Hope had no intention of slowing her roll.

He stood in the center of the cool barn aisle, listening to the sharp steel shoes quicken their pace, striking the concrete like sledge hammers on railroad spikes.

"Hope Barlow! Hold on."

The deep well of excruciating life experience Hope had fought hard to climb out of suddenly opened up in front of her. She teetered on the edge like a thirsty raccoon on the water trough. The anger she felt when Grace showed her how little humanity she had and the disgust that swallowed her whole when her own mother revealed her communication with Grace, together scheming to use her, the pained expression on Rebecca's face when she asked Hope who had gotten into the safe. It was all too much. *Why is every good-bye a shitshow?!*

She spun on her heel, startling Pirate, who squealed his protest at the sudden shift in energy.

"*What* did you call me?" Even she was surprised at the splinters of rage that came from deep in her belly.

Slade, unsure how to undo the damage he didn't create, stood still, hands on his hips, knowing his choice of words was paramount. The things John shared with him about the way Hope was raised was a heavy burden on Slade's heart. He'd seen the little girl once, aged two, when he tried to reconnect with Moose on a trip to Mount Desert Isle. The tension between the old comrades was something he never wanted to feel again, thus his subconscious decision to push anyone who came close right out the door. He had marveled at how much she looked like Moose and how she loved the stuffed animals he brought her. To his eye, she was lucky to be loved and protected by his brother-in-arms.

"Hey, I never thought in a million years, Stan was anything but a hero. I guess you just can't really know what someone is going through and what it might do to them. I think sometimes we see people the way we need to see them," Slade's voice faltered. "You know, so we can survive."

74

Slade looked at his GPS and then up at the sign: Atlantic Townhouse Apartments, Draydon Road as his heart quickened. *Seventeen years. How can seventeen years have gone by?*

He swung into the parking lot and let his truck idle, tapping his fingers on the steering wheel. He hummed the last lines of the Scorpion song as it finished. *Winds of change, no doubt.*

He cut the engine and looked at his message from Stan: **Yep, just park and come in. I'm here.**

He took his last sip of iced coffee and adjusted his ball cap, nervously.

He looked over at the passenger seat and smiled.

Waiting on the walkway in the mid-September calm, he thought for a moment about what his therapist always tried to get him to see, that everything happens the way it does for a reason, even if we can't imagine what that might be.

He heard the apartment door open but couldn't continue yet. Looking back, the passenger side truck door slowly swinging open, he smiled, waiting patiently. He watched as Hope slowly made her way up the path to him, dressed in the only sundress she'd ever owned, a gift from Eli for the occasion.

Slade realized then that all he had gone through had brought him here, to this moment. It was a chance to make things right for the man who saved him and for the child who never got to know the true man her father was long before she was born.

He stepped to the side so she could make her way. Hope,

rising above the tragedies of her past, not alone but not by force. As she stepped up to this man who appeared in her life and changed everything with just a few words and a heart filled with much love he never had the chance to share, she stopped briefly. Slade reached out to her and tapped under her chin. "Eyes up. That's where you're going. Remember?" Hope bit her lip nervously, keeping tears stationed on her waterline, like cavalry horses on a ridge.

She had prepared for this moment in her head for two weeks now. Eli and Rebecca had helped her prepare and offered to take the trip, too, but in the end she decided it was Slade she needed to go with; after all, he knew her story better than anyone.

There in the doorway stood what seemed like a smaller version of the man who raised her. Less hair, brighter eyes, and what she thought might have been a smile.

The sun chased away the chill the air conditioner had left on her tanned skin. A fragment of a recurring dream came then and time seemed to halt like Pirate when there was a deer in his sightline.

Walking up a sand dune, tiny, yet fiercely determined, leaning forward, and pulling at grass to keep herself upright, she was exhilarated, a sense of duty and pride filling her tiny chest. The hands reaching back to pull her up belonged to many. There didn't seem to be any separation. They were all gathered together in every lifetime, playing different roles perhaps, but with a common thread running through each of them and keeping them connected, no matter the storms that raged, the tides that washed away.

When she finally reached the top, she could see the woman with the dark hair on the shore, watching, waiting. She closed her eyes. *It's been Piper all along.*

Otto and Elise were making their way down the slippery sand. Hope stopped for a moment and sat with the small boy on top of the dune, his straw-colored hair dancing about his eyes as he blinked in the bright sun. He said to her, "It's your turn now. They're waiting," Philip said.

The hands reaching up to guide her down the dune were those of her mother and father. They were sober and clean. Happy and Whole. They gently took her small hands and counted, "One, two … Ready, Hope? We are going to do this. Together. No matter what. Always remember, we all chose this and one day, somehow, we will all remember why. One, two, three!"

Back on the walkway she could envision Stan now as the young grunt who sacrificed so much and suffered beyond words. *Not mine to fix, but mine,* she thought, as she stepped onto the stoop.

She turned back momentarily to see Slade wiping at his eyes and wondered how strange this must be for him.

The voice behind her, once a rushing river, eroding anything in its wake, the voice of her father, now a gentle ripple slowly reaching her, giving her time to run if she was so inclined. Like the combination to the safe back home and compass that once guided her great-great-grandfather, it was about to reveal what she hadn't known existed.

Epilogue

Leaning on her backpack in the shadow of the towering cypress trees as the sun slid through the olive grove like lattice work, comforting her, Hope opened her journal and wrote. The words came effortlessly, now, striking flint against silence, a talent she kindled from the scraps of her early life, onto which she breathed her wisdom and fanned the flames of a journey she learned to embrace. The freedom she felt was something she only ever thought she could feel on the back of a horse, racing the wind through hayfields, chasing the future over fences and fording rivers like they rushed there for her alone.

"It came like mist on the morning pasture, soft, almost kind, the way it rewrote the edges of my childhood memories. Dreaming, I revisited the rain soaked, lichen covered and rotted steps leading up to the cabin in the woods on Mount Desert Isle.

And teetering there as I often did, I came to the realization that even as they threatened to collapse, they were there to teach me balance in a place that never promised solid ground. The dry soil I was planted in only trained my roots to reach far for water to sustain me and expand my territory. I learned to read moods like a sailor studies the stars, navigating storms before they ignited. None of this was sent to destroy, only to train. I see now how it all served me.

The laughter I wore like a second skin, stitched with secret scars painted me as acceptable. Only when I learned to stop picking at them, did they go a long way toward healing. Laughing less at my own expense and saving it for things worthy of the sound of my soul.

I dug through memories like refuse, knowing there had to be some treasure, something of worth to show to a world that covets shiny things. There, I found deep taproots entangled with names and stories untold. These were family histories hidden in the quiet whispers of a tide long turned. And as time always does, she sent it all back to me as echoes, some deafening and some like beautiful, sweet smelling rooms I've yet to enter.

Love was there, yes, but not as I deserved it. Not the gentle, golden kind reserved for others, certainly not the kind that offers solace and refuge, but the kind that teaches you to survive. Harsh and demanding and sometimes brutal like the sharks that eviscerate seals down by the rocks. Learning the perspective of the shark, however, doesn't negate my deep sorrow for the seal.

I can only guess that's true because hunger is easier to bear than pain.

In the end, I suppose, I carry two truths, like mismatched reins on the same bridle. One truth that I lived and one that lived beneath the surface. And somehow I will find a way to let them both belong to me, like the breath of every horse who healed me, the love that a handful of people lent me and the courage I alone found deep inside of me.

When I awoke from that dream, I felt, for the first time in my life, that it wasn't untrue to say, "I am Hope."